SAN DIEGO PUBLIC LIBRARY UT/

~~Hinda Vista~~

DEC 2

SO-BKF-111

4

7 X "/61 ("/00)

7 X 5/02 ("/00)

STORAGE

SAN DIEGO PUBLIC LIBRARY

DEERSLAYER

Previous books by this author
Writing as M. K. Shuman

Deep Kill
The Caesar Clue
The Maya Stone Murders

Writing as M. S. Karl

Death Notice
Killer's Ink
Mayab
The Mobious Man

DEERSLAYER

A Pete Brady Mystery

M. S. Karl

St. Martin's Press
New York

3 1336 03840 9323

DEERSLAYER. Copyright © 1991 by Malcolm K. Shuman. All rights reserved.
Printed in the United States of America. No part of this book may be used or
reproduced in any manner whatsoever without written permission except in the
case of brief quotations embodied in critical articles or reviews. For information,
address St. Martin's Press, 175 Fifth Avenue, New York, N.Y. 10010.

Design by Judy Dannecker

Library of Congress Cataloging-in-Publication Data
Karl, M. S.
   Deerslayer.
     p. cm.
    ISBN 0-312-06336-9
    I. Title.
   PS3561.A6144D43 1991   813'.54—dc20   91-21570

First Edition: November 1991

10 9 8 7 6 5 4 3 2 1

This book is dedicated to the memories of Robert and Katherine Cherry of Winnfield.

DEERSLAYER

1

A COLD drizzle leaked down from the treetops, making a steady patter on the carpet of dead pine needles. The lean, dark-haired man with the rifle crouched on the little stool, waiting, as the wooden platform swayed ever so slightly in the chill breeze. Despite the forest and the wooden walls, the stocking cap, kapock jacket, and gloves, the cold cut through him like a scythe and he wondered for the fiftieth time what he was doing out here.

He looked away from the weapon and down at the thermos on the floor beside him. He'd already downed half the coffee; any more and he'd have to relieve himself, which would mean movement and the chance of frightening the prey.

He sighed and turned back to the rifle. It was a bolt action Remington Model Seven, its clip holding four .243 caliber cartridges. As he lined up the front and rear sights, he tried to imagine whether he would have the nerve to shoot if a target presented itself. With his glasses fogged, he wondered if he would hit anything.

It was the sheriff's fault, he decided. The insistence of Sheriff Matt Garitty that he come with them, participate in Scotty's first hunt. Maybe even get a buck for himself, as if it were the pinnacle of a man's existence to kill a deer.

All in all, a hell of a way to spend the Saturday after Thanksgiving, thought Pete Brady, owner, editor, and publisher of the Troy Parish *Express.*

And he'd almost been saved; Garitty had been scheduled to drive down to Baton Rouge for a political caucus, but at the last minute it had been canceled, so that late last night Brady had gotten the call: "We're on for tomorrow. Bundle up good, though. It's gonna be a cold one."

And cold was the word, Brady reflected with a shiver. The hell of it was that with Louisiana winters, one week might be below freezing and the next might be in the seventies. A little luck and he'd have been able to wait until a day when there was sun and a blue sky.

But he'd noticed that deer hunting wasn't like that; people seemed to delight in telling about the hardships they'd suffered, and the long hours in the deer stand, with the damn thing swaying under them. But even today most hunters seemed to have stayed indoors. A few distant gunshots here and there, and then, but for the rain, silence, as the hunters had retreated from the wet. All except for Matt, Scotty, and Brady, that is.

Right now Brady didn't know what he would have given the most for, the heat of the sun or the feel of solid earth beneath his feet.

Garitty had told him it was part of the local culture and that if he was going to print photographs of trophy deer in the *Express,* as everyone expected, he ought to at least know what hunting was all about. Brady had demurred at first: As a native of New Orleans, he'd never had much to do with guns and viewed hunting as left over from barbarian times. Besides, guns were something people killed other people with, and anybody who doubted that could read the *Picayune.*

But in Troy everything was different; men carried gunracks in their pickups and boys were given .22s in the fifth or sixth grade. Hunting was a religion and in late fall and early winter, during hunting season, men bragged about the size of the buck they had shot.

So Brady had reluctantly accepted Garitty's challenge. Feeling a bit foolish for a middle-aged man, he had accompanied the sheriff's thirteen-year-old, Scotty, to the range and listened intently as a deputy instructed them in safety procedures. Then, only after the range officer was satisfied, did they begin to practice on the wooden deer cutouts that Garitty had installed as targets.

At first Brady had recoiled at the idea of shooting the figures. The sheriff, taking a page from the FBI academy, had rigged a moving belt with the deer targets cleverly intermixed with targets of human beings. So Brady held his fire on every occasion, eventually becoming shamed by the sheriff's son, who, firing from the position beside him, seemed to have no such compunction. But finally the editor persuaded himself to take a chance, so that by the end of the day he was hitting the deer cutouts with gratifying accuracy and the human figures not at all.

Of course, it wasn't exactly like being a cop, he told himself. *These figures weren't supposed to shoot back, even in real life.* Which sent pangs of renewed guilt surging through him. *Because how much sport was it,* he asked himself, *to kill a creature that had done him no harm and never would?* He'd watched the range officer's demonstration of the high-powered bullets he was using. A .243 bullet left the barrel at three thousand feet per second with two thousand foot pounds of energy. That meant that when it hit a small target, like a rabbit, the animal simply exploded. When it hit a larger creature, such as a deer, it tumbled around inside and tore a gaping hole where it exited—if, indeed, it exited in one piece. The .35 caliber round Scotty was using wasn't much different.

When he mentioned it to Matt Garitty, though, the sheriff had only shrugged.

"Have to thin the deer population," he said. "And besides, Scotty's been looking forward to it for the last three years."

"But the deer . . ." Brady protested.

"Everything has to die," Garitty drawled. "At least this way it's clean and quick."

3

And Brady knew it would do no good to argue.

So now he crouched in the stand, blowing out great clouds of vapor and trying to pull the poncho back up to cover his head against the tormenting rain.

God, he thought, *I hope they get one.* Because if they didn't he had the sick feeling that he might be expected to come out here and go through this again.

Then a worse thought struck him: Suppose he were the one to see a deer? What then? He sighted down the barrel, squinting through the rear sight at the little trail below. What if a deer appeared now, picking its way down the track, searching for the grain in the bait box below? Would he have the guts to squeeze the trigger? It was easy with the pop-ups, almost reflex. But with a living, breathing animal it was different.

He took a deep breath, blinked away a raindrop, and sighted again through the gray mist. He wasn't a vegetarian. Garitty had rubbed that point in. So why was he refusing to do his own killing? After all, the deer would be eaten.

It was, Brady had argued, because hunters took such delight in what they did. What was it Aristophanes had said? "Small boys throw stones at frogs in sport, but the frogs die in earnest."

Evolution. Garitty had shrugged. Not that people around here much believed in it, but unlike most of them the sheriff had gone to college and knew it for a fact: Man was a hunter for three million years or so. It was a little late to turn things around.

Brady felt his finger tighten on the trigger and he closed his eyes as he tried to imagine his target. The trouble was there were lots of people he'd met that he'd rather have had in the sights.

He tried to envision the scene: The undergrowth would waver, blur, and a fuzzy face would peer out. For an eternal instant he would stare into those soulful eyes, and then he would become aware of the rack of antlers—antlers that made this a prize animal. So he would reach for the safety, slowly flick it off, take careful aim . . .

That was when the shot exploded across the forest.

His eyes came open with a start, and even as the echoes died away it took him a moment to realize what had happened.

4

One of the others had spotted a deer. And judging from the closeness of the shot, it was the sheriff's son, Scotty, whose stand was the next one, about three hundred yards down the trail.

He heard a faint shout. Scotty, almost certainly, yelling that he had gotten one. Anxious to find an excuse to put an end to this misery, Brady threw off the poncho and made his way cautiously down the wooden ladder, conscious of its swaying at every movement.

His foot touched the ground, his boot sinking into the soft pine needles, and he said a silent prayer of thanks. The rain filtered down on him in a steady sprinkle and he thought longingly of the poncho he'd left behind. But Matt Garitty had been adamant: the orange safety vest outside at all times, and it was just about impossible to fit it over the poncho. Besides, he was soaked through by now, anyway.

He heard the boy shout again and he wondered how long it would take them to lug the buck out of the woods on one of the three-wheelers. *Better than having to carry it by hand,* he told himself, skirting a broad puddle in the trail and feeling the dead briars grab at his sleeve.

He came to a bend in the trail and let out a "Hello" so they'd know he was here. In the distance he heard the low rumble of an ATV and knew that Matt was on his way here, as well.

Scotty stood in the middle of the trail, the bolt of his rifle open, his eyes bright.

"I got one," he said, pointing. "Right over there, in the thicket. I heard it try to run away, but I know I got it. At least a ten pointer."

Brady tried to mumble congratulations but it came out like a cough. At that moment, with a revving of the engine, Matt emerged from the other direction on the four-wheeled ATV.

"What is it, Scotty?" he asked.

His son repeated the claim, pointing at the tangle across the trail.

"It was too thick in there to go by myself," Scotty said. "I figured I'd wait for you."

His father nodded and unslung his own lever action carbine.

"Well, we'll take a look at this monster," he drawled, giving Brady a wink. "Was it a moose or an elk?"

5

"Dad!" Scotty protested.

Garitty smiled and started for the thicket, machete in one hand, carbine in the other. Brady let the boy go after his father and then followed a few yards behind. The briars scraped at his face and when he tried to push them away they snagged his clothes.

"Well, you hit something, I reckon," the sheriff said, pointing at a spot of blood on the ground. By the time Brady reached it, though, the rain had blotted it away.

A hundred yards later Brady was beginning to wonder if Scotty had seen anything at all.

"I promise it was right there, in the brush next to the trail," Brady heard the boy say, from ahead of him. "The bushes moved and when I looked—"

The others stopped and Brady emerged from the briars to collide with them.

"Oh, Jesus," he heard Matt Garitty say. The boy beside him made an unintelligible little sound between a gasp and a sob. Brady walked around the pair and stared down at what lay before them.

It was a man, his body twisted where he had fallen, surprise showing in his open, dead eyes. One hand was twisted under him and his legs were bent at the knees, as if he had died before his body had touched the ground. *It was,* thought Brady, noting the ugly hole in the right cheek, *a miracle the man had made it this far.*

Brady reached down under the orange vest, touched the man's wet shirt above the heart and then stood up again, trembling.

"It can't be," Scotty cried out. "It was a deer. I promise. I saw it."

The sheriff of Troy Parish stared woodenly ahead in shock and then slowly turned away. That was when Brady saw that Matt was trembling, too.

2

FOR a long time there was silence, punctuated only by the patter of raindrops on the leaves and the soft sobbing of the boy. Then Brady stooped back down to look at the dead man.

"I know him," he said. "This is—"

"Dwayne Elkins," Matt said in a strange, choked voice. "Runs the car dealership here."

Brady gave the blonde, slightly bloated face another look. Yes. Of course. He hadn't had many dealings with the man, except for a few ads in the *Express*.

"Dad, it can't be . . ." Scotty protested, looking from one to the other. "It couldn't have been my bullet. I saw a deer, not a man. Dad, you have to believe me."

The sheriff reached out, put an arm around his son and held him.

"Dad, you've got to believe—"

Garitty bit his lip and finally gave a little shrug. "We have to get word back to town," he mumbled. "The coroner, the chief deputy—"

"I'll go," Brady volunteered.

"You don't know how to drive an ATV," Garitty said. "Besides,

7

all I have to do is get back to my truck and use the radio. It's only a mile or so." He turned to his son. "Come on Scotty. Won't do you any good to stand around here."

Brady watched them go, a boy on the verge of becoming a man, and a grown man who seemed suddenly on the verge of becoming old.

For a long while he stood over the corpse, staring down at the glazed eyes, the swollen, purple lips, and the entry wound on the cheek, smudged red like an obscene kiss. He gently touched the other side of the head and felt blood; the bullet had exited from near the left ear, after destroying the brain. Not much chance for surviving a shot like that.

He had been at many death scenes, most of them in New Orleans when he'd been a crime reporter for the *Times-Picayune*. Always before he'd been able to distance himself. Always, that is, until his main source on a crime exposé, Ozzie, was murdered. That had hit hard, and when Brady won a Pulitzer on the strength of his work, it had only made things worse. He'd left the *Picayune,* bought the *Express* from old Emmett Larson, and moved to Troy, a quiet town in the pine hills of north Louisiana. He'd made new friends, like Matt and Mitzi Garitty, and had even managed to pair himself with Emmett's beautiful daughter, Kelly. Away from the chaos of New Orleans, with its senseless violence, he had found new structure, and now that structure was threatened by something he could not comprehend.

Because he had taken the course with Scotty. The boy knew a deer when he saw one. His father had made sure of that.

So how could he have shot a man by mistake?

And Brady sighed, feeling suddenly very weary. It was the same story every year: How many accidental shootings were there in the state every hunting season? Many of them were related to alcohol and downright negligence. But some were genuine accidents, a temporary lapse of judgment, or overeagerness on the part of a neophyte.

He wrenched his thoughts away and back to the victim.

What did he know about Dwayne Elkins? Not much, really. In his late thirties at the time of his death, Dwayne had been married

8

to Debra Penniman, granddaughter of old Garth Penniman, who had founded the dealership back in the twenties. Dwayne had more or less inherited his job as a result of his marriage. Maybe that was why Brady had heard a few rumors that the marriage wasn't a particularly happy one. He had a sudden thought and bent over the body. Putting his nose a half inch from the dead man's mouth he sniffed.

Dwayne Elkins exuded the strong odor of liquor. Brady patted the corpse's pockets, searching for a bottle or a flask, but there was nothing. Elkins must have left it at his camp, which, as best Brady could make it, was about a mile and a half away, just off the National Forest.

It was odd Elkins would be here, Brady thought, then reminded himself that if Elkins was drunk, he might do lots of odd things; it was a behavior pattern Brady recognized well from his own days as a heavy drinker, though he tried to forget that part of his life.

So the scenario was clear: Elkins had been at his camp, either alone or with friends. After a few drinks he had decided to go hunting, not realizing that other hunters were present. And he had blundered into the sights of a boy who'd never been on a deer hunt before, worse luck for both.

Except that there was no rifle nearby. *The man had gone hunting without a weapon.*

An hour later Brady still shivered in the rain, watching a pair of deputies bind the body onto a stretcher. Then he slowly walked back with them the long mile to where Garitty's truck was parked. Except that now, instead of just the truck, there was a Sheriff's Department jeep and the pickup that belonged to the chief deputy.

Garitty and the boy sat inside the sheriff's blue pickup, the motor running to keep them warm. Even through the fogged windshield Brady could make out the pallor on his friend's face.

He tapped on the window. "I think they've about wrapped it up," he told Garitty when the lawman rolled the glass down.

The sheriff nodded. "There'll be some things to do back at the office. I've handed over the . . ." he hesitated, then said it, *"investigation* to Ed Larimore." His face looked pinched, as if he had suddenly lost weight.

9

"Right," Brady said. "Well, I'll go back with one of the deputies."

Because after all, he thought, as the jeep bumped over the almost impassable road, *a man ought to be alone with his son at a time like this.*

As if there was anything either of them could say to the other that would make things right.

That night Brady sat alone in the *Express* office, while the rain dripped from the eaves and cars made slick sounds against the wet streets as they passed. Through the glass of the front door he could see the red bulbs of the Christmas lights that had just been strung over the streets yesterday. But instead of inspiring cheer the red glow reminded him of ambulances and police cars. He had returned home to take a shower and change and then gone over to Matt's house, to see if there was anything he could do. But, after making the necessary written statement, the sheriff had relapsed into gloom and Scotty had vanished into his room, with only Mitzi trying to keep up a front, so Brady had left, realizing there was nothing to be done. He'd given his own statement to a worried-looking Ed Larimore, the chief deputy, who shook his head and allowed that Elkins had been off the trail and should have known better than to mix liquor and gunpowder, as the saying went. But the implication still hung over them like a shroud: Scott should have paid more attention.

Brady started home again then, but he hadn't made it past the newspaper office. The house was empty, because Kelly was in Baton Rouge. She'd left Friday, pleading work to do in Baton Rouge on her journalism thesis that Brady was learning to hate. So Brady had gone to the office, which, while deserted on a Saturday, would still have bits and pieces for the edition he would put out Thursday. He would occupy himself with a few unfinished tasks; a story he had to write on the school Christmas pageant, a few lines on Bert Masefield's son who'd just graduated from Basic at Fort Polk, Ripley Dillon's interview with Miller Purdy, the environmentalist, who was protesting the construction of a new state correctional facility west of town.

10

But as he reached for his notes his eyes touched a photograph and attached message. The photo was of a kneeling man in camouflage, holding up the head of a deer with his left hand, rifle in his right. The message, scrawled in the hand of his assistant, Ripley Dillon, read: *Eight point buck shot by Albert Long near Pine Chapel,* November 15.

Brady stared at the picture for a long time and then shoved it away. *Damn.*

The phone rang and he jerked. He reached out from habit, then halted. Probably a wrong number. If not, then it didn't matter; everybody in town knew the *Express* office was closed today, so what did it matter? It rang four more times and kept ringing.

Maybe it was important.

Was there anything more important than what had happened today? He wasn't in a mood to listen to somebody's breathless account of some nonevent.

It kept ringing.

Finally, with a sigh, he picked it up.

"Yes?"

"Brady?" It was Kelly's voice, sounding worried.

"Oh," he said wearily. "Hi."

"Hi yourself. What's going on? I've been trying your house all night."

He hesitated, then told her what had happened.

"Oh, Jesus," she breathed, her voice anguished. "Why didn't you call me?"

"I dunno. Maybe because I didn't want to believe it myself. And maybe—"

"Maybe because you're mad at me for not staying through the weekend."

"Oh, well . . ." Brady equivocated.

"Don't hold it against me. I thought I explained how important it was for me to get this thesis done."

"Sure," he said wearily, not wanting to fight with her.

"Look," she said, changing the subject. "How are poor Matt and Mitzi holding up?"

"Well enough. I think they're still in shock." He squeezed the receiver. "Kelly, it could happen to anybody. The boy was excited, hyped up. It was one of those things."

"Is that how you're going to write it?"

"Write it?"

"Well, you're going to report it in the *Express,* aren't you?"

Brady shut his eyes and felt his temples throbbing. Of course he had known all along it would come down to this.

"Yes. I guess I have to."

"So what are you going to say?"

"I haven't seen the police report yet," he temporized.

"You were there," she pointed out. "They weren't."

"Well, it could happen to anybody," he said. "I mean, look how many people get shot in accidents every season."

"And most are preventable. At least, that's what you've always said."

"Christ, Kel, what do you want me to do? Crucify the boy? Matt's my friend!"

"I know." Her voice turned soft. "And I didn't mean to sound like a class lecture. I thought maybe if we talked it through it would help. Tell you the truth, there won't be a lot of tears shed about Dwayne Elkins's dying. I'm just sorry it had to be Scott that bears the brunt of it."

"Elkins wasn't well liked?"

"Not hardly," she laughed. "He was six or seven years ahead of me in school, but I still pick up rumors when I come back. He's got the morals of a ferret and the business ethics of a burglar. Dad bought a car from him once—ask *him."*

"It ought to make for an interesting obituary," Brady said dryly.

"It's one I wouldn't spend too much time on."

A silence settled between them and he knew they were thinking the same thing.

"You aren't coming up tomorrow," he said.

"I just got back," she said, her voice soft. "And I really have to be here Monday to meet with Jeff on my thesis."

Jeff Baxley, her adviser. Brady wondered what kind of obituary he could put together for Baxley.

"Right. Well, I hope he appreciates your conscientiousness."

He was thinking that she could drive up to Alexandria, they could meet at the Bentley Hotel, the scene of so many of their rendezvous . . .

"Don't be mad," she begged. "I'll be up again as soon as I can. You know that."

"Sure."

She heard his sigh and when she spoke again it was a whisper: "I love you."

"Love you, too," he said, thinking back of all they had been through together in the last couple of years: their meeting soon after he had come to Troy; their hunt for the killer of Frieda MacBride; their long night drives to Alexandria, sixty miles to the south, to deliver the dummy of the *Express* to the printer's. Then she had gone to the state university, a hundred sixty miles to the south for a degree he never felt she needed to begin with, and since then their affair had been long distance, limited to weekends and holidays. But now her degree program was almost completed and he sensed a moroseness about her, as if she were losing her shield. But when he tried to discuss it with her she shied away.

"Take care," she said, and he mumbled something back, replacing the receiver.

That night he dreamed he was in the forest again. He was hunched in the deer stand, waiting, and as he watched a magnificent buck stepped out of the thicket and into his sights. He squeezed the trigger and as he did the buck changed instantaneously into a man. When he awoke the night had turned into the milky gray of dawn and he knew he would get no more sleep.

3

THE funeral was Monday morning. Brady showed up at the funeral parlor out of a sense of duty—not because he'd really known the man, or even because he intended to write an extended obituary, but because he'd been there when Elkins had died and so was, of necessity, involved.

The dead man's wife, Debra, stood in the lobby, amidst a clutch of relatives and Brady waited for an opening to step forward, identify himself, and say he was sorry.

She regarded him quizzically, a small, blonde woman in her midthirties with a touch too much makeup.

"Oh, yes," she said in a far-away voice. "Of course. Thank you for coming."

He still wondered if she recognized him as he stepped back and headed for the chapel where the dead man lay.

The chapel was deserted and the publisher walked in quickly and spent an obligatory thirty seconds staring down at the corpse.

"Looks good, don't he?" a voice said from his elbow. He turned to see a man his own age staring down into the casket.

14

"Laverne Penniman, Debra's brother," the man said, offering his hand. "And you're Mr. Brady, from the *Express.*"

"That's right," Brady allowed. "But you're not from Troy."

"Well," Laverne said, "I was born and raised here, but I'm a contractor in Natchitoches now. Somebody pointed you out to me. You going to write something nice about Dwayne, there?"

Brady swallowed. "I'll probably put something together."

"Yeah, well don't go overboard." Laverne looked down at his brother-in-law and shook his head. "Look at him. After Grady Grimes finishes with somebody, they look like they could've been Saint Francis."

"And Dwayne?" Brady asked, letting the question hang.

"Dwayne wasn't a saint of *any* kind," the other man said. "No how, no way. Between us, I think Debra'll be better off. But there'll probably be a day of mourning at the Jim Beam factory."

There was a stir at the door and the two men turned.

An elderly woman was being helped forward, but it was against her wishes, judging from the protests.

"I can walk," she said, pushing away the arms that tried to assist her. "For heaven's sake!"

Laverne Penniman started forward to assist her.

"Aunt Maud."

She turned a pale cheek up to him for a kiss and gave his hand a squeeze. "Laverne, tell them I can walk by myself. Just because I have a little angina . . ."

"Well, we don't want to give Grady another one," Laverne said good-humoredly. "One from this family is enough for right now."

"This family," Maud huffed. "*He* wasn't a member of this family. Don't be hypocritical. Just because he's dead . . ."

Brady watched her make her way forward, a tall, handsome woman in her sixties who still retained a healthy appearance, despite her history of heart trouble.

She came to the side of the casket and stared down. For an uneasy moment Brady got the impression she was counting the seconds to see if the dead man was breathing.

"Well," she said finally, turning to Brady. "I hope you don't give him more than three lines."

15

"Now, Aunt Maud, we were just talking about that," Laverne assured her.

The old woman shook her head. "Do you know he didn't even put up the Santa Claus display this year? He let it rot in the storeroom. My father had that display specially made during the war. It was a part of the town. He even added a Rudolph to it after that got to be popular. You could stand downtown and look all the way down Main and see the sleigh and the reindeer, all lit up on the roof."

"We'll make another one, Aunt Maud," Laverne promised.

"It won't be the same. Poppa made that one. It was a family heirloom. And he let it go."

The old woman stumped out and Laverne shook his head.

"Going home to bed, I reckon. Probably'll have an attack. But not until after the funeral. It wouldn't be right."

Brady repressed a smile.

"I hope the preacher'll have some good things to say," he volunteered.

"He'll be the only one," Laverne snorted and stomped out.

Afterward, Brady left quickly, exchanging a nod with Matt Garity, who had come late and at the cemetery stood just outside the canvas awning, in the drizzle, on the fringe of the little crowd.

When he got back to the office, Mrs. Rickenbacker, his bookkeeper was already there.

"Been to the funeral," she observed, as he pulled off his tie and shrugged off his coat. She was a severe-looking woman who wore her hair in a bun and suffered from hysterical headaches whenever office pressures got too great.

"Yeah. He wasn't the most popular man in town."

"No. Came from those Yankee Turn Elkinses. They never were much. Married above himself."

"I got that impression from his in-laws."

"Breeding tells," Mrs. Rickenbacker pronounced. "And he didn't have any." She leaned toward her boss. "I always wondered if he was one of those Redbone people."

"Redbones?"

"Part Indian, part Negro, part who knows what? They have 'em over southwest of here, you know. Half-breeds, the lot of 'em."

"Well, whatever he was, it's too bad he had to go that way," Brady said, settling in behind his desk. "I mean, Scotty Garitty . . ."

"He'll have to live with it the rest of his life," Mrs. Rickenbacker pronounced. "I'm surprised, too. I thought his father was so heavy on safety."

"He is," Brady said, nettled at her attitude.

"Well, if that's so," she asked, "what happened?"

Brady had no answer.

He closed the office at four-thirty. The rain had stopped, finally, but the cold still held. He ate at Sophie's Kitchen, where they served steaks and seafood and bean soup, and when he drew some nods and greetings he imagined they were all thinking that he had been with Matt when it had happened. So he ate quickly, afraid that someone was going to come over to his table, and was glad once he was back in the comforting darkness of the parking lot. He drove home, passing the new Val-Save discount store on the right, where Christmas lights danced from the light poles in the parking lot, and past the State Farm office, where a string of red, blue, and green bulbs winked from the big picture window.

And beside it was a dark expanse that was the lot of the Penniman dealership, its building a brooding hulk, with a single safety light the only sign of life.

Maud was right, the Santa would be missed, he thought, turning east into the curve that led to Main Street. He was passing the courthouse now, a modern, brick structure with lots of glass and sheriff's cruisers sitting in the wide driveway at the rear. There was a Christmas tree visible through the window of Matt's office. *Yeah,* Brady thought, *Merry Christmas.*

He turned into his driveway and got out, walking wearily across the lawn to the front lock. He fumbled for his key, went to fit it into the door, and the door swung slowly open.

Brady froze, unsure whether to walk away and call the police or go in. Surely he had locked the door.

He pushed it open the rest of the way and, still outside, reached his hand in to find the light switch.

As he touched it the light flared on and he saw Matt Garitty seated in his chair, beside the reading lamp.

"Come on in," Matt said. "After all, it's your house."

Brady swung the door closed behind him and exhaled.

"God, Matt, I'm glad it's you."

"You may not be after this," he said. "By the way, I put your key back under the flowerpot. But I've got to tell you, that's the first place a burglar would look."

"You've told me before," Brady said with a wry smile, flopping onto the sofa. In the lamplight Garitty looked tired and there were new lines etched in his face.

"I walked here," Garitty said. "I didn't start to. I just started out to walk in the neighborhood, but I ended up here."

Brady nodded. Matt lived a mile away, on the other side of town, in a new subdivision of modern brick, ranch-style houses.

"I've been trying to make sense of all this ever since it happened. I keep telling myself there's sense somewhere but I can't find it."

The newsman nodded again. "How's Scotty?" he asked.

"Fine." The sheriff leaned forward, face intent. "That's just it. After the shock wore off he seemed completely normal. *Too* normal."

"You mean he ought to be brooding," Brady said.

"Something like that. But after he went to bed Saturday night, well, he came out of his room yesterday morning just like nothing had happened. At first I thought I was reading him wrong, but I wasn't. I swear to God, Pete, it's like nothing happened at all." Garitty shifted back in his chair and pressed his hands against his eyes. "I sat him down to talk, tried to explain it was okay to show he was upset, that anybody would be, and he just said he didn't want to talk about it, that he'd made a mistake, and if he had to pay for it he would."

"What did you say?"

"Well, I told him that was fine, not to admit anything just to make anybody happy. I told him if he said he saw a deer that was good enough for me, because I trained him, by God, and I knew he wasn't the kind to shoot wild."

Brady breathed out slowly. "Poor Scotty," he said. "People have all sorts of ways of protecting themselves."

Garitty jerked his head up and down in agreement. "I know. But don't you see what I'm getting at, Pete? If he were having the normal reaction, grief and all that, I'd feel better. He could work his way through that. But this way . . . I have a bad feeling about where it may end up. And besides—"

"Yeah?"

Matt hesitated, then came forward again, fixing Brady with his gray eyes.

"I don't think he killed Dwayne Elkins."

Brady blinked, trying to absorb what he had just heard.

"Matt—" he said finally, but the lawman cut him off.

"I know, I know. It sounds crazy, doesn't it? But humor me, okay? Look, Pete, we've known each other for what, three years now? You've seen me in a lot of situations. I hope you respect my judgment."

The publisher nodded.

"Well, respect my judgment once more. Pete, everything about me, everything I know, everything I feel, is telling me that something's wrong here, that Scotty's innocent."

Brady tried to find words, failed.

"And I know what you're thinking," Matt said. "He's my son, and I'm trying to protect him—"

"It's not a question of guilt or innocence," Brady finally managed. "It was an accident, for God's sake."

"An accident, but we both know that in the eyes of the law there are avoidable and unavoidable accidents. Dwayne Elkins was wearing hunter's orange. Scotty should have seen him—"

"He was keyed up," Brady said. "He didn't expect to see Elkins there. He didn't expect *anybody* to be out there. A little movement in the bushes and—"

"That's what I've been telling myself," the sheriff agreed. "But it just doesn't work." He lurched up from his seat then and Brady realized his shirt was half out. Then he noticed it had been buttoned unevenly, the wrong buttons thrust through unmatching holes.

"See, Pete, I *trained* that boy. From the time he was old enough to play cowboys and Indians I taught him about the safe use of firearms. When he saw me come home and take off my gun and asked questions about it, I took the pistol out into the backyard, unloaded it, and taught him how a revolver works and the safe handling of one. Then, later, I took him out to the range and showed him how to shoot it. When he was old enough to want a .22, I made sure he went through the NRA course first, and I checked him myself. I loaned him my old .35 to practice for deer season, but I made damned sure he didn't shoot till he knew his target. Hell, you were with him. Would *you* have shot anything you couldn't have positively identified as a deer?"

"I don't know," Brady said truthfully.

"Well, I do. The boy knew the rules."

Brady pursed his lips, trying to think of the best way to say it. When he spoke again, his voice was almost too low to be heard.

"Didn't you say he admits now he might have made a mistake?"

"We both know he's just trying to act grownup, like I taught him."

"Yeah." Brady made himself nod.

"And that's why I'm here," Garitty said finally, thrusting his hands down into the bottoms of his pockets. "You see, I'm his father. I can't take a hand in this. I mean, I've handed over the investigation to Larimore and I've stepped out. It's the only thing to do."

Brady waited, uneasy at the direction the conversation seemed headed.

"If I started asking around, people would say I was just trying to protect my son. But you're the publisher here; people *expect* you to ask questions. And, damn it, you've had more experience at investigation than any six of my deputies. That's why I came to you, Pete. You don't have to do it, of course, but I'm asking you as a friend."

"Asking me what?" Brady heard himself say, already knowing the answer.

"I'm asking you to make your own investigation of this. I want you to prove my son didn't shoot Dwayne Elkins."

4

THE next day was warm, with a clear sky. Brady made his way down the forest trail, feeling vulnerable. He had parked back where Matt had left his truck on Saturday but this morning, instead of heading left after the first two hundred yards, and toward the deer stands, he went right, on the trail that led to the Elkins camp. Or, at least, according to the sketch map Emmett Larson had made for him.

"What you want to do up there?" Emmett had asked and when Brady had explained Matt's request the old publisher had snorted.

"Sounds like Matt's got a worse problem than the boy."

"I know, but he asked me as a favor."

Emmett nodded. "Right. So you plan to go up to the Elkins place and try to find something nobody else saw."

Brady shrugged. "To tell the truth, I don't know what I expect to find. Probably nothing. I just promised Matt I'd try."

"Well, then, for God's sake, try. But don't get caught up in this, son. Matt's got to come to terms with what happened. You've got to help him realize that."

And Brady had agreed. But he had to give it his best shot. And when he turned up nothing, maybe then his friend would believe him. At least, that was the agreement he and Matt had made.

He hadn't told Ripley or Mrs. Rickenbacker where he was going, of course. Ripley would have had some choice comments and Mrs. R. would have spread it all over town. Better keep it between Emmett and himself.

But just what the hell *was* he looking for, anyway?

Damned if he knew. But the camp seemed as good a place to start as any, since Elkins had been there right before it had happened.

He stepped around puddles, left over from the rain, and halted every few steps to listen. But all he heard were the birds. No voices, no rifle bolts being pulled back . . .

The road was an old logging track, left over from the thirties, when this whole area had been cut over. Since then, the government had instituted a program of timber management, but the forest was still criss-crossed with trails and studded with stands of young pines, planted after tracts had been leveled. Very little, if any, of the forest was virgin, he reminded himself; still, it had a certain beauty you couldn't find in the flatlands.

The trees ahead bore yellow stripes and a sign on one told him he was leaving government land. He stepped past it and started up a slope. A glint of metal caught his eye and he emerged into a clearing. The camp structure was an old Airstream trailer, which Elkins had evidently hauled here years before. A wooden awning had been built out from the door and supported by two wooden uprights. As Brady approached, a squirrel stopped, bushy tail quivering, and then ran off to the far side of the clearing. A crow watched from atop the camp, then flapped away with an angry caw.

The place was deserted, just as he'd hoped it would be. He walked around it once, to make sure, and stumbled into a pile of empty beer cans; but it didn't matter, there was no one in the back and there were no lights in the windows. A small tin shed sat at the edge of the clearing, linked to the trailer by an electric wire. He opened the door of the shack and looked inside: a gasoline engine, used for generating electricity.

He shut the door and started back for the trailer, then stopped as his foot crunched on something. He bent down to see what it was and came up with a small, brass tube.

A .22 cartridge case. He scanned the ground, saw others. At the far edge of the clearing, about two hundred feet away, was a stump. Brady walked over and examined the ground around it. The grass was littered with the remains of beer cans, each showing the results of extensive target practice, and on top of the stump were fragments of colored glass.

Elkins had stood outside his camp and taken target practice at cans and bottles. And judging from the mountain of cans beside the trailer, he hadn't had to worry about exhausting his source of targets. Something silver caught Brady's eye and he plucked it out of the grass. It was round, about the size of a twenty-five cent piece, but the two sides had been pushed together by a bullet so that now it resembled a tiny, concave bowl. *Nickel,* he thought, *or maybe chrome.* Without thinking, he dropped it into his pocket and went back to the camp.

For the first time he noticed something under a tarp, at one side of the clearing. He lifted the canvas and saw a three-wheeled ATV, wheels and frame thick with the characteristic red mud of Troy Parish. *Nothing here,* he thought, and, letting the edge of the tarp fall back, returned to the camp. The door was secured by a hasp with a heavy padlock.

It took him less than two minutes to find the key. No flowerpots for Dwayne Elkins; his key was cleverly pressed into the ground, under a cement cinder block, to one side of the door. *Not bad,* Brady thought. A burglar would have to lift the block to find the key. *Except that if I could find it so could anybody else.*

He opened the padlock, unhitched the hasp, and went in.

The air reeked of alcohol and body odors. He stood in the gloom while his eyes adjusted, trying to make out the scene before him. Little by little it resolved into walls and a floor, and objects in between.

He stepped inside and his foot kicked something that shot across the floor to bang against the far wall. He reached out to keep from falling and looked down: a whiskey bottle. He scanned the rest of the room. The table held an ashtray, filled with butts, and there was a single glass beside it, still half full of amber liquid. He bent over, sniffed the glass, and recoiled. Nobody had been here to clean up. Everything appeared to be just as Elkins had left it.

For an instant he considered the consequences of violating a crime scene. Then he told himself that there was no evidence of a crime, and the worst he could be convicted of was unauthorized entry.

He went into the kitchen. The garbage pail overflowed and small, crawling things skittered away as he approached. He checked the bedroom. A double bed and dresser had been crammed into the narrow area but, while the bedspread was mussed, there was no evidence anyone had slept here recently. He stood quietly for a moment, absorbing the scene, trying to decide if there was anything unusual, any item out of place, but there wasn't. He went to the bureau and opened the first drawer.

Socks, handkerchiefs, a pair of leather gloves. And a .44 Magnum revolver, which a glance told him was loaded.

He shut the top drawer and went to the second one. It was full of magazines. He recognized most of them from his years in New Orleans, though they didn't sell them up here in Troy Parish: *Hustler* and *Penthouse* were the mildest of the lot. The rest dealt with various byways of heterosexual behavior and, from the tattered condition of the pages, they had been well-studied. The oldest had come out five years previously, the most recent was a September issue from this year. Brady slid them back into the drawer and closed it. *Let someone else, a family member, clean up the mess,* he thought.

The last two drawers held work clothes, all apparently belonging to the dead man. Brady stood upright and, opening the top drawer again, stared down at the heavy revolver. Nothing suspicious about the weapon, though—Elkins liked guns. He liked to stand behind his camp and take target practice. And the camp was in a lonely location. Plenty of people in Troy Parish kept handguns nearby for protection.

He left the bedroom, stopping at the tiny bathroom to check the medicine cabinet: an assortment of remedies, a snakebite kit, and a box of condoms. So Dwayne Elkins didn't always come out here alone. Well, no surprise there, either.

The kitchen told him nothing, except that the dead man liked cornflakes. The milk in the refrigerator was sour, but the ice box itself was still cold, which meant the propane tanks outside weren't yet empty. Judging from the three sixpacks of beer, though, the dead man hadn't been an avid milk drinker. Brady shut the refrigerator door and went back out into the main room. For the first time he became aware of the rifle rack on the wall, beside the window. It held two guns, a .30-30 deer rifle, and a .22 semiautomatic—doubtless the weapon he had used for target practice out back. The .22 would have been used for targets and campground pests because ammunition for it was cheap. The other rifle would have been reserved strictly for deer and its more expensive ammunition would not have been wasted on tin cans and bottles. He lifted down the .22 and as he did he noticed caked dirt on the barrel. He replaced the rifle and checked the .30-30. It was clean. He considered the pair of guns for a moment, then turned for the door. As he did, he saw something on the floor he had missed before, a sheet of paper. When he retrieved it he saw that it bore handwriting. He took it over to the window and held it up to the light:

Dear D:
You cant expect me to live like white trash You already got what you want from me right? I dont have a big company to pay me so please dont make me beg or feel like a whore Id like to say all I need is you but the worlds a tougher place than that isnt it? Let me know soon.
Yours (and I mean it),
J.

He stared down at the initial and tried to think who it might be but no one came to mind.

Where was the envelope? He looked around for a few minutes but no envelope turned up. Maybe Elkins had destroyed it. Or, more likely, he had left it at home and stuck the letter into his pocket. But why had he brought it out here? Or had he just

25

forgotten it was there and let it fall out while changing clothes? And where had the letter been sent? To his home? Risky, since he was married. Left at his place of work? Again, risky. Or she may have brought it here, which meant she might have been here shortly before his death.

Like the magazines, it proved nothing. But it was a place to start.

He carefully placed the letter in his own pocket, justifying himself on the grounds that if it proved to go nowhere, he had at least protected Elkins's wife. Though with a man like Dwayne, she was almost certainly aware of his infidelities.

He locked the camp and stood outside for a few minutes, enjoying the sun. The squirrel was on a limb now, loudly protesting Brady's presence, and a woodpecker was drumming a nearby pine. Everything seemed peaceful, deceptively so. And yet only three days ago Dwayne Elkins had walked out of this camp and been shot dead by someone who should have known better.

Damn it, if that someone had just been anybody but Scotty. Brady could then build a scenario based on murder or, at the least, manslaughter: Elkins had popped into a hunter's sights at the wrong moment. The hunter was someone who bore him a grudge, a person who had been cheated by the dealership, a boyfriend of Elkins's mysterious *J...* But Scotty had no motive at all. It was as if he were the instrument of an inscrutable fate.

He started back down the trail, his eyes on the ground. Not that he expected to find anything, but you could never tell. *Maybe,* he thought somberly, *the hypothetical killer had dropped a signed confession.*

It was ten minutes after he started out that he realized the danger of letting his mind wander while he was on unfamiliar ground. Because when he looked around him he realized he hadn't come this way. He vaguely recalled a fork in the trail; he must have taken the wrong direction. There were fewer hardwoods here, the occasional oak and sycamore giving way to exclusively longleaf pines. Ahead was another fork, and he decided to follow his innate sense of direction and take the trail to the right. Surely it led eventually back to where the car was parked.

26

Except that after another half mile he seemed more lost than ever.

Hell. He should have known. Matt always said that in the woods you backtrack instead of taking unfamiliar shortcuts.

Well, the good thing was he couldn't be more than a mile from the road no matter what. He'd beat around looking for it and waste a couple of hours but there was no chance of becoming really lost.

That was when he heard the footsteps in the brush.

He froze, listening. There was silence, and then the steps started again.

An animal? Too big for an armadillo, he decided. Maybe a wild hog. If so, better to give it a wide berth.

The steps stopped and he had an eerie sensation of being watched. It wasn't an animal. It was human.

He started to call out, and stopped himself. If it was human, why didn't the person hail him? Or had he been followed all the way from the camp?

He took a few cautious steps and halted. A crackling of leaves sounded in the forest. All at once he had the urge to run, get away from whatever it was that was tracking him, but he forced back the panic.

If they meant him harm they could have killed him by now.

Nevertheless, he ought to have a weapon. He scanned the ground for a stick, found one, and bent swiftly to pick it up. As he did so, he heard the steps again, only now they seemed closer, behind and just off the trail.

He stepped forward, turned to check his back, and stumbled against a fallen branch. He went sprawling in the center of the trail, his stick flying out of his hand to land out of reach in the thicket.

The steps were right behind him now, a few yards away, no longer hesitant, but inexorably approaching.

He turned over, hands doubled into fists, and froze.

The man looking down at him smiled. "Are you lost, or are you the Bigfoot we hear so much about?"

5

THE man was in his midthirties, muscular, with dark longish hair and a closely cropped beard. At first, from the khaki shirt, Brady thought he was a ranger. Then he saw the jeans and remembered that Forest Service employees wore green uniforms.

"Here," the man said, reaching out a hand to help Brady up. He watched Brady dust off his clothes, squinting slightly.

"Hey, I know you. You're—"

"Pete Brady, Troy Parish *Express*," the publisher said. And then the other man's name sprang into his mind: "And you're Miller Purdy."

"Mad Miller Purdy," the younger man laughed. "Yeah, you've caught me out. And right when I was about to get one on film."

For the first time Brady noticed the videocam resting on the ground by Purdy's foot.

"Get what?" Brady asked.

"*Picoides borealis,*" Purdy replied. "The red cockaded woodpecker. An endangered species. There're about twenty-five colonies of them in the forest."

"I don't think I've ever seen one," Brady mumbled.

28

"Most people haven't. You have to be looking for them. They're small and fast. You mostly run 'em down by finding their trees; they only nest in mature pines, sixty or seventy feet tall, never in the younger stands. The Forest Service has let the lumber people cut over so much acreage it's a wonder there're nesting stands left at all. But this is my land, here, and I've kept the timber people out. As well as the public as a whole."

"Well, I wouldn't have ended up here if I hadn't been lost," Brady told him. "I guess I took a wrong turn back there."

"No problem," Purdy said. "You're not the kind I worry about. It's more people like Dwayne Elkins and his friends. The kind that like to spotlight their game, shoot guns out of car windows, leave their trash all over the place."

Brady nodded. "Well, I don't think you'll have that problem with Elkins anymore."

"No. And I can't say I'm sorry." He leaned down, picked up his camera. "People around Troy think I'm a little odd, Mr. Brady. I stay by myself in the cabin over there, on the land my family owned, and I don't mix a lot. I've got a degree in biology from SMU, enough of an inheritance to live on, and I write letters to the Forest Service and the Police Jury about environmental issues. In Troy, that makes me a troublemaker. Worse, I won't put up with the likes of Elkins and his friends on my land. That makes me a real public menace."

The editor folded his arms. "You had some run-ins with him?"

Purdy chuckled. "Run-ins? More like a feud. I told him if I caught him trespassing again I'd shoot him and skin his carcass. Just like the carcass of the doe I found on my land in July. I know he shot it. It was a .22 bullet I dug out. It ran all the way to my side before it died. Two laws broken, right there: a doe, out of season, and using a rimfire gun. But I couldn't prove it." Purdy spat in the dust.

"You figure he went hunting with his .22," Brady asked, "or did the doe just walk past the camp while he was out back?"

Purdy shrugged. "Who knows? But I doubt anything living would go anywhere near that place. All Friday I heard him there, morning and afternoon, plinking away with that Marlin of his. He liked to sit out back with a bottle and drink till he was shit-faced, and then, when the bottle was empty, he'd take target practice at it and go inside and get something else." He screwed up his face. "A real sportsman."

"Tell me something," Brady said. "You see or hear anything odd Saturday?"

Miller Purdy's brows rose slightly. "Odd? Saturday? You mean the day Elkins was shot? Well, as a matter of fact no, but then I wouldn't have."

"How so?"

"I was in Natchitoches all day. Didn't get back until late. In fact, I didn't hear about what happened until the next day."

"I see."

Purdy shifted his weight from one side to the other.

"Why? Is there something more to all this? I heard Elkins's death was an accident."

"As far as I know it was," Brady said. "I guess I'm just inquisitive."

Miller Purdy smiled. "I guess that's your job." He shook his head. "Sure didn't like me and I didn't care for him."

Brady started to speak but the other man held up his hand and frowned.

"Hear that? It's the one I was tracking."

The newsman listened, but all he heard was a distant, reedy chirp.

"Well, he's gone now." Purdy hefted the camera. "Come on, I'll show you the trail."

Ten minutes later Brady caught a glint of windshield and saw his car.

"Thanks a lot," he said, sticking out his hand. "And I'm sorry if I scared away the woodpecker."

"He'll come back," Purdy smiled, giving the editor a firm shake. "But if I were you, I'd be careful in the future. Lots of folks out hunting right now. Fellow wandering around on these trails could get killed just like Brother Elkins."

"Yeah," Brady said, watching the other man walk away. "I'll remember."

* * *

30

When he got back to the office he drew a stern gaze from Mrs. R., but he must have radiated a warning, because she said nothing, not even commenting about the mud on his pants. There were some routine matters on his desk and a pay voucher to sign. When he'd finished he rested his chin in his hands, thinking.

Evidently, nobody had liked the dead man. That was what made it so ironic—with everybody who had known Dwayne Elkins to choose from as a possible suspect, it was the one person who had no motive at all who had killed him.

Life was like that: not a Bach fugue, elegantly ordered, with everything in its place, more like hard rock, chaotic and sometimes dissonant. He turned to his bookkeeper.

"Mrs. R., do you know a fellow named Miller Purdy? Lives out near New Gideon?"

"Elmer Purdy's boy," she said with a knowing nod. "Inherited all that money and now he goes around making a fool out of himself."

"So I hear."

"He's against hunting, you know, and he once got arrested for sitting down in front of the Royal Pine gate after they did that big timber deal with the Forest Service. That was before your time, of course. But he spent ten days in jail. He wouldn't even put up his own bail—and they say he's worth a million."

"Where did he get it?" Brady asked. "You say his father was rich?"

Mrs. Rickenbacker smiled thinly. "Elmer Purdy got it by selling timber." Her laugh emerged as a cackle. "Young Miller is living high off the hog on the very thing he says is wrong with everybody else. He's a hypocrite, that's what he is." Her eyes darted around the room, as if she were afraid there might be someone else present. When she spoke again, her voice was a half-whisper.

"And that isn't all he is. I have it on excellent authority that Miller Purdy, for all his put-on about being some kind of Mark Trail, is really—"

The door came open and Ripley Dillon breezed in, slamming it after him. Mrs. R.'s face fell and she turned back to her books. The pair didn't get along and whatever gossip she had been about to impart would have to wait until Ripley was gone.

"Mr. Brady," Ripley half-shouted. He was a thin, curly haired boy with glasses, whose brashness was generally overlooked as enthusiasm. "I was over at the courthouse and I heard something interesting at the DA's."

"Oh?" Brady's belly did a flip. The district attorney, Joe Gant, was a political enemy of Matt's and there was no telling what he might have cooked up.

"I heard Gus Forbes talking to one of the clerks," Ripley went on. "You know Gus—assistant DA's the only kind of job he can get. Couldn't win a case with a guilty plea."

Mrs. R. sucked in her breath and Brady wondered if she might not be distantly related to the hapless assistant prosecutor.

"I know him," Brady said. "Get on with it. What did he say?"

"He said that Gant's calling the grand jury to hear evidence in the Elkins case. Only he called it the *Garitty* case."

It was Brady's turn to flinch.

"Goddamn," he muttered, not caring whether the bookkeeper heard him or not. "Orville Jordan is behind this. If he gets elected sheriff, he and Joe Gant'll have a lock on the parish."

"Always wanted a sheriff who was in the Million Dollar insurance sales club," Ripley cracked.

"Anything else?" Brady asked.

"No. That's it. Isn't it enough?"

"Yeah." Brady thought for a moment, then remembered the letter he had found at the camp. He started to ask Ripley if the dead man was known to have a steady girlfriend, but decided against it, at least so long as Mrs. R. was in hearing distance. Instead, he motioned his two assistants over to his desk.

"Let's work on Thursday's issue," he said.

Within an hour they had come up with a tentative dummy. Where stories had already been written they inserted them, and other spaces they left blank. When they had finished, the front page bore a left-column story about the proposed new state prison west of town, while the all-important right-hand column was blank.

"You *do* intend to put something there, don't you?" Mrs. R. asked.

Before Brady could answer Ripley spoke. "Look, I'll do it, I don't mind. After all, for what I know about Elkins, it won't take much. And the obit on the inside won't be any big deal."

Brady started to nod and then caught himself.

"No," he said. "Thanks. But I'll do it."

He was still staring at a blank page at closing time.

It would have been easy to let Ripley do it, of course. But that would have been taking the easy way out. It wasn't that it was a hard story to write. He'd made several attempts:

LOCAL CAR DEALER DWAYNE ELKINS, 38, WAS KILLED IN A HUNTING ACCIDENT ON SATURDAY, NOVEMBER 24.

That much was simple. It was what followed that he choked on:

SHERIFF'S DEPUTIES SAID ELKINS WAS KILLED BY A BULLET FIRED BY SCOTT GARITTY, SON OF SHERIFF MATT GARITTY.

It was the truth, but it was also an evasion. Brady had been there: Could there be any doubt whose bullet had done the work? Was it excusable to use an impersonal style when he should, as a newsman, give an eyewitness report? But what could he report. He *wasn't* an eyewitness, just one of the first on the scene.

He ignored the lead sentence and went on to the next part:

ELKINS WAS ALONE AND APPARENTLY DID NOT KNOW THERE WERE OTHER HUNTERS IN THE AREA.

No, damn it, he had to say that the man was wearing a safety vest.

He slapped the pencil back down onto the desk and called the hospital, which told him that Dr. McIntire had just arrived to begin his evening rounds.

Well, he thought, *time to go see the coroner.* Maybe there'd be something to report there. After all, it would be the height of

33

irresponsibility to quote the chief deputy on the death bullet if the coroner had another idea.

Brady closed up the office and drove to the hospital. The Christmas lights had been put up and on the lawn three plywood kings stood before a smiling Christ child. Brady took a quick look at the hovering angel, shook his head at the thought of how innocent it all looked, and headed in through the front entrance. He caught up with McIntire outside the Intensive Care Unit.

"Busy night," McIntire said good-humoredly. "Traffic accident on eighty-four and a cardiac from out in Ward Six. What can I do for you, Pete?"

"Just some information," Brady said, following the physician over to the nurses' station. The doctor was a young man whose prematurely gray hair made him seem older than he was. He'd come here a couple of years ago, to replace Doc Sanborn, who had been here forever. People liked him, and when he'd agreed to accept the onerous burden of coroner, the police jury, which was the parish governing board, had been relieved. Now Brady waited while McIntire made a few final notes on his clipboard, then laid it on the counter.

"So," the doctor asked. "Is this about the Elkins business?"

" 'Fraid so. I guess you did an autopsy?"

McIntire nodded. "Under such circumstances there wasn't any choice. You're welcome to a copy of it."

"Maybe you can just tell me what you found."

The physician shrugged. "Sure. Death was due to a high-velocity gunshot wound to the brain. You don't want all the technical language, do you? Struck the right cheek and exited just above the left ear. No bullet, because it went through, but the entrance wound was approximately thirty-five one hundredths of an inch across, give or take a little. In other words, consistent with a .35 caliber weapon."

"Did the bullet fragment?"

"No, it seems to have stayed in one piece."

"What about the angle? The boy was in a deer stand, above Elkins."

"Well, the wound is consistent with that. I mean, Elkins probably had his head bent slightly, his right side toward the stand, when the shot hit him." McIntire frowned. "But look, you were there, weren't you? Is there some doubt about who shot him?"

"I didn't see it," Brady said. "And I guess, technically, there can always be some doubt in a case like this."

The coroner shook his head.

"Not unless there was somebody else with the boy I haven't heard about."

Brady's face fell. "I see. Well, thanks anyway, Doc. Oh, by the way, did you do a check of the amount of alcohol in Elkins's blood?"

McIntire smiled. "No surprise there, either. It was point one two. Not enough for him to be staggering drunk, but just over the legal range for operating a motor vehicle."

"Anything else in his blood?"

"Lots of red cells," McIntire joked. "Hey, maybe if you told me what you suspected I could help you more." He scratched an ear. "But, on second thought, I doubt it. I looked him over pretty good and he was in good health. Overweight, with too much cholesterol in the arteries, but that goes for half the parish. Other than that, he was a perfectly normal physical specimen. Except that he had a .35 caliber bullet hole in his head and a brain that had been destroyed by its trajectory."

Brady frowned. "What about *that,* Doc? Isn't it odd that he managed to go a hundred yards with that kind of wound?"

McIntire nodded. "Odd but not unheard of. He was running on empty, you might say."

"Well, thanks, Doc. I appreciate your help."

"What help?" McIntire asked. He was about to say something else when a nurse hurried up, her shoes clap-clapping on the tile floor.

"Doctor, we just got a call from Debra Pennimen. They're bringing in Miss Maud. She's had an attack."

6

MAUD *Penniman. The aunt of the wife of the dead man.* Well, maybe the strain had been too much for her. What had Laverne Penniman said? *Probably'll have an attack. But not until after the funeral.* Brady decided to wait and see if anything interesting turned up.

Five minutes later a car sped up to the emergency entrance and he watched a pair of nurses rush out with a wheelchair. Debra Elkins came around from the driver's side and helped her aunt from the car into the chair and followed her in.

As the sick woman passed Brady got a look at her face: pale, with her lips pressed tightly together, her expression a mask of pain.

They took her into one of the cubicles and Brady lingered near the admissions desk, waiting for Debra to reappear. When she did he turned away, as if he were just another relative or friend waiting for word on a loved one.

"It's the angina," he heard Debra say. "There was all this with Dwayne and then she went into the office today and . . ."

Her voice caught and he heard the receptionist soothing her.

"I'll get Dr. McIntire to give you something," the woman behind the desk promised. "You poor thing, you've been through so much."

At which Debra buried her face in her hands and began to sob.

Brady tiptoed out of the hospital, making a mental note to drop by the hospital tomorrow and see if Maud was receiving visitors.

The next morning he confronted the blank page again. He toyed with words like "alleged" and "reportedly" and finally gave up. He drove over to the dealership, identified himself to a red-faced, perspiring salesman, and said he was gathering material for an obituary.

The salesman nodded a lot and said that Dwayne Elkins would be missed. No, he had no idea what changes would be made. It had always been a family run operation, with Dwayne only getting the job because he'd been a salesman here when he'd met Debra. As for Mr. Laverne, he was content to take his cut and stay in Natchitoches. No, he didn't know anything about the finances; Miss Maud handled that, but he was sure the business would stay open and anytime Brady wanted to trade in his old Ford . . .

Brady thanked him and started out, passing a petite, brunette woman who was headed in. He got into his car and waited a minute, watching through the big plate-glass window. The woman, who looked not over thirty, was talking to the salesman and he saw the salesman shrug. Brady started his car and drove out to Penelope Martingale's place, on the north edge of town.

She was waiting on the porch as he pulled up, dressed in the kind of long skirt that was popular in the sixties, her graying hair in Indian braids.

"How did I know you were coming?" she asked, letting him kiss her cheek.

"Telepathy, I guess," Brady said, playing the game.

Penelope held the door open for him and her big yellow cat ran in ahead of them.

"Oh ye of little faith. Come in and have some orange pekoe. Your aura's a little dim. You must be working on that terrible business about Matt Garitty's son."

Brady started to ask how she knew but realized it didn't take a psychic. "When else do I come see you?" he asked.

"When indeed? And after all we've been through. That whole business with Cory Wilde. So sad."

Brady nodded. A year or so ago Penelope had rented a house to an ex-convict, despite the collective wisdom of the town. And she had been right, though it hadn't helped Cory Wilde any.

He relaxed against her sofa while she went into the back for the tea. One end of the room was a virtual greenhouse, with a jungle of plants and shrubs, many of which, Brady knew from experience, were medicinal. Penelope was what would have been called a witch in the old days. Now she was simply regarded as an eccentric, a spinster of odd proclivities. What fewer realized was that, beneath the talk of spirits and auras, there was a shrewd business sense, which had allowed her to start with little and by middle age become comfortably off.

She returned with the tea and sat down across from him on the ottoman, her knees almost touching his.

"You know," she began, "when it happened I was so sad. I felt a dissonance, the kind of break in the universal harmonics that happens when something is terribly wrong. I still feel it."

"I feel it, too," Brady said, sipping his tea. "That's why I'm looking into it."

"Yes. I thought you would be."

Brady sighed. "You see, Matt wants me to prove his son didn't do it."

Penelope nodded. "Of course." She leaned forward, touching him lightly on the knee. "Peter, don't expect too much. When I said something was out of the ordinary I didn't mean Scott didn't shoot Dwayne Elkins. Just that Elkins was the kind of person who attracts trouble. Sometimes the innocent are instruments of retribution."

"Maybe so," the editor allowed. "But that's not really why I came to see you, Pen. I came because I was wondering how the dealership is doing these days."

Penelope blinked and then smiled.

"Peter, you never cease to surprise me." She turned her cup

around in her long, thin fingers. "Well, you know it isn't a public issue. It's always been a family business, ever since old Garth Penniman founded it in the twenties. When he died his son Jack managed it. He and his wife were killed in that terrible car crash about ten years ago. That's when Dwayne Elkins took over. He was just a salesman then, but he was married to Debra. He wasn't even thirty years old. I remember there was a lot of talk about somebody that young running the business, but Maud kept the books. I guess they figured she'd keep him from making any bad mistakes."

"You think she was successful?"

Pen chuckled. "I doubt it. Even a person as strong as Maud can't win out against stupidity. One day she was walking past the house here and we stopped and talked. She said the doctor had ordered exercise for her heart problem. I remember thinking a weak heart's a small obstacle compared with somebody like Dwayne Elkins. None of those Elkinses was very smart. But you've got to realize I'm not tuned in to all the gossip in this town. For that you'd do better to talk to your own Mrs. Rickenbacker. Or that old fool, Emmett Larson."

Brady sipped on his tea, letting the silence fold over them. At last Penelope spoke again.

"But you know the American car industry is sick. The only dealerships that are making any money are the ones selling imports. GM is on the skids and Ford isn't all that healthy, either."

"And Troy-Penniman hasn't ever considered imports?"

"Do you see any Toyotas in their lot?"

Brady got up, smiling.

"Thanks, Pen. You always help put things into perspective."

"I don't know how. You're a total unbeliever when it comes to the other spheres."

"Not an unbeliever. Just an agnostic," he said, moving toward the front porch. He halted: "By the way, do you know Miller Purdy?"

"A fine young man," Penelope averred. "Naturally, people around here think he's odd."

"Right."

Brady went back to the office. Mrs. R. raised her brows meaningfully and Brady knew she was letting him know there was nothing more anyone could do about tomorrow's issue until he wrote the story on the Elkins affair. Gritting his teeth, Brady sat down and forced his pencil to spell out the few essential facts:

DWAYNE ELKINS, LOCAL CAR DEALER, WAS SHOT SATURDAY IN AN APPARENT HUNTING ACCIDENT. THOUGH WEARING A SAFETY VEST, ELKINS, WHO HAD A CAMP NEAR THE FOREST BOUNDARY, WAS IN AN AREA WHERE THE UNDERGROWTH IS ESPECIALLY THICK. SHERIFF'S OFFICERS QUESTIONED A JUVENILE IN CONNECTION WITH THE INCIDENT. THIS WAS THE SECOND HUNTING FATALITY REPORTED STATEWIDE SINCE DEER SEASON OPENED EARLIER THIS MONTH.

He ripped the sheet from the yellow pad and slapped it down on Mrs. Rickenbacker's desk.

"Please input this," he said, turning around before she could react. On the next sheet he scribbled out a purely pro forma biography of Dwayne Elkins, leaving blanks where he lacked data.

"You can call the funeral parlor for the rest of this," he said and went out the front door. Standing alone in the sunlight, he realized his right hand hurt. When he looked down he saw he was still gripping the pencil. He forced his fingers to relax and put the pencil in his pocket.

So what was wrong with his story? Scotty was a juvenile and hence entitled to protection, even if everyone in the parish knew who was meant.

That night he drove the dummy to Alexandria, sixty miles away. When he'd bought the *Express* he'd learned that the day of the small-town printing shop was past and the weekly issues were jobbed out to a printing operation in the city, which handled the work of a number of other weeklies. So each Wednesday evening, whenever the master copy was finished, he drove south to leave it at the printer's. The first year he was here he'd had Kelly to go with him. They'd take a room at the elegant old Bentley, Alexandria's historic hotel, built by a timber baron in the early days of the century. Since she'd been at the university, in Baton Rouge, the Bentley usually served as a meeting place, where they could spend the night before each hurried back to their respective work the next morning.

Now he felt especially lonely, boring through the dark tunnel of highway with pine forest on either side. It was so damned important for her to get that degree, and he wondered if the degree really meant much at all. Or was it just an excuse for distancing herself after the unhappy marriage that had caused her return to Troy three years ago? It was only a few weeks after her return that she'd met Brady, and in a short time they'd become lovers. Then, though, she'd left for Baton Rouge to work on her degree. He had tried to discuss it with her but she had always deflected him.

"You got something against professionalism, Brady?" she had asked and there was nothing more to say.

So he had tried to ignore it and live with the situation, but at times like this his insecurity came to the fore. He was so much older than she, he could hardly believe she had fallen in love with him to begin with. And now she was down at the university, among twenty-four thousand other students and God knew how many eager male faculty, some of whom doubtless preyed on beautiful graduate students.

Damn. It was not a good time to indulge his frustrations. He had to keep his temperament on an even keel if he was going to help Matt at all.

But what good, really, could he expect to do?

Pen had said it right: "Sometimes the innocent are instruments of retribution."

So all Brady was really doing was spinning his wheels. Because he could rake up dirt on Dwayne Elkins, but in the end what would it prove? Facts were facts and the fact was that a bullet from Scott Garitty's gun had killed Elkins. There was nothing different in this case than in any of the others that happened. Except for one thing. Matt was his friend. But even Matt would have to bow to the truth.

God, how was he going to get him to accept it?

It was eleven-thirty when Brady came off the Pineville bypass and onto US 71. The two lane wound past Forest Service headquarters and the first site of the state university, where a retired army officer named Sherman had served as superintendent for a few months until called to the army again in the Civil War. At eleven-thirty-five Brady crossed the Red River on the old bridge and emerged onto the floodplain.

The town was named for the infant daughter of a man named Fulton, who, early in the last century, had set up a trading post and gotten the Indians so far in debt they were forced to sell him their land. His daughter had died the year before and he had named his new town in her honor. A melancholy story on all counts, Brady reflected, turning left toward the business district of Alexandria.

Half an hour later he had finished with the printer. The copies would be printed overnight and delivered tomorrow. Except, he realized, checking his watch, it already *was* tomorrow.

He thought about the long trip back and drove down the soft-lit streets to the Bentley. He found a parking place in front and went up the steps and into the ornate lobby. From central fountain to mosaic floor to marble columns, Brady had always considered the hotel a monstrosity. And for that very reason it had always seemed a special place for Kelly and him—a structure too baroque to be true, hence an ideal fantasy setting.

He went to the desk and the clerk greeted him by name.

"A room for tonight, Mr. Brady?"

Brady exhaled. "Yeah. I don't guess—"

"Haven't seen her," the clerk said, handing Brady the registration card.

The publisher filled in the required information, handed the clerk his Visa card, and took the key. He was already in the elevator when he looked at the number on the key. His heart did a little jump: It was the room he and Kelly had first used, almost three years ago.

The elevator stopped and he emerged into a maroon-painted hallway. He came to the room, inserted his key, and went inside.

He had just turned around, after flipping on the light, when he realized there was a naked woman on the bed.

42

7

KELLY giggled, enjoying his surprise.

"I asked the clerk to give you this room and call me when you were on the way up. It was worth twenty dollars just to see your face."

Brady coughed, unable to tear his eyes away from her bare form, knowing how much he wanted her, yet still unable to believe she was here.

"I . . . You're going to catch cold," he said finally.

Kelly stretched, her black hair spreading to reveal one breast.

"I love it when you're like this," she said. "Well, I could put on some clothes."

Brady tried to suppress a leer.

"Well . . ."

"After all, you're tired, I know, and it was a long day, and then you had to make that drive and—"

"Oh, shut up," he ordered, flicking out the light and moving toward the bed.

* * *

Afterward, he lay back, staring at the ceiling, her head pillowed on his shoulder.

"You really shouldn't do that to me," he said. "I might have a coronary."

"Don't you want to die happy?" She ran her fingers through the hair on his chest. "Besides, I think there's some life in the old boy yet."

She touched him in a particularly sensitive spot and laughed when he jerked.

"I didn't want you to stay mad at me," she said. "And, besides, I couldn't wait till the weekend."

"It could always be a weekend," he said, and quickly added, "after you get the thesis in."

"Yes," she said, and looked away quickly.

"Kelly . . ."

She shifted onto an elbow, so that her hair fell down onto his shoulder.

"How's Matt getting along?" she asked, and he knew she wasn't going to discuss it with him any further, at least not now.

"I haven't seen him for a day or so. But it's hurting him. He's worried about Scotty. He seems to be acting like nothing happened."

"That *is* bad. The boy needs to talk it out."

"I agree. It's a bummer all the way around." He told her about his story and saw her nod gravely as he talked.

"You keep asking yourself if you wouldn't have written it differently if it had been somebody else," she said, verbalizing his thoughts.

"Hell, I was *there,*" he said, his voice suddenly anguished. "Most of the stories I get these days are somebody's wedding, or the police jury meeting on a new road tax. I take what I'm given and I print it. But here I was, just by blind luck, on the scene. In New Orleans . . ."

The sentence hung half-finished.

"But this isn't New Orleans," she said softly. "And this isn't the *Picayune.* Isn't that what Matt's been trying to drum into you all this time? Sure, in New Orleans you'd have gotten statements from everybody there and added your own observations, and maybe you'd even have won another Pulitzer. But is that what you really want? Is that why you came to Troy?"

Silence again and then he sighed.

"Good question. And I don't know the answer. I just know I didn't stop being a journalist when I bought the *Express.*" Then he told her about Matt's request.

"You see? Matt doesn't want me to stop being one, either."

"Matt wants you to walk on water," Kelly said in a flat voice. "It doesn't have anything to do with journalism."

"No, I guess not. I guess I just have this old-fashioned notion that a good journalist turns over all the stones and eventually the truth emerges."

"That *is* old-fashioned," she chided. She touched his lip with a finger.

"Listen to me, Brady, you care about Matt and Scotty because they're your friends, and I wouldn't want you any other way. But there're some things you can't do, even for them. What happened, happened, and just because you got a Pulitzer for crime reporting, Matt can't expect you to prove the impossible. You know, he's got as much of a problem accepting this as Scotty."

"I guess. But it's not so simple. I mean, I was with Scotty at the range. Matt trained us both. The boy knows a man from a deer."

"The range is one thing," she said. "I've been in those woods. Your imagination—especially if it's an active one—can play all kinds of tricks."

Brady thought of the image he had almost convinced himself he had seen and nodded.

"Maybe."

"So do what you can, but don't buy into something that can't work out," she advised. "And especially not right now; I still have plans for you tonight."

She touched him and his body responded. He turned to her, feeling her hardened nipples against his bare chest. His mouth came against hers, their tongues met, and she rolled slowly over onto her back, inviting him.

45

He looked down at the pale outline of her face, barely limned by a pencil of light falling through the curtains.

"By the way," he asked, "did you know Dwayne Elkins was having an affair?"

She groaned, shaking her head in dismay. "I couldn't even say if Pete Brady is having one."

The next morning he forced himself awake, hating the thought of the hour's drive back alone. He lay in bed, listening to her shower in the bathroom, and finally swung himself to sit on the edge of the bed.

He resented having to get up, resented having to go back to Troy, resented her leaving. Of course, he'd see her again tomorrow night and they'd be together for the weekend, but sometimes he felt like a truck driver, always on the move, with no time at all.

The shower stopped and Kelly came out of the bathroom, wrapped in a towel.

"Well, he's finally up." She went to the closet and began to take out her clothes.

He watched her tall form, with the long hair splayed down her back.

"Come here," he said, aroused once more at the sight of her smooth flanks and firm breasts.

"No time for that," she said over her shoulder. "I've got to be back to teach a class at ten-thirty and it's almost eight. Jeff had a sinus operation and I promised I'd take over for him. I *am* his assistant, after all."

Jeff, Brady sneered inwardly. Well, maybe the operation wouldn't take. Maybe . . . Then he caught himself: That was a hell of a way to feel. He'd never even met the man yet he was as jealous as a fifteen-year-old kid. All because Jeff was Kelly's adviser and had an access to her Brady lacked.

He reached for his own clothes and dressed. Then he put his hand out for the change he'd left on the bedside table and his eyes came to rest on something odd.

It was the little chrome-colored object with the bullet dent, that he had found at the camp. He'd been carrying it around in his

46

pocket ever since, unsure what to do with it. He picked it up and turned it over in his fingers. Yes, it definitely had two sides. Or was it simply that it had been round once, before the bullet had done its work?

"What's that?" Kelly asked, coming over to pick up her gold necklace. "A lucky charm?"

"I'm not sure what it is," he said. "I found it at the Elkins camp."

She took it from him and held it up to the light.

"You think this means something?"

"Probably not. Just another straw I was reaching for."

She nodded good-humoredly. "Well, good luck, whatever it is." As he watched her put the rest of her things in her overnight bag it suddenly came to him how very tired he was.

When he reached Troy it was just after nine. He didn't feel like facing the office so he drove over to the hospital and asked for Maud Penniman's room. The old woman was watching a television quiz program with her niece when he came in.

They both looked surprised to see him.

"Is this about some kind of remembrance for Dwayne?" Debra asked, her voice quavery. She wasn't a bad looking woman, Brady reminded himself, just a little washed-out, with hollows under her eyes. Not surprising, considering what she'd been through.

"Well, I do always like to get as much as I can," he said. "And I didn't know your husband very well."

Maud's lips pursed and Brady sensed that she was biting her tongue.

"But how did you know I was here?" Debra asked.

"Oh, well, you weren't at home," Brady equivocated.

Debra nodded vaguely. "Of course. Ever since Aunt Maud had her attack—"

"I'm fine," Maud said then. "Nothing to concern yourself about, I told you. I have them two or three times a year. I guess one of these days the old heart will quit . . ." She gave a half-smile. "But not for a while yet. It was all my fault for forgetting my medicine, anyway."

47

"You poor thing, you've spent all your time trying to take care of us, arranging the funeral and—"

"Now, somebody had to do it. I was happy to be there," Maud declared.

Debra got up and walked to the window.

"We met in high school, you know. Dwayne was quarterback on the all-state team back in nineteen seventy. He could have had any girl he wanted."

Maud's eyes darted to Brady's, held for a second, and he knew what she was thinking: He probably *had* had any girl he'd wanted.

Debra twisted a handkerchief. "It was really a kind of storybook thing. I always thought I was the luckiest girl alive." She sniffed. "Until now."

"Now stop that," Maud ordered. "It won't do a bit of good. Dwayne's gone and you're young yet, plenty young to find somebody else."

Debra gave a little sob and Maud sighed.

"I know it sounds terrible but you'll get over it. Life does go on."

Brady turned to the sick woman.

"What about the dealership," he said, "will it go on?"

"My father founded it in 1925," Maud said. "That was over sixty-five years ago. It definitely will go on, as long as I have a breath of life."

"It's in pretty healthy shape, then?" Brady asked, trying to sound nonchalant.

"You tell me a business in this part of the state that's in good shape," Maud countered. "We were in a depression even before oil collapsed. But we'll make it." She reached over, took her niece's hand and squeezed it. "We'll make it just fine. After all, I don't think people are willing to give up their cars and start walking anytime soon."

Brady smiled. "Never thought about selling foreign cars?"

"Pshaw," Maud muttered. "And have to get parts from Japan all the time? And look at those things. I rode in one the other day, one of those little bugs not much bigger than a bicycle. All I could think about was what would happen if somebody hit us."

"Yes," Brady agreed. "There's that."

Maud straightened until she was sitting upright and Brady could tell he'd touched a nerve.

"There has to be somebody with class in this town," she continued. "I may drive a gas guzzler but when people see it they know who I am."

"That's for sure," said a male voice from over Brady's shoulder. The editor turned and saw Laverne Penniman, with another man just behind him.

"Last time I saw you on the streets," Laverne went on with a grin, "people were running for their lives."

"Now that is a lie," Maud declared, but Brady thought her voice was noticeably softer. "In forty-odd years of driving I've never gotten a traffic ticket."

"No," Laverne laughed, "the cops are all afraid of you." He bent down and pecked her cheek. "But I'd better shut up." He winked at Brady. "You don't ever want to get on Aunt Maud's bad side."

"*Laverne!*" the sick woman complained.

"Just trying to get you well," Laverne told her. "I figure if I get you mad enough you'll get up out of that bed and—"

"You see what I have to put up with," Maud told Brady, but the editor thought there was pride in the way she said it. Laverne was clearly her favorite.

"Well," she asked, sighing, "did you at least bring me some cigarettes? You know they won't let you do anything in this hospital. Not even a cup of coffee in the morning. Just that old decaffeinated stuff. Ugh."

Laverne shook his head sadly. "No, all I brought you was Mr. Steptoe here. Mr. Steptoe's from Natchitoches, helps me with my business affairs. He's—"

The other man came forward quickly, a business card in his hand.

"Arthur Steptoe," he said quickly, "of Givens, Lovett and Steptoe. You may have heard of us."

"No," Maud declared, "but you look like a lawyer."

Mr. Steptoe blinked, obviously taken aback. He was short, with a Fuller-Brush moustache, and closely set eyes.

"Yes ma'am."

"There're some things—family business—that Mr. Steptoe

agreed to help with," Laverne said. "If Mr. Brady would excuse us?"

"Sure," Brady agreed, secretly sorry he couldn't stay and hear what was about to be said.

He started for the door but Maud's voice caught him before he could leave. "Mr. Brady, that poor boy, the one who fired the shot, how is he? I hope this doesn't ruin him for life. It wasn't really his fault—these things happen all the time."

"Now, Aunt Maud, that's something I was talking to Arthur about," Laverne said. "He says there's a serious question of liability."

"Oh, for heaven's sake," Maud said.

Brady closed the door behind him, feeling slightly sick. That was all Matt needed: a lawsuit instigated by a greedy lawyer.

He turned the corner into the lobby and almost bumped into a woman. He mumbled an apology and watched her hurry past. It was five seconds before he realized it was the young woman he had seen go into the dealership as he was leaving.

What the hell was she doing here?

Well, it wasn't a large town. Somebody could have business at both the dealership and the hospital. But there was something furtive about the way she had rushed by him.

Why did he suspect she might be the mysterious *J*?

He started after her, passing the IC unit and ending up in the Emergency Room. Now he was sure she was evading him, because even as he watched she went out the automated doors of the emergency entrance and into the parking lot. He let her have a few more seconds, then went out himself in time to see her head up the street, around the side of the hospital, toward the front parking lot.

Brady ducked back inside, ignoring the stares of the nurses, and walked quickly back down the hallway to the front lobby. She was getting into a gray Plymouth in the second row and as she backed out of her place he went out into the lot and got into his own vehicle, to follow.

She jumped through the stop sign, into the street, and then turned right at the traffic signal. Brady slammed into reverse, almost nicking an Olds, and then spun after her. Even in the business district she was accelerating, and he caught a glimpse of her as she sped up the overpass that crossed the train tracks.

Brady edged the speedometer up to forty, cursing as a bread truck emerged from a side street to block his way. He toiled up the overpass, found an opening on the straightaway, and passed, ignoring the double yellow line. She was headed for the highway now, but he'd had a little luck of his own—a log truck had blocked her, giving Brady a chance to close the distance.

Then, unexpectedly, the log truck pulled to the side of the road and she zoomed past, leaving Brady to stomp his own accelerator pedal.

He took the curve by the lumber yard at forty-five, bouncing dangerously on the railroad tracks, and saw her half a mile ahead, leaving him steadily behind. His own speedometer went to fifty, then sixty, and sixty-five. The car had just started to vibrate when a warning siren blasted behind him and he cursed under his breath. He eased off the pedal, recognizing the flashing lights in his mirror as a sheriff's cruiser. His tires crunched onto the gravel shoulder and he glided to a halt. The deputies got out and Brady fumbled for his wallet, to get out his license.

One of the deputies leaned down, smiling.

"In kind of a hurry, aren't you, Mr. Brady?" His name tag said Larkins and Brady remembered seeing him around the courthouse.

"Yeah, I'm sorry," Brady said, extracting his license and holding it out.

Larkins waved it away.

"That's not why we stopped you," he said. "We were just trying to catch up with you to give you this."

He handed Brady a folded sheet of paper.

"Grand jury subpoena," the deputy said with barely veiled disgust. "They're meeting tonight."

8

IT was seven-thirty that night when District Attorney Joe Gant came out of the grand jury room and greeted Pete Brady.

"Appreciate your coming, Pete," he drawled, a toothpick dangling from under his brown moustache. "I hope you understand about all this: Just want to protect the rights of everybody involved."

"I've been to grand juries before," Brady said tersely.

"Sure you have," Gant nodded. He was a medium-size man of fifty, whose belly slopped over his belt, and the Hawaiian shirt made him look like he belonged on the beach. "Down in New Orleans. You probably know all about grand juries."

He led Brady through the doors into the jury room.

Brady nodded to the jurors, who lounged in their chairs showing varying degrees of boredom. A few smoked and a couple chewed gum, but most simply looked resigned. Brady counted fifteen present, which meant the other nine had managed somehow to dodge the summons. Agreement by any twelve was needed for an indictment, and since the district attorney ran the proceeding, it meant that his satisfaction was usually a foregone conclusion.

The clerk, a woman Brady knew only slightly, administered the oath, and asked Brady his name. Brady replied and took his seat. Across the room, half-asleep, slumped the assistant district attorney, a man named Gus Forbes, whose main job seemed to be making coffee for the office staff.

"Now," Gant declared, clearing his throat, "I'm sure everybody here knows Mr. Brady, from the *Express*. I've called Mr. Brady because he was on the hunting trip where the fatal event, the shooting of Dwayne Elkins, happened. It's your duty, as jurors, to decide, after hearing everything, what happened and whether there was likely any criminal negligence involved. But I'll get to that later. Just want to say now you're here as much to protect the innocent as punish the guilty. That's why I called you in the first place. Something happens, especially involving somebody as prominent as Sheriff Garitty, lots of rumors start. People believe what they want. For the sake of protecting everybody involved, it's best to do things in a legal way. Sheriff Garitty understands that. And so does Mr. Brady. As you know, in this state the witnesses are asked to appear without legal counsel, except in a case where they're actually under suspicion of something. Since Mr. Brady isn't accused of anything, he doesn't come with counsel."

He gave the editor a nod and then turned to face him.

"For the jurors, Mr. Brady, would you mind telling just where you were on the morning of Saturday, November twenty-fourth, at, say, ten o'clock?"

Brady took a deep breath. He'd been before a couple of grand juries in New Orleans, in connection with criminal investigations, and each time had refused to reveal his sources. He'd been calm, firm, and unwavering then, so why was he starting to tremble now?

"I was in a deer blind, south of town, in the National Forest." He hoped they didn't see his nervousness.

"Are you a hunter, Mr. Brady?" the DA asked mildly.

"I never have been. Never cared for it, that is." He sensed the curious eyes of the jurors probing him. He was sure the men on the panel were all hunters and his reluctance to hunt would only confirm whatever suspicions they already harbored of him as an outsider.

"So why did you decide to go hunting last Saturday?" Gant persisted, leaning back against the green, flaking wall.

"I . . . Well, that is, Matt Garitty and I had discussed it and . . . Well, I thought I ought to try my hand—"

"Think you'd have tried it without Sheriff Garitty encouraging you?"

"I don't know. Maybe. Maybe not."

"You own a rifle, Mr. Brady?"

"No. Matt loaned me one."

Gant chewed the toothpick thoughtfully.

"You know how to use it?"

"He took me out to the range. With his son. We went out there three or four times and practiced."

"Practiced," Gant said approvingly. "What you shoot at?"

"Targets," Brady said, and a ripple of amusement ran through the jurors.

"Yeah. Didn't reckon you shot at your own feet. I mean what kind of targets?"

"Matt had gotten some plywood and had somebody cut out outlines of deer, and also some outlines of people and livestock. They popped up different ones, so we'd learn to tell the difference between them."

Gant nodded. "And?"

"I hit the wrong ones at first a couple of times but I managed to learn the difference," Brady said dryly.

"Glad to hear it," the lawyer said. "And Scott Garitty?"

"He was better than I was," Brady said. "I mean, he didn't take as long to tell the difference. He could snap off a shot and . . ." He stopped, suddenly aware of the way it sounded.

"Yes?" Gant urged. "Go ahead. You said he could snap off a shot."

"Well, I just mean he was more certain than I was. He'd been hunting before. Small game."

"Umm."

"And we both went through the NRA safety course," Brady added quickly, sensing that many on the jury would be members of the gun organization.

54

"Right." Gant walked slowly to the other side of the room and then turned quickly. As an observer Brady would have considered it clumsy courtroom theatrics, but it caught him by surprise and he felt sweat trickling down his back.

"Let's get back to the hunting blind. This was National Forest, you say."

"I think Matt, that is, Sheriff Garitty, has a hunting lease on that particular strip."

"He assigned the stands you'd each take?"

"Correct. He was at one end, Scotty was in the middle, I was on the other end. But the trail curved, so it was more like a triangle, with Scotty at one point and Matt and I each at a corner of the base. There are a lot of game trails and Matt said it was about as likely deer would come from one direction as from another. He'd put out some grain as bait, to attract them."

"Yes, I think everybody here knows the procedure." The DA exchanged a smile with several of the jurors.

"These stands, they were how far apart?"

"Maybe two or three hundred yards for each one," Brady estimated.

"Okay. Now tell us what kind of day it was."

One of the jurors on the front row, a man named Payne, shook his head.

"Come on, Joe, everybody knows what kinda day it was. Can we get on with this?"

Gant chuckled, but Brady saw that his timing had been disrupted and breathed a prayer of gratitude.

"Charlie, lemmie ask the questions, okay?" Gant said, with a sterile attempt at humor. "You'll get your chance." He turned back to Brady. "Want to answer the question?"

"It was cold," Brady said. "And there was a fine rain. It was a lousy day."

"Sounds like it. How was visibility?"

"Poor. My glasses kept fogging."

A few jurors laughed. Gant managed a smile.

"Scott Garitty wear glasses?"

The question threw Brady and he had to think. "No," he said finally. "He doesn't."

"Well, did you see any deer?"

"I . . . No. Nothing."

"Nothing at all. No animals of any kind?"

"A few birds. I guess. I don't really remember."

"People? You see any people?"

"Not until I came down, after the shot."

"What time was that?"

Brady hesitated, wondering if Gant was readying to spring a trap. "About ten o'clock," Brady answered.

"You fire any shots?"

"No."

"Anybody else in your group fire any, except the boy?"

"No."

"Any other shots from nearby, say, either before or after?"

"None that I heard."

Gant nodded. "But you did hear a shot. Where did it come from?"

"From my left," Brady said. "Then I heard somebody yelling. It sounded like Scotty, so I came down out of the stand."

"Yelling," the lawyer repeated, then faced Brady melodramatically. "What was he yelling exactly?"

"Well—"

"Think carefully, Mr. Brady. This is important."

Brady frowned. The truth was that he hadn't thought about it since the shooting. Everything prior to the accident had been submerged by the horror of the event itself and now, for the first time, he tried to resurrect Scotty's words.

"Well," he began hesitantly, "I think he was saying something about getting one. I don't remember his exact words."

"Getting one. Like, 'I got one,' maybe? Something like that?"

"Something like that."

"You sure? He didn't say, 'I got something'? Or 'I got a deer'?"

Brady shook his head, helpless. "No. I mean, definitely not a deer. Maybe 'something.' "

"How about," Gant suggested, " '*I got somebody*'?"

56

Brady gulped. "No. He didn't say that."

"You're certain of that?" the district attorney demanded, finger aiming at Brady like an accusation.

"Yes."

"From three hundred yards away, you can swear under oath, he didn't say those words."

"I'm not swearing to his words," Brady said in a low voice, anger starting to take over. "I'm only swearing to what I heard. Like you say, it was three hundred yards away."

"Fair enough," Gant agreed. He then led Brady through a recapitulation of the discovery of the dead man and asked a few questions about Brady's observations at the death scene. Just at the point where Brady was afraid he would start prying about Matt's refusal to believe what had happened, though, the DA gave a final nod and thanked him.

"The grand jury can now ask any questions it wants," Gant said.

The men and women in the chairs looked at Brady with a combination of curiosity and weariness. At last the man on the front row, Payne, raised a hand.

"Mr. Brady, you didn't hear anybody say they *meant* to kill Dwayne, did you?"

Brady managed a smile, aware that Payne was on his side.

"No. Of course not."

The newsman snuck a glance at the DA, who looked surprisingly unruffled by the question. Then a man in the back spoke: "You against hunting?"

Brady shot a look at Gant for help but the DA's back was to the jury and he was busy picking his teeth.

"Well, no," Brady managed. "I've just never liked to do it."

"You against guns, too?" the juror persisted. He was a thin, wiry fellow with a droopy moustache whom Brady did not recognize.

"Not guns as a class of things," Brady said. "I don't have much use for assault rifles."

"You want to register firearms?" another man asked, squinting.

"Look," the publisher said, "I'm not against people owning hunting weapons. But I don't see why anybody needs a gun that can knock down a house, or why anybody can't wait a couple of days after they place an order for a gun. Or why there shouldn't be a law requiring people to take a course in gun handling safety."

His clothes were sticking to him now and he wondered how they had managed to stray so far afield.

"What if the communists was to take control of the government?" the moustache demanded. "And you had all the guns locked up?"

The district attorney finally turned back around to face them.

"Okay, okay, we're not here to investigate whether Mr. Brady is a member of the NRA or whether he's got socialistic views. Does anybody else have any questions that are *relevant*?"

The man with the squint shook his head.

"I thought we was supposed to ask the questions, Joe."

"Well, you are and you did." Gant turned to the witness. "Mr. Brady, on behalf of the parish of Troy, and of this grand jury, I want to thank you for coming here tonight. You're excused, but remember that everything that's been said here, including your testimony, is secret and cannot be revealed under penalties of contempt." He winked. "In other words, you can't publish it in the paper."

Brady accepted his handshake and found himself being guided out of the room.

As he came into the anteroom he stopped short.

Matt Garitty and Scott were both standing in the waiting area, and when they saw him their faces went white.

58

9

THE two men shook hands and Brady felt his friend's eyes questioning. Brady gave an apologetic shrug and turned to Scott.

"You doing okay, fellow?"

"Fine, Mr. Brady. I just want to get this over with."

The publisher turned back to Matt Garitty.

"They aren't going to . . . ?"

"He wanted to come," Matt said, "but, no, they didn't subpoena him."

The door to the jury room opened and all at once Gant was there again, motioning to the sheriff.

"Sheriff, you want to step this way?"

"Good luck," Brady said and then walked out into the hallway, through the big glass doors, and into the night.

Five minutes later Emmett Larson, Kelly's father, was listening to Brady's story.

"Of course, I can't talk about the questions they asked," Brady said, "but you can imagine."

"Sure," Emmett agreed. "Loop Wilson, the one with the Wyatt

59

Earp moustache? He's got the brain of a guinea pig. Charlie Payne's okay. He can see through all that political crap. Don't know about the others except in sixty some-odd years here I've learned not to ever overestimate the gullibility of the people of Troy parish."

Brady raised his coffee cup and sipped. They were in Emmett's house, where Kelly had lived before she'd left home to go north, and even now Brady felt closer to her by being here, knowing that if he went down the hallway to the second bedroom he'd see her stuffed animals and Elvis poster and the frilly bedspread.

"Emmett, what I can't figure out is what Gant's up to. He can't mean to indict the boy?"

The old publisher shook his head.

"He'd be a fool. Everybody in town'd jump him for picking on a kid. Naw, way I read it he wants to accomplish two things. One, he wants to make sure what happens is stuck in people's minds real good, with the election just a year away. And second, he wants to come out of this as the fair, upstanding DA who did everything the proper way and made sure a thirteen-year-old kid didn't get railroaded. You know what I mean: 'Terrible accidents happen but you can be sure your son won't get dumped on as a result. Even if his father's a political opponent.' " Emmett took a last draw on his cigarette, then stubbed it out in the ashtray.

"No, Pete. My guess is the grand jury won't do a damn thing. But he may draw it out for a little while. Make Matt worry."

"Bastard," Brady swore. "Scotty and Matt don't deserve that, or Mitzi, either."

"Somebody said human beings don't *deserve* anything," Emmett drawled, stretching. "Is that girl of mine coming up here this weekend?"

"She said so."

"Saw her last night, did you?"

Three years ago Brady would have choked, but he'd come to realize that under the curmudgeonly exterior Emmett Larson was one of the few truly broad-minded people in town.

"Yeah," Brady answered.

Emmett ran a hand through his red thatch, which was finally starting to turn white.

"I don't guess she said anything about her plans after she finished this degree."

"She didn't want to talk about it," Brady said ruefully.

"Damn." Emmett reached for another cigarette, thought better of it, and tossed the pack back onto the table. "Well, I know it's not your doing, Pete. You're the best thing ever happened to that girl. But she's always been that way, sort of wild. Only she calls it independent. I just wish she'd get her act together. You do reckon she's coming back, don't you?"

The question stabbed into Brady like a spear. It was the only question he had been afraid to articulate, always preferring to pretend the issue was settled between them.

"Well, I expect so," he said lamely. "She hasn't said anything else."

Emmett reached over to pat the younger man's shoulder.

"Well, it'll work out."

"Yeah."

When Brady left he drove around for a while, trying to avoid going home. He wondered if Matt was still with the grand jury. Then he thought of the lawyer who had showed up with Laverne Penniman. That was all Matt and Mitzi needed, a lawsuit for wrongful death. He felt guilty because he hadn't come up with anything, but what was there to come up with? The Christmas lights hanging over the streets belied his feelings of hopelessness and when he finally went home he lay in bed a long time, agonizing. Four or five years ago he would have drunk himself to sleep. Now, it was different. He had given up drinking for facing reality squarely. Sometimes, like tonight, he wondered if the choice had been worth it.

The next morning Brady woke feeling like a railroad track after a hundred cars of freight. It had turned cooler again and when he opened his front door he had to step back in for a windbreaker.

He drove down to the office, wishing today were Saturday instead of Friday, and attended to a few chores. Mrs. Rickenbacker had asked for the day off and Ripley wasn't due in until afternoon.

Sitting at the desk was more than he could face, so after half an hour he flipped on the recording machine, put the Back Soon sign on the door, and left.

This time he went out to the range, a couple of miles west of town, off Highway 84. He had no idea whether it would be open or not, but there were some cars when he arrived. One of them was a sheriff's cruiser and even as he got out of his car he heard shots.

He went over to the deputy who served as range officer and they exchanged greetings. The range was divided into two parts—a standard half, where shooters could practice using normal bull's-eye targets at different distances, and the half Matt had converted into a practice portion for hunters. It was the first part that was in use by a couple of men Brady recognized as members of Matt's department.

"Time to requalify," the deputy explained. "Everybody waits till the last minute."

Brady tried to smile.

"Look, you wouldn't happen to have a rifle, would you?"

"What kind?" the deputy asked.

"A deer rifle," Brady said. "I wanted to practice some. I'll pay for the ammunition."

The deputy nodded, went over to the patrol car, and came back with a lever action carbine.

"Know how this works?" he asked Brady. "I was going to sight it in myself, but you're welcome to use it." He placed the weapon on the range table, with the action open, and put a box of ammunition beside it. "This ammo is old. I was gonna shoot it all up anyway. But you're welcome to use what you want."

Brady watched him load the weapon.

"This is a .308," the deputy said. "Good deer load. It was developed for NATO back in the early sixties. Idea was everybody would use the same round, so if there was a war in Europe, there wouldn't be problems of supply. The U.S. came out with the M-14 and adopted it and then jumped into 'Nam in a big way and decided to drop the M-14 for the M-16, that fires a smaller, faster bullet. But there are still a lot of .308s around."

The deputy pointed to a knob on the right side of the trigger.

"This is the safety. When you press it in, the weapon's ready to go. Five shots, you need to chamber the first."

"Thanks," Brady said, gingerly accepting the carbine. He walked over to one of the positions, feeling like a man holding a wildcat that might wake up at any second. He took a supine position and raised the weapon so that the end of the range lined up in the sights. This was different from the rifle he'd had on the hunt. The first had been a standard, no-nonsense weapon you had to cock for each shot by pulling back the bolt. This one, while it had to be cocked, was like the Old West rifles you saw in cowboy movies: You just pulled down the lever and it was ready again.

"You want me to start the targets?" the rangemaster asked.

Brady took a deep breath and flicked off the safety. "Please."

He frowned, trying to imagine the way it had been last Saturday, with a low haze that fuzzed everything and a dripping rain. His fingers had gone numb and everything around him seemed painted in unrelieved tones of gray.

The first target popped up at the end of the row, moving slowly toward the corner.

Brady shifted his aim, squeezed the trigger, and then released it before the weapon fired.

His sights showed a cow.

"Good eye," the range officer said. "Next one coming up."

Brady gritted his teeth, waiting.

This one was at the opposite end and even as he swung the weapon over he could see that it was a deer figure. He brought the sights to bear, tracking its motion, and forced himself to fire. The gun slammed back against his shoulder and the bullet thudded into the back dirt two feet from the target.

"Good eye again," the deputy said from behind him. "Don't worry about being off. I need to check the sights myself and there's a little breeze out here."

Brady levered a second round into the chamber and waited.

This time the deer jumped up squarely in front of him and he squeezed off a round that punched a hole right through the painted neck.

63

"Good shooting," the deputy said. "You'd have brought home the venison that time."

Brady tried to shut out of his mind the thought of what the high impact slug would have done to flesh and bone. He chambered the third round.

A cow again and he held fire. Then a deer, which he missed, followed by a deer he grazed.

He worked the lever, chambering the fifth and final cartridge.

The target flew up midway between the center of the course and the right end. He swiveled, started to press the trigger, and stopped midway.

He was looking at a man in camouflage green, with a rifle cradled in his arms. The man was wearing a vest of bright Hunter's Orange.

For an endless moment Brady let the figure ride on his sights, as it moved inexorably toward the end of the alley. As it vanished around the corner he flicked the lever, ejecting the final round.

He drove back to town, feeling worse than ever.

Even he, a rank novice, could tell the difference between a cutout human and a deer.

But, of course, that's all there *were:* cutouts. You couldn't call the range real life.

What the hell was he trying to do? Convince himself of what he wanted to believe, of course. But would that do Matt or Scotty any good in the long run? Wasn't it better to help them confront the truth?

When he got back to the office Matt was waiting for him in the parking lot, his eyes bloodshot and his face unshaved.

"Pete, I just wanted to tell you I understand about last night. I heard you were subpoened."

"Yeah." Brady clenched his fists in frustration. "It's a crappy deal, Matt. If there was anything I could do—"

"Just keep doing what you're doing," the sheriff said firmly. "Have you come up with anything yet?"

Brady shrugged. "I don't know. Maybe. I can't say. Nobody liked the man except his wife. But, damn it, Matt, that doesn't have anything to do with what happened."

"You never can tell," Garitty said. "Keep digging."

"Sure." As Brady watched his friend get back into his car and drive away, he felt particularly hopeless.

Keep digging. Sure. But *where*?

He spent the rest of the day in the office, leaving only to interview one of the merchants about the imminent arrival of Santa. Brady promised to be on hand tomorrow, with camera, and hoped there would be a better Saint Nick this year than the baggy-eyed, red-nosed specimen of last year, who even the kids knew was one of the loafers from the hotel. He also took a call from a member of an antihunting group in Baton Rouge, who wanted to know more about the accident.

"The sheriff's office wasn't very helpful," the woman complained in a nasal voice.

"Well, I don't have anything more than what you heard," Brady said shortly.

"I guess you're a hunter," the woman said.

"Does it matter?"

"Do you know how many people died from gunshot wounds last year? Over twenty thousand."

"Are you against hunting or guns?"

"Do we need either?"

Brady felt his blood pressure rise.

"Hunting's part of the culture up here," he told her. "Boys grow up accepting it as a normal part of life. Game is an important part of the diet."

"And twenty years ago everybody accepted segregation and lynchings," she declared snidely.

"It's not the same thing," he snapped. "People and animals are different, in case you didn't know."

"Yes, they are. Animals don't despoil the environment, commit rape and robbery, or make war."

"Good-bye!" Brady said and slammed down the phone.

Was this the kind of person he needed badgering him? She was as bad as some of the diehards of the NRA.

He went into the room next door, which served as an archive for past issues, and dug out a set of topographic maps for the parish. He thumbed through them until he found the right section for the hunting lease and carried it back into the main office.

The topography hadn't changed much in the quarter of a century since the maps had been made. He saw the green shaded area that was the forest lapping over onto the Elkins and Purdy tracts. Various dashed lines showed where trails led to the camp, the hunting stands, and to what must be Purdy's house, indicated as a small black square at the edge of a clearing.

Purdy was a strange character, living out there all by himself. What did he do for amusement, besides photograph birds and write angry letters?

Still unsure what he was looking for, Brady rolled the map back into a tube and carried it back to the storage room.

At four he called Kelly to see if she'd left yet. He got her on the third ring.

"I'm on my way," she told him.

"Good." He felt better, hearing her voice. "Look, be careful."

"Don't worry. Remember? There's a new interstate all the way from Opelousas to Alec."

"It's a lonely stretch," he said. "So be careful anyway."

He was hanging up the phone when Ripley came through the door.

"Scored another one," he said breezily, holding up an advertising form. "One I've been working on for six months."

"Great," Brady said, trying to show enthusiasm. "Who is it?"

"Troy Sporting," Ripley replied. "They have a new line of rifles and shotguns. I told 'em there wasn't a better time, with Christmas and deer season and . . ." He stopped short, his face flushing. "I'm sorry. I didn't mean—"

"It's okay," the editor said, heaving himself up from his chair. "You did well." He went to the coat hook and took down his windbreaker. "Lock up, will you? I'm going home early."

But instead of going home and listening to the echoes of the empty house, he drove back out toward the hunting tract. Here and there he saw pickups and Land Rovers parked beside the road, where hunters had gone into the woods, and once he saw a pair of men walking back, empty-handed, rifles over their shoulders.

Hunting really was part of the culture and people took it for granted, as an essential element of life. He might as well hit his head against a brick wall as tell people they shouldn't do it.

When he got back at six it was already dark, with a vicious little wind bending the treetops, and he found himself thinking of the streets of New Orleans, with their mixed odors of food and exhaust fumes, and the hurrying shadows that were its people. Suddenly he found himself missing it in a way he found difficult to explain to himself. Finally he decided it was because chaos was a normal aspect of existence in the city, with things happening for no apparent reason and people accepting this as a quality of existence there. But in Troy there was supposed to be order, and when something unpredictable happened it cast doubt on his fundamental assumptions.

He checked his watch: it would take Kelly another hour to get here, so he might as well buy some steaks. He went to the A&P and loaded up with the essentials. A couple of men in jeans were standing in an aisle and one nodded to him. He nodded back and a second later heard the men laugh.

He tensed up, then realized he was being oversensitive. Why had he assumed the men were laughing at him, and his view of hunting? Most people in town didn't even know his views, because he hadn't editorialized them.

The whole business was making him paranoid.

He drove back toward his house, glad that he would soon be seeing Kelly, but still pricked by anxiety over his conversation with Emmett. During their lovemaking she was completely abandoned, but at other times there was always a tiny niche she kept to herself, a secret hideaway for her plans and schemes.

Passing through the intersection by the courthouse, a flash of light caught his eye and he looked down the street, toward the Police Department.

A patrol car was pulling away from the curb, its emergency lights on, and when it zoomed through the intersection behind him he instinctively made a U-turn and headed after it.

Probably nothing important, but long years of habit had taught him never to pass up the possibility of a good story. And since it was a city police car, it meant the call was within city limits.

It raced through the light by the A&P, headed west, and he squeezed after it as the light went amber. It swung into the curve on the edge of town, headed north, then disappeared from view. Traffic blocked him now and there was little he could do but wait until he pulled out of the curve, onto the highway.

A road led left from the highway and into one of the newer subdivisions. On a chance, he turned into it, only realizing after he had done so that it was the subdivision where Matt Garitty lived.

Sudden fear shivered through him.

Why would they be going to Matt's?

He swung right, onto Matt's street, but everything seemed quiet: the house, when he passed, had the usual lights on and all three vehicles—station wagon, pickup, and Matt's unmarked Olds, were in the drive.

Brady came to the turnaround at the end of the street and drove slowly back, away from his friend's house.

It was at the next street that he caught a glimpse of the police flashers.

The cruiser was stopped halfway down the block and Brady strained to think who might live there, but no name came to mind.

He pulled over, across the street, and got out of his car.

These were city cops, he reminded himself, not sheriff's deputies; his relationship with the city force was tenuous, at best. Some of them remembered him from a run-in a year or so before, an episode that had cost the police chief his job. They'd give him the time of day and very little more.

He ambled across, toward the house, the collar of his windbreaker pulled up to shield his neck. The front door of the house was open and light spilled out onto the lawn. Both officers were inside but the hollow voice of the police radio made the night seem alive.

In vain Brady sought for some sign of who lived here. It was a nice house, he noted—not more than ten years old, with closely clipped shrubs and a well-tended appearance.

He came to the door and stopped. One of the policemen was coming out. He stopped short when he saw Brady.

"Who the hell?" he demanded, raising his flashlight, and then lowering it as he recognized the editor. "What are you doing here?"

"Covering the news," Brady said as pleasantly as possible.

"Well, there ain't nothing here for you," the officer snarled. "Just a routine burglary."

That was when the woman came through the door, eyes blazing.

"Routine?" she shrieked, voice teetering on the edge of hysteria. "You call what was done here routine? You call somebody breaking in while I was at the hospital routine? Somebody taking the things that belonged to my dead husband *routine*?"

That was when Brady recognized her.

Debra Elkins.

10

BRADY quickly made his apologies and walked away. There would be time tomorrow to come back and see her and find out what had been taken.

Why would anyone be interested in Dwayne's things?

It was the same question he asked Kelly an hour later, after she had washed off the dust of the road and they had sat down in his living room to eat.

"Honestly, Brady, every time I think you're about to get romantic you manage to come up with some cockamamie question." Her green eyes glittered in the candlelight and he couldn't tell whether she was teasing or whether he'd touched a nerve.

"Well," he asked, tracing a line on the tablecloth with his finger. "Doesn't it seem a little odd to you?"

"Odd? That somebody would wait until they know Debra and the kids are at the hospital and then clean her out? What's odd about that? In case you didn't know, Brady, there are some bad people in this world. Some of them even live in Troy."

"I gather. Look, no need to fight."

"No, of course not. I'm just tired. It's been a hard week and, believe it or not, this business with Matt's affected me, too. God, Brady, you don't know how much I wish you *could* prove Scotty didn't do it. But all this running around seems like just so much grabbing at straws."

"I know," he admitted. "But it's all I've got."

She nodded, her raven hair falling forward as she eyed him over her wineglass. "Well, let's just pretend that tonight all you've got is *me.*"

The next morning he drifted in and out of dreams, listening to her voice. It seemed to be coming from a distance. At first he thought she was talking to him but it seemed too muffled, somehow far away. He turned over to move against her and touched bare sheets.

She was gone.

He dragged himself upright, blinking at the sunlight that slanted in around the corners of the windows. The clock on the nightstand said nine. He had slept almost ten hours.

He relaxed against the pillow, his mind enjoying the memory of last night. After dessert they had danced to big-band music on the stereo and then she had taken his head between her hands and stared into his eyes and when he was about to speak she had touched his lips with her finger and given a tiny shake of her head, as if this were enough, for him not to ask any questions, just to take what was offered. And she had offered everything.

Everything, he thought now, *but an explanation.*

He forced the memories back and heaved himself out of bed.

Her voice was coming from the other side of the bedroom door: She was in the living room, talking on the phone.

He threw a towel around him and padded toward the doorway, rubbing his eyes. She was probably talking to her father. Of course. She hadn't had time to call him last night and he was expecting her today.

He started to open the door and then stopped.

No. There was something about the tone of her voice, something almost furtive.

71

He pulled the door open and she wheeled around, surprised. Her hand went over the mouthpiece and she tried to smile.

"Oh, Brady, you scared me." She lowered her hand. "All right," she said into the phone, her voice still almost too low to be heard. "That's fine. I'll see you then."

She replaced the receiver and tried to laugh.

"I was trying to let you get some sleep. I guess I woke you up, though. I'm sorry."

"Somebody I know?" Brady asked, trying to sound casual.

"Nothing important," she said with a wave of the hand. "Look, I've made you breakfast. Eggs Benedict. I thought I'd try to make you feel at home. It's not exactly Brennan's, but maybe I can come close."

He tried to act grateful and the eggs did taste good, but he wanted to ask her more about the call. Before he could finish eating, though, she was already to the door.

"Have to go somewhere," she said with a wave. "I ought to be back this afternoon."

By the time he got up from the table she was out the door. He watched her go, black hair flowing behind her.

"What's going on?" he called after her, as she opened the door to her car.

"See some folks," she said obliquely and blew him a kiss. He watched her pull out of the drive and disappear down the street.

What the hell was the girl up to? When they'd first met she'd wanted a job on the *Express,* and he hadn't known who she was, because she was using her married name, Maguire. After he'd found out she was Emmett's daughter, she'd insisted on working independently to solve a killing, just to show him that she was competent. Now he wondered if she was working on the Elkins business, just to prove her independence. But what could she be finding that he *wasn't*?

No, it wasn't the Elkins business that was driving her. It was something else, and the more he thought about it the more the answer seemed clear—she'd been talking to someone about a job. That had to be it. She was planning for when she got her degree; planning to leave.

A morose Brady put away the dishes and drove over to the Elkins house. The dead man's children were playing in the front yard, a blond boy and a girl, both grade-school age. Death seemed to be the furthest thing from their minds and he wondered if it had registered yet. No, that would come later, probably in adolescence, when they most needed a father's help. At least, that was how it had been for him.

He went up to the door and was about to knock when they squeezed in ahead of him to shout his arrival.

Debra appeared at the door, dark smudges under her eyes. "Mr. Brady. What's this about?"

"The business last night," he explained. "I'm sorry to bother you but it seemed odd. I know the police have looked into it, but I was wondering if there was anything that came to mind since then?"

"I wouldn't know," she said wearily. "Except that they mainly seemed interested in Dwayne's things. He has a sort of little office set up in the den and they wrecked it. The police said it was probably some drug addicts who knew I was at the hospital. You'd think people would have more decency. How much do they think one family can stand?"

"I'm sorry," he said.

"You can come in if you want," she said suddenly. "I've got some coffee on the stove. I've been drinking it ever since . . . to stay awake, you know? Everybody keeps telling me to sleep, but I don't want to. I guess I'm afraid of what will happen if I do."

He walked inside, noting that the living room appeared to be in good order. If the burglar had been here, the mess had been cleaned up.

The view he caught through the doorway into the den was another matter: a welter of papers and overturned furniture attested to the destructiveness of the intruder.

She shook her head. "I just left it that way. I couldn't face it. Not today."

"I understand," he said and went over to view the mess. "Mind if I look around?"

She shrugged. "Sure. It's all Dwayne's stuff. I don't need it anymore." She turned away quickly and went into the kitchen, where he heard her fussing with pots and pans.

He stepped over a fallen chair and thumbed through some papers in the open desk drawer. Check stubs, some family photographs that had never been mounted, a pocket version of the New Testament.

He turned away and came face to face with a huge, stuffed deer's head, staring down at him from the wall. He avoided its accusing glass eyes and scanned the items below it, on the floor. Nothing unusual there, either, just some old *Sports Illustrated* magazines that had been pulled down from the shelf, along with some *Readers' Digest Condensed Books,* and some issues of the official NRA publication, the *American Rifleman.*

"Here," Debra said, "I didn't know if you wanted cream or sugar, so I left it black." She handed him a cup and her hand briefly touched his own, then darted away.

"Thank you. It's fine."

"He always took his black. The stronger the better. I got him a new coffeemaker for the camp, for a Christmas present."

Brady raised the cup, uncomfortable with her standing there. He shouldn't have come. It was a time of grief and he was in no position to offer solace.

"Maybe they'll catch who did this," he said finally.

"It doesn't matter," she said. "You know, I guess I ought to make some kind of list, though, don't you think?"

"A list?"

"What was his. The children get half, don't they? Isn't that how it works in this state? I mean, when Grandpa Penniman died, Pop and Aunt Maud got half each, and when Mom and Pop died, Laverne and me inherited a fourth. I guess Dwayne, Junior, and Sue Felice'll each get a fourth."

"Well," Brady said, "I think they changed that law a couple of years ago. You really need a lawyer for that."

"Yes, that's what Laverne said. He brought that friend of his, whatever his name was, from Natchitoches, but I'm not sure I trust him. Do you know anybody here, a lawyer, I mean?"

"There're four or five," Brady told her. "Ashton Phelps, Buddy

Flynn, Brewster's boy, Mike . . . You might want to go to Judge West, though, and get his advice."

"West." She nodded. "Yes, maybe I'll do that."

She was standing there, slightly disheveled, as if she was waiting for something and he didn't know what more to say, so he made a pretense of turning around to examine the contents of the desk again. That was when he saw the corner of paper sticking out from under the Bible.

"May I?" he asked.

She nodded, her eyes never leaving him, and he pulled the paper until he held it in his hand.

A shiver of excitement coursed through him. Just as he had thought, it was a copy of a parish map. But someone, presumably the dead man, had scribbled on it in red ink.

It was the southern portion that caught his eye. Across the hunting tract, the camp site, and the land beside it, which now belonged to Miller Purdy, Elkins had printed his last name in inch-high letters.

He held up the paper. "Does this mean anything to you?"

Debra shook her head slowly. "It was Dwayne's. I think he had an eye on some land out there. He was always talking about buying land."

"Would you mind if I take this and get a copy made?"

"Why not? It doesn't matter now."

He carefully folded the map and put it in his shirt pocket.

"Do you want some more coffee?" Debra asked. "I can make some more real quick."

"No, thank you," he said, moving toward the door. "This is fine."

She followed, moving like a dream-walker.

"I haven't been able to sleep. Did I tell you that? Without him there I just can't make myself. The doctor gave me some pills, but I couldn't get myself to take them. Isn't that funny?"

He set the cup on the coffee table and tried to smile.

"Thank you, Mrs. Elkins. If there's anything I can do . . ."

"Do you want to come back and look at the curtains I put in the kids' rooms? I got the material in Alec, last week. I've wanted to do that for a year now . . ."

He stepped through the front door and back into the sunlight.

"I hope your aunt gets to feeling better."

"She's supposed to go home today. But I may bring her here. It's so lonely, even with the kids."

He left her standing in the doorway, a forlorn figure still unsure of what had happened, and headed back toward his office. As he came into the curve he saw the car dealership to his right, with people in the parking lot, and remembered that it was open until noon. He pulled in, got out of his car, and halted. Something wasn't right, but he wasn't sure what.

He shrugged and went inside, where he found the salesman he had spoken to before.

"Show you a new model, Mr. Brady?" the man asked, trying lamely to be jovial.

"Not right now, thanks," the publisher said. "I just wanted to check something with you: there was a woman in here the other day, slight, dark-haired, good-looking, young. She came in right when I was leaving."

The salesman nodded slowly, as if he were unsure where this was headed.

"Yeah, I remember."

"Know who she was?"

The man shook his head. "Never saw her before in my life. She was asking about Dwayne, said she left something with him, a car registration, I think she said. Wanted to go in his office and look for it. I told her no way."

He chuckled. "But you're right; she was some looker, okay."

Someone cleared their throat from behind one of the display vehicles.

"I heard all that," Mitzi Garitty said, stepping out. "Are you sure it wasn't me?"

The salesman tried to laugh but it came out as a croak. Brady, after his initial surprise, went forward and gave her cheek a peck.

"Come to think of it, there was a resemblance. Just a little bit of an age difference."

"You're saying I'm mature," she laughed.

"I'm saying she was a child," Brady countered. The salesman, sensing there was no business here for him, managed to fade into the hallway, leaving the two friends alone.

"What are you doing here?" Brady asked. "A new car?"

"I wish," Mitzi said. "The wagon's been acting up. I had it in all last week, made them promise it for Friday so I could have it while Matt was in Baton Rouge and then felt like a fool when I had to admit he wasn't going. I should have let them keep it another couple of days. Matt says it's the carburetor, but I can't get him to take a look, himself."

Brady nodded. "How is he, Mitz?"

"Holding on, I guess. Or pretending to. It's Scotty that bothers us."

"He told me. I wish I could do something."

"What can you do? I keep telling Matt it's unfair to expect you to pull some kind of rabbit out of a hat. He has to accept the truth, but he's like a stone wall. He just keeps saying, 'I taught the boy, it couldn't be the way it seems. Pete will find out.' "

Brady closed his eyes and exhaled. "Damn. You don't know how helpless I feel."

"I know. And then, when he heard about the break-in at the Elkins place last night, he was all excited. He walked over when he heard the siren and he saw you leaving. He didn't say anything, but there was something in his eyes, a sort of spark, something I haven't seen since this happened." Mitzi reached forward, put a hopeful hand on Brady's arm: "Pete, is there anything to it? Was the break-in connected?"

Brady looked into her eyes and stifled the urge to tell her what she wanted to hear.

"I don't know, honest to God."

"But you *are* checking on it."

"Sure."

"Well, for all you're trying to do, thank you." She leaned forward, kissed his cheek, and then, before he could see her cry, walked back toward the repair shop.

He went back to his car, feeling worse than ever. They were both depending on him, yet it was an impossible task. He was like a blind man in a mirror maze, without even reflections to guide him.

77

Well, there wasn't anything else to do but plunge forward. He went back to his office and called the assistant parish assessor, Douglas Troy.

The official answered just as Brady was getting ready to give up.

"This is Peter Brady. I need your help," the newsman said. "I'd like to get into the office today to check some records."

The man on the other end snorted. "Today's Saturday, Pete. Office is closed. I'm fixing to go to the camp. Can't it wait?"

Brady was in no mood to be patient.

"Doug, I'm asking as a favor."

"Is this connected with some investigation you're doing?"

"Just some things I need to check out. *Please.*"

Troy sighed. "All right. For you, just this once. But it won't take long, will it?"

"Ten or fifteen minutes," Brady lied.

"I'll meet you there in half an hour."

Actually, it only took half that long. It was almost eleven when Brady, standing just inside the glass doorway of the courthouse, saw the figure of the bald little official hurrying up the walk like someone jealous of his remaining time on earth and loath to part with an instant of it.

"Appreciate your doing this," Brady said as Troy shoved through the doorway, keys in hand. "I'll try not to be long."

Troy grunted and halted before the door to the assessor's office. The door came open and Troy flipped on the lights and shut the door after them.

"Now, Pete, you do what you've gotta do, but I'm telling you if anybody else sees us, they're all gonna want to start coming in here on Saturdays to check hunting leases and I'm not about to put up with it."

"I understand," Brady said, moving over to the ownership map on the wall. Each tract in the parish bore a coded number and the name of the owner at the time the map was made, which was 1965. According to the map, the land ownership in the area Brady was researching had not changed in that time except through normal inheritance. The tract now owned by Miller Purdy read *Succ. Elmer*

Purdy, while the piece of land that now held the Elkins camp bore the name Stafford Elkins.

Brady copied the code numbers and went to the property tax books, while Douglas Troy leaned on a filing cabinet, watching.

From the tax book Brady got the dates of the last time the tracts had changed hands, but that was as far as he could go; the conveyance records, which contained chronological lists of the owners of each piece of land in the parish, were next door, in the Clerk of Court's office. And Brady knew for a fact that Wilson Creswell was not about to come out on a Saturday on a newspaperman's whim.

"You finished?" Troy asked, as Brady shut the tax book.

"I guess so," Brady allowed. "You don't happen to have a key to the clerk's office, do you?"

"Do I look like the janitor? What the hell are you looking for, anyway, Pete?"

Brady took out the map he had found in Dwayne Elkins's desk and spread it on the table in front of the other man.

"See how ELKINS is written there? I just thought I'd check, on a hunch, to see . . ."

"To see what, for Christ's sake?" Troy grumbled, shaking his head. "If you'd just asked me on the phone it would have saved me all this trouble. The Elkins family owned all that land back in the twenties, before the depression. Then along come *Elmer* Purdy and bought it cheap, at a sheriff's sale. Made a million selling to the lumber companies and then to the government. There were hard feelings between Dwayne and Elmer Purdy's boy, Miller. But it ain't because of Miller's love for nature." The bald man hawked and turned off the lights, closing the door behind them.

"It's because Dwayne figured the Purdys stole his inheritance."

79

11

BRADY was still trying to digest the import of what he had learned when he heard the carillon from the First Baptist chiming the noon hour. With a shock he realized he had promised to be on hand at Troymart to photograph Santa.

He drove the two blocks, swinging into the vast parking lot where a small crowd waited. He got his camera out of the trunk and hurried forward, toward the anxious store owner.

"There he is," the merchant exclaimed as he saw Brady coming toward him across the asphalt. He gave an assistant a dig in the ribs and Brady saw the younger man stride quickly away, toward the store itself, probably, Brady decided, to call Santa.

"I was starting to wonder if you'd forgot," the storekeeper said with relief.

"Sorry," Brady apologized, looking over the assembled people. Small children dribbled ice cream down their shirts and women in blue jeans held infants in their arms, while a clown with a pressurized tank inflated red and green balloons at the edge of the gathering. One balloon—lost by its owner—floated skyward, two hundred feet above, but no one seemed to notice. A scratchy record played "Jingle

Bells" through a jury-rigged PA system but it had to compete with the drive-in intercom from the Dairy Bar, fifty yards away.

Brady checked his camera to make sure he had enough film and scanned the crowd to check the light conditions. He noticed that a few of the people in the front were perspiring and even the red and green crepe banners looked wilted. *Christmas in Louisiana was an anomaly,* he thought, *where people watched* White Christmas *on TV with their air conditioners running.* There was always the record cold snap of eighty-nine of course, but that was the exception to the rule and this year looked to be another warm one, with a few little flurries of bad weather, but nothing really messy hitting until mid-January.

"Makes it hell on Santa," a voice commented from his elbow and he saw a man he vaguely recalled meeting at the Forest Festival. "Them pore reindeers—not only hot as hell but people around here'd just as soon shoot 'em."

The newsman turned to respond, but at that instant there was a racket in the street, near the Dairy Bar, and an excited murmur ran through the crowd.

"There he is," a woman cried. "See, here he comes now."

The din resolved into the loud ratcheting of an internal combustion engine and Brady caught a glimpse of red through the bodies.

Brady raised his camera, stepping back to get a better shot.

And froze.

Because Santa, when he emerged, was riding a four-wheeled ATV instead of a sled. And even under the false whiskers he looked disappointingly familiar.

"Hell," the man from the Forest Festival chuckled, "that's Duffy Malone."

No doubt about it, Brady thought, as the ATV made three circles around the lot and the figure in the red suit threw favors from his gift bag. It was the mayor of Troy, followed by three other ATVs, each driven by an elf otherwise identifiable as the clerk of court, the assessor, and the chief of police.

"Mom," Brady heard a small boy protest, "that's not Santa, that's Mr. Malone."

"Hush," the mother ordered, jabbing him in the ribs. "That's Santa."

"Mama, Mr. Duffy?" a toddler asked from a few bodies away.

"No, honey," said a plump woman who overflowed her jeans. She glared at the first child. "That's Santy, coming from the North Pole."

Her husband shrugged. "Jesus, Willianne, kids ain't stupid. You may think that's Santy Clause, but Chester's right. That's Duffy, trying to get hisself reelected."

"Bubba, shut up," the fat woman commanded. "Wasn't you ever little?"

A piece of candy landed a foot away from Brady and three children struggled for it on the warm asphalt. The winner peeled off the paper, grimaced, and threw it back down on the ground.

"Aw, I got this Halloween."

"Hey, Santy," a man called, "you gonna bring us a new tax?"

The circling Santa reached into his bag and, with a snap-throw worthy of the National League, propelled a gumball in the heckler's direction, eliciting a yelp of pain.

"Merry Christmas, ho, ho, ho!" the red-clad figure intoned.

The vehicle finally jerked to a halt in front of the store and Brady got his pictures. The store owner stepped up onto the four-wheeler.

"Now if everybody'll come inside, Santa here will listen to the kids and take orders for Christmas."

"Ho, ho, ho," said Santa.

Brady lowered his camera and started away, the jingle of sleigh bells ringing behind him from the PA system.

And stopped after a few steps.

What was it the man from the Forest Festival had said? *"Makes it hell on Santa"*? Yes, that was it. And so Santa had showed up on an ATV, in keeping with the weather. What was Brady's sub-conscious trying to tell him? He gave up and went back to his car, the jingle bells fading as he started his engine.

Maybe, later on, it would come through.

* * *

It was midafternoon when Kelly returned, breezing in with a wave and hugging him as he sat in front of the TV, watching a football game.

Much later, after dinner, she asked him how his investigation was proceeding.

He started to ask where she had gone, as a quid pro quo, then abandoned the idea; he would only get an oblique reply. So he told her about the visit with Debra Elkins and what he had found out from the deputy assessor.

"There was a lot more than Elkins just getting on Purdy's nerves by hunting on his land," he finished. "There was bad blood between the two families. It may be Elkins figured the land was his by rights all along."

"And you think Purdy may have killed him to make him leave him alone?"

"If Elkins had been murdered, it would be a motive." He raised his hands helplessly. "But there's no evidence that he was."

"I read a story once where somebody with a rifle waited until somebody else was getting ready to shoot and then fired at the same time."

"It was a movie," he said. "John Wayne shot Lee Marvin but everybody thought Jimmy Stewart did it." He rose from the sofa to pace back and forth. "But that doesn't make any sense. I mean, there was only the one shot. How could anybody fire at the same time as Scott? The odds are a million to one."

She tossed her hair out of her eyes. With her creamy skin and dark brows she looked especially beautiful tonight, almost too beautiful to be real. He had a sensation that if he touched her she might slowly dematerialize before his eyes.

"Are you going to see Purdy?" she asked.

"He doesn't seem very sociable," Brady said. "And I don't know what I'd expect to find."

She smiled enigmatically and got up to embrace him, swaying back and forth to a little tune she hummed. With a shock he recognized "As Time Goes By."

"They ended up apart," he said finally.

She lifted her face from his shoulder. "What?"

"Rick and Ilse, in *Casablanca.* They ended up going back to their worlds."

"But they got back together afterward," she murmured.

"What do you mean? The show ended with . . ."

"But they got back together. Her husband died in a plane crash and after the war she and Rick met again. I have it all worked out."

He smiled in spite of himself. *Strange girl,* he thought, as they circled the room in their soundless little dance. *But right now there's only us and maybe that's enough.*

That night he dreamed of Santa Claus. Only it wasn't the jolly figure of childhood, but a maniacal figure in red on a three-wheeler who chased him up and down forest trails, echoing insane laughter. It was only when Kelly awoke him that he finally shook off the nightmare and lapsed back into something like a restful sleep.

When he woke up there was a note from her on the bedside table: *Back in a couple of hours. Not to worry. Have gone to see Miller Purdy.*

His mouth opened but no sound came out. *Miller Purdy.* For God's sake, he might be the killer. If, that is, there *was* a killer. At the very least he was an odd man and he lived in a remote area. There was no telling what he could do to her before anybody found out.

Brady threw his clothes on, wiped his face with a wet rag, and half ran to his car. As he passed First Baptist a trickle of people were already heading in for Sunday worship and he waited impatiently for them to get out of the street.

It would take half an hour to get to Purdy's and who could tell when she had left?

He made it there in twenty-five minutes, spinning off the black-top onto the gravel access road and past the mailbox with Purdy's name on it.

My God, was she insane? Purdy might be perfectly harmless, but then again he might not be . . . Brady should never have mentioned the man's name. She was trying to be helpful, of course, and set his mind at rest, but her vaunted independence was only making things worse. There was something about Purdy that bothered Brady. . . .

The road wound through an open field and then through pine woods, a lone power line indicating that there was a human being at the end of the journey. He urged his speed up to forty-five, swerving to avoid potholes, and hoping the cloud of dust that plumed into the air after him would not give him away.

He should have called Matt's people. It would have been better to come here with a deputy, but it was too late now. He'd have to brazen it out, hope that he was being alarmist.

The woods had just given way to another field when he came around a curve and slammed on his brakes, skidding sideways across the road.

There was an iron bar blocking the way, with a No Trespassing sign on the metal post to which it was hinged. And parked just off the road, hugging the soft red earth of the shoulder, was Kelly's car.

Brady backed up and then pulled in behind her. He looked through her windows. The car was locked and everything seemed in order. She had obviously stopped here and gotten out to walk the rest of the distance.

He ducked under the bar and started walking, wishing now he had paid closer attention to the topographic map in his office. Purdy's house was at the end of this road, but was that in half a mile? A mile? Even two?

A bluebird skimmed over the high grass of the pasture and he saw a hawk circling high above on the wind currents. Things seemed so peaceful, yet it was deceptive. Anything might have happened by now.

He had been walking for fifteen minutes when he saw the house ahead.

It was a handsome, two-story structure of logs, with a garage to one side and, adjoining that, what looked like a storage shed. On the other side of the yard was a tin-roofed building that probably housed farm machinery.

A blue pickup was in the garage and a horse grazed in a corral just visible to the rear.

85

Everything seemed peaceful, even idyllic. A Sunday morning in the country.

He forced back his fears and started forward. He could leave the road when he passed through the enclosure fence and use one of the outbuildings for cover. After that, there'd be a lot of luck involved.

He came to the fence and walked over the cattle guard, then angled off quickly so the metal roofed outbuilding was between him and the house.

So far, so good. He looked around a corner of the structure, toward the house, but all was tranquil—the only sound coming from the rusted pulley of the old well out front, squeaking in the breeze. The house itself was forty yards away. He could make it to the near corner, and then hoist himself up onto the porch.

He checked again for anything out of the ordinary, took a deep breath, and sprinted forward, bending over to make himself a smaller target.

If his foot hadn't hit the old axle in the grass he would have made it. As it was, he shot forward, off balance, and went down headlong in the grass. Pain radiated up from his right arm, which was under his body; his glasses had flown off to lie several feet ahead of him in the grass.

He groaned and sat up. His arm tingled, but it didn't seem to be broken. He flexed his fingers several times and then reached for his glasses. The house, miraculously, was still quiet. He hobbled to his feet and propped himself onto the porch.

The front window was curtained but there seemed to be a light on inside. He ducked under the window, to avoid showing his outline, and stood up again on the other side.

He thought about breaking down the door, but that was foolish; he had no proof yet that any crime was being committed. Instead, he looked around for a weapon and saw a flowerpot. He would knock, holding the pot behind him, and if Purdy opened the door, he would try to inveigle his way in. If Purdy was belligerent, or if Kelly yelled, he'd use the pot as a club.

It didn't seem like much of a plan, but he couldn't think of anything better, so he picked up the pot.

That was when the dog hit him. Middle sized and furry, it flew out of nowhere, barreling onto the porch and into him with a cacaphony of snarls and barks. Brady fell backward, the pot flying out of his grip. His attacker, some kind of sheepdog, fastened itself to his pants legs and began to pull. Brady swore, trying to warn it away, but it only pulled harder. he kicked out, freeing himself long enough to scramble to his feet, but the dog dove back; this time its teeth found his calf. He gave a cry, at the same time realizing there was no way now to keep his presence secret. The dog bore him backward, against the doorway, and just then it opened, so that he stumbled backward, into the house.

He only stopped when he felt the cold metal barrel jab him in the back and heard the voice telling him to be very still.

Miller Purdy was clearly at home.

12

THE dog backed off when it saw its master and began to wag its tail.

"Turn around slowly," Miller Purdy said.

Brady obeyed, moving very carefully.

Even before he'd turned completely he heard a gasp.

"Brady," exclaimed Kelly, from her place on the divan behind the standing Purdy.

"Brady, the newspaper man?" Purdy asked, lowering his carbine. "What in hell?"

The editor tried to summon up a smile.

"I guess I miscalculated," he said.

"I guess you did," Kelly echoed, her eyes shooting fire. "Didn't you get my note?"

Brady nodded. "I thought it was another one of your wild notions. I was scared you were going to get into trouble."

Miller Purdy stared at his unexpected guest and broke into a grin.

"Like maybe robbed and raped and left for dead in the woods by the wildman of the forest," he laughed. "Oh, Gawd, Brady, you really *do* belong in Troy, don't you?"

"Well . . ." Brady began, aware that he was blushing.

"Well, to ease your mind," the bearded man told him, "Kelly and I were classmates at Troy High. She decided to come out here and pay me a visit. I've got to admit I was a little surprised to have a visitor early on a Sunday morning." He winked at the girl. "But I can't think of one I'd rather have. We've been catching up on old times."

"I feel like a fool," Brady said.

"You ought to," Kelly accused. "You'd think I didn't have any sense at all."

"I think she was just trying to help you with your investigation," Miller Purdy said. "We've been batting around the possibilities, as well as swapping stories about old classmates." He uncocked the carbine and set it back in the corner. "I've got to say I can't see anything except what's obvious. Unless you want to charge people with their wishes." He leaned down to give the dog's head a pat and then shut the door. "Have a seat," he invited. "I'll get some salve for your leg."

Brady hiked his pants leg and saw that the dog's teeth hadn't penetrated the fabric.

"I'm okay," he said.

"Get you some coffee, then? Or juice?" Purdy pointed to a pair of glasses on the coffee table. "I squeeze my own oranges."

"Thanks, but I had some before I left home," Brady lied.

"Suit yourself." Purdy took a seat on the other side of the room, his sandals flap-flapping on the wooden floor.

"Now," he began, "about my family. I hear from Kelly that was what was bothering you."

Brady bit his lip.

"Well," he began, sneaking a glance at Kelly. She was clearly enjoying his mortification.

"No secret," the other man said, waving a hand. "The stories are true. My father *did* buy it all up cheap. He was a smart man. Worked like a dog back in the twenties. Didn't marry till late, because he was busy socking away money. My mother was twenty-six years younger than he and he was fifty-five when I was born.

Died when I was in college and left me everything. All this land and enough money to live on."

"I understand he got it from the Elkinses?" Brady asked.

Purdy nodded. "True enough. And he made a million or so selling timber to the lumber companies. Not just here, but in other parts of the parish. Sometimes, Mr. Brady, I lie awake at night, listening to the screeching of the owls and the cries of the bobcats, thinking, *They wouldn't be so scarce today if it hadn't been for my father*. You see, in those days all kinds of game roamed these woods. Right over at Savage Creek they reported bears as late as 1955, the year I was born. And the Forest Service recorded a pack of wolves not five miles from here in 1947." He leaned forward, eyes aglow. "Can you imagine that? Wolves." He slumped back into the chair, shaking his head. "Twenty years before that they were too plentiful to record. In those days . . ." His voice lowered and he drew out his words so that they hit each pool of silence like a falling raindrop in water. "In those days people were afraid to go very far unarmed. There are accounts of wolves attacking humans. Not many, and they may be exaggerated, but it happened, there's no doubt. In those days this forest was one carpet of longleaf pines from horizon to horizon, all the way from Driskill Mountain in the north, to the Red River. A couple of gravel roads: those were your highways. Cars were few and far between; most people still used wagons and horses. If you wanted to go from Shreveport to Alexandria you might just as well go down the Red River."

Brady listened, his eyes taking in the room. For the first time he noticed there was no TV set or stereo and he wondered if the black potbellied stove in one corner was meant as a statement.

"People were more in tune with themselves then," Purdy went on, his tone scornful. "The family meant something. People read books and enjoyed the sky. They didn't spend all their time in front of the screen on Sunday, watching some illiterate giants bang their heads together." He slumped even more. "And my father helped bring all that to an end."

"I imagine it was more than just your father," Brady said quietly. "There are things nobody can stop. And some things that *have* to be stopped."

90

"Wars that have to be fought?" Purdy asked sarcastically.

"Wars that have to be fought," Brady agreed. "A month or so ago I was up at Pine Chapel, in Ward Eight . . ."

"I know where it is," Purdy interrupted.

"Right. I walked in the graveyard. I couldn't help but notice some of the stones. There was a whole line of them for one family, the Blounts. You know, I can still see them in my mind: Samuel Blount, born 1890, died 1952. Eliza Blount, born 1901, died 1963. And then four other stones that were older. William; Samuel, Junior; Ellen Mae; and Sarah, all dead in a single year, 1937. In the same month, August. And within twenty days." He closed his eyes for a few seconds. "It didn't say whether it was typhoid or cholera or diphtheria. Maybe it doesn't matter, because whatever it was could probably be prevented now."

Purdy's features hardened.

"At least they died without being exposed to drugs, serial killers, child abuse, and racial prejudice."

"Maybe," Brady said mildly. "It *is* a sort of trade-off, isn't it?"

"That's right," Purdy snapped, "except that society doesn't allow most people a choice about what to trade." He gave a contemptuous wave. "Oh, I've heard all the arguments. The lumber companies, the Forest Service, and the oil conglomerates are full of them. They have a rationale for every barrel of oil they spill in the ocean, for every seal and whale they kill, for every ton of chemical they dump in the rivers." His voice was trembling now and Brady sensed Kelly's surprise, but he kept himself quiet.

"Do you know this state is the sewage pipe for the country?" Purdy thundered. "Do you know we take chemicals from every other state and bury them in our soil? The water you drink, the air you breathe, the food you eat . . . they're all deadly. And my father was a part of that. He was part of what made it happen, and it's something I've had to live with all my life, and, by God, I'll do anything I have to to set things right!" His palm hit the arm of his chair, the sound echoing off the walls.

"It must have been difficult living next to Dwayne Elkins," Brady said.

He felt Kelly stiffen, but Purdy's body seemed to relax.

Purdy smiled suddenly. "Yes, it *is* ironic, isn't it? If Elkins had had this land he'd have done the same as my father. The only difference between his family and mine is that my father had better business sense." Purdy shook his head. "Elkins was a stupid man. A yahoo. And the world's better off without him. The trouble is that there're plenty around here to take his place."

Brady got up slowly, reaching for Kelly's hand again.

"I expect you're right there. I'm sorry for disturbing you."

The other man nodded and got to his feet.

"No harm done. It was *your* leg got bitten."

"It probably should have gotten bitten harder," Kelly said, pulling her hand free.

Purdy walked over to the door with them but Brady halted halfway out and pointed to a stick leaning against the inside wall.

"Interesting," he said.

Purdy reached over and picked it up. About three feet long, it was essentially a wooden strip about a quarter of an inch thick that was doubled at one end and tied with leather thongs to form a circle. A couple of strings of leather were threaded through this oval to make what resembled a net.

"My lacrosse racket?" Purdy asked. "Yeah, I played it in college." He grasped the round end of the stick and waved it through the air. "Never was much good at the game, though."

He replaced it against the door. "Just a keepsake from quieter times."

Brady pushed open the door and went out. The dog, sleeping at the edge of the porch, raised its head and regarded him with interest.

"It's okay, Bruno," said its owner. "They're going."

Kelly turned. "Well, Miller, I'm sorry we bothered you, but it's been nice. And I was glad to see your house. I've heard how you built it all by yourself."

"Well, most of it," Purdy said. "I'd ask you to stay, but I have a field trip planned. The other day I found what looked like panther tracks out by Dry Fork. I'm anxious to see if there are any more."

"Be careful," Kelly said, extending a hand.

"You be careful, too," he said, giving Brady's hand a pump and looking him in the eye.

They were out of the yard before Kelly spoke.

"That was the dumbest thing you've ever done," she accused.

"Funny, I was kind of thinking that about you," Brady said. "You didn't tell me he was an old friend."

"Do I have to tell you everything? Can't I get credit for any brains at all?"

"I'm sorry," he said, reaching for her hand. "I guess I did jump the gun. I just worried when I found out where you'd gone."

"And now?"

"I'm not worried, if that's what you mean. But I can't say I feel real comfortable around your friend, either."

"Why, because he's got convictions?"

"Well, I won't pass on the convictions. But it seems funny to me that somebody so much in love with the old ways has a new truck, and an electric line leading right to his house. That must've cost a fortune."

Kelly jerked her hand away again.

"That's ridiculous. He doesn't have to be a hermit in a cave."

"No. But he doesn't have to tell us lies, either."

She stopped to stare at him.

"What are you talking about?"

"That so-called lacrosse stick. Didn't that seem odd to you?"

"No. Should it? He said he played the game in college."

"He went to Southern Methodist. I never knew there was a big lacrosse contingent there. Lacrosse is a northern game. Dallas is part of the South: it's all football."

"You can find almost any sport, anywhere. They have lacrosse at LSU. And soccer and probably polo," she retorted. "He didn't say it was big time, just that he played it."

"But with *that* stick? That was handmade."

"What about it? So he's good with his hands."

He shook his head, knowing it would be useless to argue.

"Maybe," he said, "but I've seen one like it before and it wasn't on a lacrosse field. I just wish I could remember where. Then maybe I'd know why it was so important for Miller Purdy to lie about it."

13

THEY drove back in silence and when they reached his house she went directly to the bedroom to pack. He wasn't sure if she was still angry with him or just chagrined at having missed his observation. When she finished she loaded her bags in the backseat as he watched from the lawn.

"Leaving already?" he asked. "It's not noon yet."

"I have things to do back at school," she said. "The final chapter to write and I promised to get the whole thing to Bax so he could read it during the holidays."

"When do they start?" he asked. "It's already December."

"Classes end the seventh," she said. "But then there're exams."

"Of course. Well, call me when you get in."

"Sure." She turned and touched her lips quickly to his own.

He watched her get into the car and start the engine. "Kel . . ."

But she was already backing out and as she left he felt as if a part of himself had been wrenched away.

He saw a small piece of white flutter to the ground and bent over to pick it up from the driveway. It was a gas receipt from a filling station in Jena, a town twenty-five miles to the east and it bore yesterday's date. So that was where she had gone when she'd left in such a hurry yesterday morning. But why? What was there in Jena, of all places, for Kelly?

Whatever it was all about, it was an indication that something was fundamentally wrong with their relationship—that she would always be proving something and he, for his part, would never be able to quell his pangs of insecurity.

His mind wandered back to the man he had visited earlier.

Now he was sure there was more to Miller Purdy than just the eccentric environmentalist. Why invent some kind of story about playing lacrosse at school with something that resembled a folk artifact? It was not only a lie, but a gratuitous one. And there was something else that bothered him about Purdy: despite the man's seeming love of nature, Brady could not shake the feeling that he was essentially unbalanced. He remembered a case from New Orleans where an assistant prosecutor had goaded a pleasant, smiling witness into a peak of fury that led to an admission of murder. Why did Purdy remind him of that man?

Even so, it still cast no light on the matter he was trying to investigate. That was what was so damned frustrating—at every turn there was another thread, leading back to the dead man: he was disliked by his neighbor, his brother-in-law, and most of the town. Someone had even burgled his house. Yet each thread went straight into a cul-de-sac.

He was still trying to make sense of it when his doorbell rang and he got up, wondering who was visiting him at midday. *Maybe,* he thought, *it was a missionary delegation from one of the churches.* He never knew quite how to handle them. In a small town you couldn't shut the door in their face the way you did in the city.

He lifted an edge of the window curtain and groaned inwardly. It was a woman. Surely a missionary.

Already composing his refusal he pulled the door open. And blinked.

The woman on his doorstep was Maud Penniman.

"Mr. Brady," she said, her breath coming in little gasps, "please excuse me for bothering you, but I just had to come."

95

He reached out to take her arm and guided her inside.

"Miss Penniman, I thought you were in the hospital."

"A body can't get well there," she said, sitting down in his armchair. "And the food is terrible. I'd rather be at home, where I can eat what I want and smoke my cigarettes. I know, they're killing me, but I figure I've lived long enough to beat the odds."

"But how did you get over here?"

"I drove, of course. I don't think I'm in any shape to walk." She managed a titter. "This condition isn't as serious as it seems. I have these little attacks but I'm all right in a couple of days. This one just lasted a little longer than usual. Stress, I suppose."

Brady nodded sympathetically. "What can I do for you, then?"

"Get me some water, so I can take one of these." Maud held up a little tablet. "Then we can talk."

The publisher went into the kitchen and came back with a glass. Maud put the pill in her mouth and took a swallow, closed her eyes a second, and then exhaled.

"Thank you. You don't know how helpless you feel when your whole life depends on these things. Sometimes I feel like I own a drug company." She handed Brady back the glass.

"What I came for was to tell you that I spoke to my nephew about this business and I wanted you to know I've convinced him to leave things alone. We don't need any lawsuits to make things worse. Of course, he just meant well. I'm sure he was thinking of poor Debra and the children, but they'll make it. Suing that poor young man's family isn't going to accomplish a bit of good."

"I'm glad to hear it," Brady said. "But why are you telling *me* instead of them?"

"Well, because you were in the hospital room when Laverne brought that lawyer in. I thought you might have told somebody."

"Right. Well, I think it's a good decision," he said. "I know Matt Garitty and Scotty feel badly about it, as it is."

"Of course they do. This will scar that poor boy forever. And Dwayne just wasn't worth that, as horrible as that sounds. I'll never know what Deb saw in him. But they say love is blind."

Brady tried to smile. "By the way, Miss Maud, have you ever seen a young, good-looking woman with close-cut black hair hanging around?"

"You mean Mitzi Garitty? She was into the dealership last Friday when I was working on the books . . ."

Brady fought back a chuckle.

"A little younger than Mitzi, ma'am. Say by about fifteen years."

"Oh, good heavens. You mean a child. Why, no, I don't remember anybody. Should I?"

"I don't know. She was at the hospital the other day, outside your room. She left in a hurry when she saw me."

"Really." Maud reached into her purse for a pack of cigarettes, then let them slide back into her bag. "That's right. You don't smoke. I forgot."

"Does Debra know you're over here?" Brady asked.

The old woman made a face. "I think I'm old enough to do things without her permission. I promise not to die on you, Mr. Brady. As my mother would say, that wouldn't be ladylike."

"Thank you," Brady said with a smile.

"Anyway," Maud said, "whoever it was you saw was probably one of Dwayne's women. He had all the morals of a tomcat. I can't tell you how many times I've seen his car parked outside that joint on the highway, the one where they have all the knifings. I frankly don't know how Debra's put up with it all these years. You know, they broke up once seven or eight years ago. But then he came on his knees and cried on her and she took him back. Worst mistake she ever made, after marrying him. He just isn't in her class." Maud shook her head. "Now doesn't that sound awful? I just can't help it, that's the way we old-timers feel."

"I understand there was unpleasantness between Dwayne and Miller Purdy."

"Purdy?" Maud frowned slightly. "You mean that young man that lives all by himself down there near the camp? Well, I suppose there is, since you mention it. Something about somebody getting the land from somebody else. I don't know how many times I've heard the same story in this parish, Mr. Brady. It seems like somebody's family always swindled somebody else's family out of some-

97

thing. And if not a family, then the government. But if you ask me, any land the Elkinses owned they frittered away. When Dwayne married my niece he didn't have the usual pot, if you know the expression."

Brady smiled.

Maud pushed herself to her feet.

"Well, I've bothered you long enough. How is old Emmett doing? I don't see much of him anymore. Do you know we were in school together, before the war? He was ornery even then. He once glued the pages of the teacher's gradebook together and that wasn't the half of it." She sighed. "But he surely did manage to marry the most beautiful woman in the whole class. Lord, I hated her!"

Brady laughed and helped the old lady to the door. But as she reached the porch she swayed slightly and reached out to him for support.

"I'm dizzy. Can you hold onto me for just a second? I'll be all right."

Brady eased her into a rocker and she took a few deep breaths. "It's passing now, thank you."

"Can you make it home? You shouldn't be driving in this condition," Brady advised. "Why don't you let me take you?"

"And leave my car over here?"

Brady did a quick calculation.

"Why don't I drive your car?" he suggested. "I can walk back."

"But it's so far. I live on the other side of town."

"Half a mile tops," he said, "and it's a beautiful day." *Besides,* he thought, *I've already done a couple of miles, so what's another one?*

"Well, it might be best. Are you sure you don't want to call Debra?"

"She has her hands full," he said and helped her out to her car. She slumped down in the passenger seat, invisible from the road.

It took him a few moments to adjust his own seat correctly; the car was a new, luxury model, all buttons and switches, and he felt uneasy as he made his way slowly out onto the main street and over the tracks, as if at any moment lights might start flashing and voices might begin booming out at him from the dash. He was sure that

98

the other drivers were watching him with curiosity, wondering what was going on.

Isn't that that Brady fellow, the one that bought the paper? What's he doing in Miss Maud's new car? Do you figure he's taken up drinking again?

He gritted his teeth and soon was on the west side of town. But instead of heading north, around the curve where the road split, which was the way that led past Matt's subdivision, he kept straight, taking Highway 84. He passed the Forest Service office and then came to a left turn, with a sign that said Woodland Hills.

"Turn here," Maud told him. "I always miss this turn, myself. I'm used to the old house, where the MacVeys live now. But Poppa thought it would be so wonderful to move out here. This was the first subdivision, you know."

They went up a hill and past houses set back on shaded lots. Here, pickups shared driveways with Volvos and Mazdas, and on mailboxes Brady saw the names of bankers and several of the town's lawyers.

"This one," Maud said, indicating a two-story house on the left. Brady turned into the drive and stopped the engine. The house was among the older ones, probably dating from the midfifties, but it was well-kept, with a fresh coat of paint and what appeared to be a new roof.

"It was always too big for me after the folks went," Maud sighed. "What can you do with a big old house like this one but pay and pay and pay? But every time I think about moving into an apartment I just can't do it. Too much of the folks is still here. And too much of their things. What would I do with it all? I couldn't sell it and let strangers have it." She managed a laugh and Brady got out and went around the car to help her.

"I feel so foolish," she said, as he walked her across the lawn. "But I guess that's one of the privileges of old age." She fit her key into the door and turned to face him.

"Thank you for putting up with an old fool, Mr. Brady. You're very kind. Are you sure you don't want me to call Deb?"

"It's not far," Brady said.

"Then thank you."

The door closed behind her and Brady started back toward town.

A car passed, heading in the opposite direction, and somebody waved. He waved back, not knowing who it was. Now, he supposed, people would wonder what the editor of the *Express* was doing afoot so far from his own house on a Sunday morning. Well, it would make good gossip.

I heard he has a woman out there. Do you know whose wife? But I thought he was going with Emmett Larson's daughter. Yes, but she's almost never there. Something funny, if you ask me.

Well, the hell with them. It was a nice day, not as hot as yesterday, and the air smelled good—like pine trees—and, besides, it didn't do him any good to sit inside and brood about Kelly.

He started down the hill, his feet slipping on the pine needles. When he got to the highway he stopped for a second to catch his breath. It was farther than it looked, and now he had to walk back through town. He was suddenly aware of how little exercise he got and resolved to do something about it. After he got over his aches and pains from today.

Across the highway a man was hitchhiking, heading in the opposite direction.

Except that as he looked he saw that it wasn't a man at all, but a boy. And the boy was Scott Garitty.

Brady waited for a truck to pass and then started across the road, but where Scott had been standing there was nobody now.

"Scotty!" he called, wondering for an instant if his eyes had played a trick on him.

Then he saw him again, walking away quickly into the parking lot of the Trucker's Cafe.

Brady jumped the ditch, fell to his knees on the other side, and scrambled back to his feet. The boy was walking alongside the cafe now, heading for the woods to the rear. Brady brushed off his knees and trotted after him, dodging through the few cars and trucks in the lot.

He came to the side of the fake-log building and stopped. Pots and pans banged together in the kitchen and the smell of grease frying floated out on the breeze. A black woman in an apron came out the back door, flung a pan of something onto the ground, then went back inside.

Brady darted into the woods, trying to think which way the boy would head. When he'd seen him he was obviously trying to leave town, because after the trailer park a half mile down the road there was nothing for twenty miles but woods. But now that Brady had seen him, his plans would be altered. So was he just trying to get away now? Or would he head back for his house?

The editor listened, to see if he could hear any movement through the leaves, but there was nothing but the chattering of a squirrel a few yards away and the scamper of some of its family as they rummaged for nuts long buried.

On a hunch, Brady headed right, at an angle. His direction now was northeast. This patch of woods backed up to the subdivision where Matt lived. Though Brady had never been in these woods before, he knew that if he kept in that direction he would eventually come out where there were houses. Or, at least, that was the theory.

He skidded down a creek bank to the dry bed, glad the water table was low this time of year, and clambered up on the other side. A fence confronted him and he was about to duck under it when he heard what was unmistakably a human voice.

It was the sound of somebody who had been hurt.

He hurried forward, brushing away dead briars and limbs and halted. There, a few feet ahead of him, his shirt caught in the barbs of the wire, was Scott, twisting like a rabbit caught in a trap.

Brady walked over slowly, careful to keep the smile from his face.

"Looks like you could use some help," he said, reaching down to pluck the fabric from one of the prongs.

Scott looked away, obviously embarrassed, and waited until Brady had finished before he straightened up.

"I . . . I didn't know that was you, Mr. Brady. I thought it was somebody else." He gulped. "I thought they were after me."

"Sure. Do your folks know you're out on the highway thumbing rides?"

Scott shrugged. "Don't know. They went to church. I wasn't feeling too good and I stayed home."

101

"But you started feeling better," Brady said.

"Something like that."

"Well," the newsman said softly, "they're probably back now, so don't you think we ought to go back so they won't worry?"

Scotty shrugged. "If I have to."

Brady found a log and sat down on it.

"You know, your father and mother are worried about you," he said. "They love you."

"I know. But there's nothing for them to worry about. I'm fine. I was just hitchhiking out to Sand Springs. I was coming back."

"I know. But how do you think they must be feeling to come back and find you're gone? Did you leave a note?"

"I'm old enough," Scott said. "I'm old enough. Isn't that what my dad said when he took me out?"

"Come on," Brady said, rising to put an arm over the boy's shoulders. "Let's go back and let 'em know you're okay."

The boy seemed to shrink slightly and Brady sensed his defeat. They walked back to the cafe and used the phone and five minutes later Matt pulled up in his pickup.

Scott climbed in docily and then Matt drove Brady back to Brady's place.

The sheriff walked with his friend to the front door.

"Pete, I don't know what the hell you were doing out there; all I can say is thank God you were." Garitty's eyes clouded and he looked away quickly.

"I'm glad I could help," Brady said. He put a hand on the other man's shoulder. "I just wish I could do more for the boy."

Garitty nodded. "His mother wants to take him to Natchitoches, to a psychologist. I've got to admit I've got some doubts about those kinds of things, but . . ." He shrugged. "If it'll do any good, I'm for it."

"I think it's a good start," said Brady.

"I hope so." The lawman kicked the ground with his foot. "Look, Pete, I don't guess you've turned up anything yet?"

Brady cleared his throat. "I've looked at a couple of things," he said, "but all they show is that nobody much liked Elkins. It would've been easier if we had a bullet, or at least fragments."

102

"Yeah. Well, this is kind of hard for me to say, Pete, but I was talking to Mitzi, and maybe . . . Well, maybe I expected too much. I mean, maybe I haven't been able to look at things squarely. Maybe I need to face up to things so that boy'll have some support."

Brady waited, saying nothing.

"I've got to say, I still don't know how it happened. But I guess it did. And maybe I've got to live with the fact before I run everybody around me crazy."

"Look," Brady said, sensing the other man's embarrassment. "You take care of that boy and I'll keep looking. If anything turns up, I'll tell you."

"Thanks, Pete."

Brady watched them drive away, sensing his friend's hurt and chafing at his own frustration. For the rest of the day he waited for Kelly to call, letting him know she'd arrived, but she never did. He called her, finally, at nine o'clock, but no one was home. When he at last went to bed his sleep was fitful, as he waited for a phone call to rouse him, telling him she had been hurt on the highway or killed.

When the phone finally did ring the bedside clock said it was five in the morning. He yanked the receiver away from the cradle, groaning inwardly at what he was about to hear.

"Pete?" It was Matt Garitty's voice and Brady felt his muscles go weak.

"Matt, is it Kelly? Is something wrong?"

"Not Kelly," Matt said. "It's somebody else. The trailer park west of town. You'd better come out here. I want you to look at a body."

14

TEN minutes later Brady pulled off the highway and into the trailer park. Several people huddled in the chill grayness, in various stages of dress. To the rear of the park were a couple of sheriff's cruisers and an ambulance, their flashers painting the mist with streaks of red and blue. Brady stopped behind Matt's white Olds and got out.

Matt appeared in the doorway of one of the trailers, a flashlight in his hand.

"Pete. Thanks for coming."

Behind him a light flashed and Brady realized the photographer was taking pictures. The sheriff led Brady over to the ambulance, whose back doors were open. Inside, on a stretcher, a form lay covered by a sheet.

"Got a call from the trailer park manager," Matt explained. "Said he got up to chase some dogs away from the trash and noticed her lights were still on and the radio was playing. It wasn't like her to be up so early so he knocked on her door."

Matt gestured to one of the paramedics, who lifted the sheet, to expose the face of the victim.

"That's when he saw her through a crack in the curtain, lying on the floor."

Brady stared down at the woman's face, pale now in death, the black hair limp in the beam of the sheriff's flashlight.

"Is this the woman you told Mitzi about?" Garitty asked.

Brady nodded. "Yeah."

The sheriff nodded at the corpsman, who flipped the sheet back over the dead woman's face.

"When I saw her I wondered," Garitty said. "Her name is Jean McInnery. She's been living here a couple of months. The manager thinks she's one of the McInnerys from over in Jonesboro."

The J. *of the letter,* Brady thought. Jean.

"How did she die?" he asked, feeling a cold that didn't come from the morning chill.

"Pills," Garitty said. "Or, at least, that's how it looks now. There was an empty bottle of them on the floor next to her." He turned to the paramedic. "Okay, you can take her to the hospital. Doc McIntire ought to be there by now to do his thing."

They watched the ambulance pull away.

"You think she killed herself because she couldn't go on without Elkins?" Brady asked.

Garitty hunched his shoulders. "Stranger things have happened. I've got people inside sifting her things, but so far nobody from this place admits seeing much since she's been here. All I could get from the manager was that he saw a dark-colored, new pickup truck leaving here just after dark, but it could have been from any of the trailers. Or somebody just turning around." Garitty exhaled a faint white vapor. "So I guess as far as the Elkins business goes this doesn't really help any."

"You figure she broke into the Elkins place?" Brady asked.

"Sounds logical. The way I read it, she wanted to get back anything that might compromise her. To the extent somebody like her can be compromised."

"Did you find anything in there to suggest that?" Brady asked. "A letter, or a notebook?"

Matt's laugh sounded like a dry cough. "That may be the way they do it in the city, but out here in the country it's a lot more

105

informal. She seemed to have a lot of cash on hand, about a grand from what we counted, but I figure anything she got from his place has long since been burnt. The way I see it, she had her hooks into him for all kinds of money and she just didn't want the family to know how much. They might've made things hot for her around here. She doesn't seem to have worked for a living, at least not lately. I think the manager there said she did a stint at the Dairy Queen for a couple of weeks after she came here, but then she left."

"Because she was riding the gravy train after that," Brady said. The sheriff smiled lewdly. "Or the gravy train was riding *her.*"

Brady walked back toward his car, his friend following.

"I'll call you when Doc's got some results," Matt said, leaning on his car door. "Meanwhile, I guess I'll get on back to the house. I feel like I'm asking for trouble whenever I leave these days."

"Things that tense?" Brady asked.

"Yeah. After today we're afraid to turn our backs. But I'm hoping that shrink'll be able to do some good. Maybe for all of us."

"Hang in there," Brady said.

He was at the newspaper two hours later when Matt called him from the hospital. Outside, the town was coming alive and soon the offices and stores would be open to begin a new week. Brady had gone straight to the *Express* office after leaving the trailer park because he knew that he would never go back to sleep. But he had accomplished nothing and now he was glad to be placing the Closed sign back on the door and leaving things to his assistants, who would be in just after eight.

He went in through the emergency entrance, drawing stares from the nurses.

"Excuse me, but are you all right?" one of the women asked. "You're limping."

Without thinking, he rubbed his hand across his jaw and felt a matt of whiskers. With dirt on his pants and his hair uncombed, he probably looked like some accident victim in shock.

"I'm okay. Thanks," he said. "Where's the morgue?"

"The what?"

"I'm here to meet Dr. McIntire," he told her. "Pete Brady."

Surprise battled recognition in her face.

"Yes. Of course. I think he's in one of the examination rooms at the end of the hall. Try Number One."

He thanked her and stopped before a door with a frosted window. Did he really want to go in? He turned the knob anyway and stepped into the room.

The body of Jean McInnery lay on a metal examination table, still draped with a sheet. Matt Garitty sat in a chair while the doctor leaned against one of the cinder-block walls, looking haggard.

"That was a fast autopsy," Brady said, trying to keep his voice steady.

"What I have is just preliminary," McIntire said. "Lab analysis will take a while. But I think I've got enough."

He whipped back the sheet and Brady flinched at the sight of the dead woman.

"The pills were a tranquilizer prescribed by a doctor in Jonesboro. I called him and he confirmed it. Said she was high-strung."

The physician turned the corpse's head and pointed to the back of her skull.

"But if you'll look close you'll see there's a wound in the occipital portion of the skull. I might have missed it if Matt hadn't told me to be especially careful."

Brady bent his head and saw a small, encrusted wound.

"Maybe she hit her head when she fell down, after she passed out," he volunteered.

"I don't think so." The doctor lifted one of the pale arms, his gloved finger pointing to a bluish stripe on the wrist.

"See that? I think she was tied up. *After* somebody hit her. Now, she was dead about two hours, judging from body temperature. That puts her death at about three o'clock this morning, maybe a little before." He eased the wrist back down and tilted up the dead woman's chin. "See those?"

Brady nodded. He had seen such marks before on the throats of strangle victims. "You think she was choked?" he asked.

"No. At least, not on purpose. The lab tests'll tell the story, but my guess is somebody hit her to knock her out, then tied her up and shoved the pills down her throat. The marks on her neck and chin are from fingers; her killer was forcing her mouth open and making her swallow. I talked to Matt. He said the floor was wet where she was found. Granted, some of it may be vomitis, but my guess is that somebody slopped water down her throat to help her wash the pills down."

"Jesus," Brady muttered. "That means she could have been given the pills a lot earlier, then."

The coroner nodded. "That's right. How much earlier will depend on how much of the chemical turns up in her blood and stomach contents. I'd say, just guessing, mind you, that it was some time before midnight, maybe as early as ten. But there's one other possibility I have to mention."

"What's that?"

"Well, it's always possible she choked swallowing the pills." He shook his head. "God, I hope she thought it was worth it."

"How's that?" Brady asked.

McIntire made a face. "Well, the examination showed she'd had sexual relations earlier in the evening. We'll get blood type and all from the sample we collected from her body. All Matt has to do is find a man to match them."

"Yeah," Matt said, getting up, "that's all."

It was noon before Brady could convince himself it was time to go back and see Miller Purdy.

He'd tried for nearly four hours to find some way around it. But the blue pickup the park manager had seen was something he couldn't ignore.

He was about to leave when the phone rang and he heard Kelly's voice.

"Brady, I'm sorry I left the way I did. I was mad at first but I felt badly about it all day. I was kind of thinking you'd call, but I don't blame you for not doing it."

He started to tell her nobody had been home when he'd tried but decided to maintain the advantage.

"I guess I shouldn't be quite so demanding," he finally managed.

"I've got to admit I half expected to have a state trooper drag me out of class to explain why I wasn't dead on the highway."

Which, Brady thought, *was really what she'd expected.*

"I thought about it," he said. "But, like you say, you're a big girl."

"Right." Was there a trace of disappointment in her voice? "Brady, please don't be mad. I love you."

He melted. He glanced around, reassured himself that neither of his co-workers was in the room, and said, "I love you too. But what were you doing in Jena on Saturday?"

"What?" When she spoke again her voice was low, filled with suspicion. "How did you know I was in Jena?"

"I have eyes and ears everywhere," he said, trying to make a joke of it.

"Do you?" There was a long pause.

"Kel? Look, I didn't mean it that way. I—"

"It's okay," she said in a tone almost too low for him to hear. "Look, I'll tell you about it later, okay? Please trust me."

He found himself nodding. "All right."

"I love you, Brady. Believe me."

"I love you, too."

Then the phone clicked and the line went dead.

Miller Purdy couldn't do worse to him than this.

He still hadn't decided how he was going to find out if Purdy knew the girl. Keep his eyes open, ask the right questions. His excuse for coming again so soon would be a story he was doing on conservation. Surely Purdy would be glad to help him with that. But once inside Purdy's house, it would be sheer luck to turn something up.

Even if Purdy was the murderer he wouldn't kill an editor. That would be too obvious.

Except that as he considered it, his pretext sounded more and more feeble.

As a leading conservationist, your views are important and so I thought I'd come out unannounced again and try to dig up whatever I could before you killed me.

Because Miller Purdy wasn't a conservationist, as he tried to make people believe; but a madman, obsessed with his own family background.

It wasn't too late to turn back.

He slowed, wondering if his decision to come here hadn't been the result of fatigue and desperation. He was still considering it when a blue pickup shot around the curve ahead of him, heading back the way Brady had come.

The pickup was already almost out of sight in his rearview mirror when he realized it was Miller Purdy. And Miller Purdy was in a hell of a hurry.

15

BRADY made a U-turn and followed. When he got to the main highway he saw Purdy's truck half a mile away, headed south, toward Alexandria. If he followed he might lose Purdy. Maybe he should go back, use this opportunity to try to get into the deserted house and rummage for evidence.

Sure. And give the dog another meal.

Besides, he had caught just the briefest glimpse of Purdy's face and there was something about his expression that made Brady want to know more. Something was on Purdy's mind, something that must have an answer someplace on this highway.

If it hadn't been for the roadwork near Bentley there wouldn't have been a chance, but as Brady slowed for the long line of cars he saw Purdy's blue truck ten vehicles ahead, half coated with dust from the construction.

He wondered for a moment if Purdy had seen him, but dismissed the idea; Purdy had his mind set on whatever was ahead of him, not what was behind.

A few seconds later a bulldozer backed onto the shoulder and the roadguard began to wave traffic through. There was a log truck ahead of Purdy's pickup, and an RV ahead of that, so that for the next five or six minutes, until they reached the outskirts of Pineville, Purdy and all the cars behind him limped along, following the two behemoths. But once at Pineville there was a traffic signal, where the road divided. To the left was the old route, through the community of Tioga, a winding two-lane that took fifteen minutes. None of the cars went that way, preferring instead the four-lane that looped around the northern edge of Pineville like a half-moon, leading at last to the bridge that fed into Alexandria, on the opposite side of the Red.

Brady followed the stream of traffic, watching the blue truck whip out at the first chance to pass the slower traffic.

What was there in Alec that was so important Purdy had to get there this quickly? It was almost as if he was running from something . . .

Then, to Brady's surprise, he saw the pickup slide off the four-lane and down the exit toward Highway 71, which was the old way. So he was headed for the business district.

Wrong again. Brady following, lost the pickup on the curves and hills when he came to the old white three-story on the left that was Forest Service Headquarters and slammed on his brakes.

The blue truck was in one of the visitors spaces in front of the building.

Brady turned in quickly and found a parking spot discreetly removed from Purdy's truck. Then he went up the walkway and through the big glass doors.

"Yes, sir?" the receptionist looked up. "Are you here for the meeting?"

"Meeting?" Brady asked.

"The rehearing on the land exchange. It's in the conference room on the third floor. It's already started."

"Thank you." Brady headed for the steps, falling in behind a pair of men in business suits.

The room was an auditorium at the end of the hall, with metal folding chairs, and some of the attendees spilled out into the hall. Brady slipped between the bodies and when there was an opportunity he edged his way inside the room.

Several men, some in Forest Service green, were seated at a conference table at the front of the room. The man in the center, who wore a business suit, was speaking into a microphone.

". . . plan was submitted for environmental review and duly approved at the level of the Secretary of the Interior, and contracts were bid. The bid from Mid-State Contractors was accepted, based on accepted standards of state bidding procedure. The land to be used is currently nonproductive due to the forest fire of 1988 and will not be productive for at least fifteen years to come. The need for the new correctional facility was established by an act of the state legislature, passed, let's see . . ."

The new prison. Of course. The one the state planned to build in the western part of Troy Parish. Brady had heard about it, of course: The Forest Service was trading some land with the state, and the deal had been finalized. But then the environmental lobby had gotten a couple of congressmen to intervene, so that a rehearing had been scheduled.

The bureaucrat went on: ". . . expected to provide enhanced employment opportunities, in the form of between seventy and one hundred jobs; ancillary economic advantages in the form of approximately three million dollars of additional business . . ."

"Pssst. Mr. Brady . . ."

The editor jerked around at his name. Ripley Dillon was seated in one of the folding chairs, not ten feet away, a press badge prominently displayed on his shirt.

Now Brady remembered: Ripley had agreed to cover the hearing for the *Express* and Brady, with his mind elsewhere, had forgotten all about it.

He gave his assistant what he hoped was an approving smile and scanned the gathering.

Miller Purdy was three rows up, standing along the wall.

Brady swore under his breath. Of course Purdy had been in a hurry. He had been on his way to this hearing. It was a hotly debated issue and it was hardly surprising that someone who considered himself an environmentalist would want to attend.

Well, Brady thought, *an afternoon wasted.*

The man finished his statement.

"Now, if there are those who would like to speak in favor of or against the plan, we'll be happy to listen to them."

Miller Purdy strode across the room to the podium.

With his dark beard bristling, Brady was reminded of portraits he had seen of John Brown, the abolitionist leader.

"This plan," Purdy thundered, "is an abortion that will have absolutely no positive effects besides making politicians and their cronies rich. And to declare the land that's being traded worthless just because there was a forest fire a couple of years ago is like saying let's build a high-rise in Yellowstone because it burned, too."

A murmur ran through the audience and Brady saw the men at the table exchange glances. They had heard it all before and their faces showed resignation at having to hear it again.

"I know the Forest Service has carried out environmental studies," Purdy went on. "I've seen them. You people are very good about that. A lot of trees had to die to make paper for all your documents. But the fact is that asking the Forest Service to look after the environment is like asking the fox to take care of the chickens."

"Mr. Purdy . . ." the chairman said but Purdy cut him off.

"There were days when panthers and wolves and bears roamed the woods," Purdy declared. "Now you want to change them for convicts. The cities have sent us their trash, their chemicals, their dirty air, and now they want to send us their human trash, as well."

There was a sprinkle of applause. The diatribe lasted another five minutes, then the chairman called time.

"Mr. Purdy, we appreciate your views, but there are others who would like to be heard."

A reluctant Purdy returned to his place against the wall, his eyes briefly touching Brady and moving on. Fortunately, Brady told himself, there was nothing strange about the editor of the *Express* being here and Purdy appeared unconcerned.

Another man had risen from the front row of chairs and was advancing to the podium now. Brady started for the door, knowing that his assistant would take all the notes necessary, but then he stopped.

He knew the man who was about to speak, had seen him only a few days ago.

It was Laverne Penniman.

"Mr. Chairman, you know me, Laverne Penniman, of Mid-State Contractors. We have the contract to build the facility and I've got to say we're just a little upset that now that the contract's been signed suddenly there's all this stir to throw it out. We bid in good faith and we put a hell of a lot of our money into it." Penniman waved his hand dismissively. "You folks did all kinds of studies, they were accepted by everybody in Washington, and now we have to come here and listen to how it ought to all be done over again." He turned to stare at Purdy. "You know, I like nature just as well as the next man. I hunt and fish and I believe in conservation. But this isn't 1930. And anybody who thinks it is is living in the past."

"Despoiler!" cried Purdy.

"Can I talk?" Laverne asked.

"Profiteer!" Purdy shouted back.

The chairman banged his gavel furiously.

"Mr. Purdy, if you don't keep quiet, I'll ask you to leave."

Miller Purdy's face went red and his beard bristled.

"You don't have to. I can't listen to any more of this garbage." He swept the room with an accusing finger. "You'll all have to answer to your children!"

He stormed out and Brady followed. Purdy was angry, and angry men were sometimes careless.

Purdy's truck jumped backward out of its parking place as Brady reached the front door and by the time the editor got to his own vehicle the other man was at the highway, gunning his engine impatiently as he waited for a break in the long line of traffic.

To Brady's surprise, Purdy went left, toward the city, instead of back the way he had come and Brady, risking a collision with a van, nudged into the string of cars three back from the other man. They passed Lake Bulow, on the right, and went over the bridge into Rapides Parish. A macabre whimsey seized Pete Brady: What if Purdy were headed for the Bentley Hotel. What if he also had a rendezvous?

But Purdy passed the turn-off, staying on 71 until a traffic circle, one of the pair for which Alexandria was justly infamous. Here he swung right, heading onto Highway 1, which ran alongside the Red, toward Shreveport.

Wild goose chase, Brady told himself. The man was probably just driving until he got over his anger. If, that is, a man like Miller Purdy ever got over his anger.

They had gone just over a mile, almost to the gates of England Air Base, when the blue pickup slid into a gravel parking area, in front of a convenience store. Brady passed the parking area and pulled to the side in front of a house that advertised, Madame Zena: Problems Solved Palms Read. In his mirror he saw Purdy walking across the gravel, still angry, and Brady relaxed—he hadn't been seen. Purdy went to the payphone at one end of the building and put in a coin.

At that point a woman came out of the house, smiling. She wore a multicolored skirt and a gypsy blouse. A cigarette hung out of her mouth, and gold jewelry jangled on her hands and arms.

She bent low and motioned for him to roll down his window.

"You want your palm read?" she asked.

"I don't think so," Brady said.

"Twenty dollars," she said. "I'll tell you what to be careful of. You look like a man with problems."

"Thanks anyway," Brady told her.

"That air crash they had at the base last month?" she said. "I saw it before it happened. If that boy had come to me I could've saved him."

Brady managed a smile. "Too bad."

"Fifteen bucks," the woman said. "I'll tell you about your love life. You got a problem, I can tell. You got some things you've got to resolve."

"Look . . ."

"Can't ignore them," the woman said. Her hair was done up in a bun and, unlike Penelope, her eyes were hard and probing. "You got a chance for everything you want but you're gonna screw it up, the way you're going."

"Thanks, but I've got my own fortune-teller," he said, checking his mirror again. Purdy had finished his call and was heading back to his truck. The engine started and the pickup made a fast circle in the parking lot, heading back the way they had come.

"Wise ass," the woman said.

"That's me," Brady agreed, starting his own engine.

"You remember what I told you," she called after him. "You had your chance."

By the time Brady had managed a U-turn the pickup had vanished.

16

EMMETT Larson listened to Brady's experiences, slumping back in his frayed old easy chair with his eyes half closed. Outside it was dark, with a chill wind building.

"So Maud had her eye on me, did she?" he chuckled. "Well, she was too mean for me. In eleventh grade she got jilted by Sam Anderson, you know. Made his life miserable after that. Too much like me, I guess." He shifted, grimacing slightly from his rheumatism. "But it sounds like Kelly's the one making you miserable, right now."

"We'll work it out," Brady said.

"Sure." Emmett shook his head. "I should of put her over my knee a few more times. Trouble is, the last time I tried she ran away. Guess there's only so much you can do."

Silence drifted back over them, the low mumble of the TV forming a background noise.

"I expect right now her parents are saying the same thing about Jean McInnery," Emmett speculated. "God, you never know, do you?" He fixed Brady with a squint. "You figure Purdy killed her?"

"He's got a blue pickup. But so do a lot of people."

118

"Well, if it *was* him, there's got to be a motive. If she was having it on with Elkins, it could be jealousy, though kind of late in the day. On the other hand, maybe she was blackmailing him. There was bad blood between the Elkins and Purdy families over that land. Come to think of it, Purdy doesn't much like anybody to have *any* land."

Brady sighed. It was at moments like this that he most missed alcohol.

"Well, since the bullet went through Elkins, there isn't any solid proof Scotty shot him, so I guess there's still hope."

The old editor snorted. "I know what you're thinking: The Elkins killing could have been an accident, but it could have led to the death of the McInnery girl. A sort of catalyst."

Brady nodded. "Yeah. If I could just nail down the links in the chain." He paused, remembering something. "The other day Mrs. R. said she knew something about Purdy. She was about to tell me when somebody interrupted and I forgot to ask her later on. Any idea what it might be?"

Emmet waved disparagingly. "His family, probably. People like Mrs. R. resent the fact that his father wasn't the 'right kind of people,' if you know what I mean. He married some barefoot girl from the country, who was young enough to be his granddaughter and yet he ended up with all that money. Sticks in people's craws. It's an offense against the order of things, way they see it."

"I can see that," Brady said, rising. "If I could have followed Purdy today I might have been able to find out more. I can't shake the feeling he's a dangerous man."

"Most fanatics are." The old publisher shook his head and blew out. "Comes from his upbringing. Living with old Elmer must have been like living with the Old Testament God."

Brady put a hand on the door and turned.

"What about the new prison, Emmett? Almost everything I've heard so far has been in favor of it."

Emmett nodded. "Save this parish. Hell, Pete, you know how it is with employment. The big lumber companies aren't hiring like they used to. The state economy is flat. The young people just want to get out of here. This has always been a poor area, since before

119

the days of Huey Long. Even the Indians couldn't make a living scratching out this soil. People look to the prison as a place they may be able to get jobs. So it means a jailbreak every couple of years; they'll pay an extra penny of taxes for a few more deputies if it comes to that. But you can't talk to the Miller Purdys. It's like talking to these antigun people."

"Or the NRA," Brady added quickly.

"Them too," Emmett agreed. "Most definitely them too."

He was still thinking about Miller Purdy and the man at the bar the next morning when his office door opened and Laverne Penniman came in.

"Mr. Brady," he said, shaking the editor's hand. He turned to the bookkeeper, seated at a table to the rear. "And how is your beautiful young associate today?"

Mrs. Rickenbacker blushed and looked away, but she was clearly pleased.

"Really, Laverne . . ."

"I'm sorry. You know me too well to be taken in." He gave Brady a smile. "She used to chase me out of her backyard for shooting acorns with my slingshot. A few years back." He winked.

"Just a few," Mrs. R. acknowledged. "I told my husband you wouldn't come to any good. I said, 'That boy will wind up in the prison.' "

"And here I am building it, instead."

They laughed together and Laverne turned to the publisher.

"Mr. Brady, I saw you at the hearing yesterday. I guess you heard what went on."

"I heard a lot of it," Brady said.

"Right. Miller Purdy's sermon."

Mrs. R. made a disapproving sound from her desk at the rear.

"He's forceful, all right," Brady said.

"Well, he's opinionated and there're others like him," Laverne drawled. "They got this whole question reopened after it was a done deed; that shows how much power they've got in some quarters. Hell, I know that land. Ain't nothing on it but dead pine beetles."

"Nonsense," Mrs. R. fulminated. "Just terrible, that one man can hold up progress for a whole parish."

"Well, he won't hold it up much longer," Laverne Penniman assured her. "The hearing took care of that. I'm sure they'll see him for what he is."

"I certainly hope so," Mrs. R. huffed.

"But I've got to admit," Laverne went on, "we can't take any chances. My whole business depends on doing this job and every day that idiot holds it up costs more money. That's why I'm here, Mr. Brady. I want to put an ad in your paper."

"An ad?" Brady asked.

"Right." Penniman held up a piece of paper with typing on it and Brady saw that it was the letterhead of his company. "I just wanted to publish something about the benefits to the parish from this project. See, I've listed the number of new jobs, the economic input, all the projections. A full page spread, whatever it costs. I want people to know what's at stake."

Brady took the page and read over it.

"You want people to write their legislators," he said.

"Sure," Penniman laughed. "That's the idea. If a nut like Miller Purdy can get people to write letters so can I."

The publisher nodded. "We'll put it in Thursday's issue," he said. "If that's okay."

"That's fine," Penniman said. "How much will it be?"

"Mrs. R. will take care of you," Brady said. "You can pay her and make out the usual form."

He stood by Mrs. Rickenbacker's desk while she took a check and helped Penniman make out an ad order form. When she was finished Laverne turned back to Brady.

"I feel better now," he said. "If Miller Purdy wants a fight, by God, he'll get one."

Brady watched him walk out to his carryall and drive away.

He had an uneasy feeling, that this might be exactly what Purdy wanted, and wondered just how far Miller Purdy was willing to go.

17

THAT afternoon Brady drove west along Highway 84, past the trailer park and the local Forest Service office. In ten minutes he came to a warning light, where a side road intersected with the highway, but he kept going, taking the dips at sixty miles an hour and then laboring up the steep hills at a sedate fifty.

Twice he passed green Forest Service trucks and he told himself that he probably should have stopped in to let the District Ranger know where he was heading. But it was too late now and he'd just have to take a chance.

He saw the green road sign ahead and flicked on his turn signal. A narrow two-lane threaded away to the left and he turned onto this road. He had a topographic map from the office with him and every minute or so he referred to it, but there was no need; a line of orange survey flagging on the right side of the road led inevitably toward his destination.

No one lived out here now; it all belonged to the government. But once, before the establishment of the Forest, there had been an occasional farmstead, occupied by people too hardheaded to let the sandy soil win out and chase them away. He had checked a soil map before he had left and it had characterized the earth here as largely unfit for anything except pine growth.

But Miller Purdy thought it was worth saving.

Ten miles south of the highway he came to a gravel road and went left again. The line of orange flags followed.

An escaping convict would have a long walk, he observed. Not as bad as the impassable Tunica Hills that guarded the state penitentiary at Angola, but Angola was a maximum security facility, one of the toughest in the nation; this was to be a medium security prison. Inmates who had only killed once, somebody had wryly observed. A real country club, Brady told himself, looking out at the thick pine growth. Right.

The orange flags came to a halt at a sign and Brady stopped.

Site of the New Louisiana Medium Security Correctional Facility.

Brady looked down at the map he had gotten from his files, from when the project had originally been proposed; the map had drawn on it a square nine acres on each side. Brady folded the map and put it into his pocket and got out.

The wind was colder now, razoring down the road like a whipsaw, and the newsman zipped his windbreaker up to cover his chest.

He considered the pines around him—definitely not first growth, he noted; this part, at least, had been harvested and then replanted ten or twelve years ago. He locked his car and started into the woods, following a logging trail.

The roadside flags were for the power and gas lines, of course. And it was possible they might disrupt wildlife. He had heard of objections to the North Alaska Pipeline on those grounds. But this would be considerably smaller, about four inches in diameter, buried, and it would be laid alongside the road. The power line would require a corridor of sorts, but, again, that would merely be an extension of the existing road, except for a few places where it took shortcuts across the woods.

Miller Purdy hadn't said anything about the power or gas lines, though. He seemed more incensed by the prison itself.

Brady stepped over a fallen limb and halted; there was a trash pile beside the road, full of aluminum cans and old bottles. The single eye of an old television stared at him accusingly and he bent over to pick up a piece of tarpaper, then tossed it away. The dump was recent, not more than five years old and probably still in use. He considered it for another second and then, hands buried in his pockets, started forward again.

It would be nice to have a dowsing rod, he thought, *so I could just follow it to whatever the hell I'm looking for.*

And that was just it: he didn't know what he was looking for. If he had expected to find a pine forest, he had found it. But if he had expected to see anything out of the ordinary here, he had so far been disappointed. He'd called the Forest Service earlier and they had even told him an oil well that had been sunk nearby ten years ago had come up dry.

The trees parted and he found himself standing in a vast, charred field—all that was left from the forest fire. What was it Laverne had said? "Ain't nothing on it but dead pine beetles."

Brady took a deep breath and stepped forward, into the field. In the last few years the secondary growth had started again and he felt dead briars clutching at his pants. He came to a charred log and had to make his way around it, the thorns pricking him as he moved.

Then he had an idea and climbed up onto the log to get a vantage point. There was nothing in the field except blackened earth and burned vegetation. He climbed down again and started back the way he had come.

A wasted afternoon, he told himself. After all, hadn't all the environmental studies been made? What could he expect to find that the experts hadn't?

He left the woods, driving back the way he had come. He found the District Ranger at his desk, struggling with paperwork, in the small building that served as the local Forest Service office.

"How do I find out about that property?" Brady asked.

The ranger, a round-faced man of forty with a crew cut, put down his pen and leaned back in his chair.

"We did the woodpecker survey ourselves, and I'm glad to say there weren't any. As for the archaeology, I reckon they'd know in Pineville," he said. "There's a fellow there who keeps track of all that." He checked his watch. "He's probably still in his office if you want to call him."

It took Brady five minutes and several offices before he was finally given the name of the forest archaeologist.

"But he's not in his office," the receptionist told him. "He's due back before leaving time, though, if you want to call back."

Brady thanked her and consulted his own watch. It was three o'clock now and Pineville was fifty miles away. He had time to make it before four-thirty.

It was just a hunch, of course, but it was worth it, even if it was a long drive, and the second time he'd made the trip in as many days. But at least it provided the illusion of doing something and that was what he badly needed now.

He decided to drive to Pineville and at four-fifteen he was seated in the lobby of the Forest Service building when a man in green uniform came out of the hallway.

"Mr. Brady? I'm Phil Griffin, the forest archaeologist. They told me you were out here. I just got in from the field, myself. I hope you didn't wait long."

"Just got here," Brady said, shaking the man's hand. The archaeologist led him down the hallway, toward an office at the end. The room Brady entered was occupied by a desk and filing cabinets, with a huge poster on one wall that read Protect Your Heritage, and photographs of the profiles and trenches of an archaeological dig over the desk. A door to the side led into what appeared to be a lab.

"Have a seat," Griffin said, waving to a chair, and sat down behind his desk. Griffin looked about thirty-five, wore a dark, closely clipped beard and glasses, and his black eyes seemed to be sizing up his visitor despite his apparent friendliness. "Now what can I do for you?"

Brady spread his topographic map out on the desk.

"I was curious about why Miller Purdy is so opposed to the new prison being built here, so I drove out there this afternoon to look over the site. I didn't see anything, but I was wondering if your studies had turned anything up."

The archaeologist got up slowly like a spring unwinding and

125

went through the doorway into the next office. He pulled out a drawer of the map cabinet, withdrew a map, and brought it back with him, laying it on the desk. Brady saw that the prison area had been shaded and marked with some numbers.

"Well," Griffin drawled, "we surveyed this tract in 1986, as part of a timber sale, according to the map. Nothing reported or it would show up on here." He gave Brady a hard stare. "What did you expect to find?"

"I don't know. It just seems like Miller Purdy is awfully interested in seeing that nobody uses that land."

Griffin made a sour face.

"Mr. Brady, Miller Purdy is attached to *all* the land on the Forest. You know, there are preservationists and preservationists. *I'm* a preservationist myself. And I'll be the first to admit not everybody in the Forest Service *is*. Some consider archaeological surveys a nuisance. But when we get somebody like Purdy, it just gives them fuel. They figure we're all that way."

Brady got up and the archaeologist handed him back his map.

"Thank you, Mr. Griffin. You've been a big help."

The official gave him a parting handshake. "Glad to help, Mr. Brady. Anytime."

As Brady started into the hallway, his hand went into his pocket and his fingers curled absently around the little piece of metal he had found at the Elkins camp. On an impulse he brought it out and held it up for the other man to see.

"By the way, got any idea what this is?"

Griffin took the tiny object and held it to the light.

"This come from the site we're talking about?" he asked.

Brady shook his head. "No. A hunting camp eight or ten miles away. I found it lying on the ground."

The archaeologist grunted and handed it back. "Well, there's not a lot I can say. If it had been part of a burial, say, or in the ground, at least, where it could be placed in stratigraphic relationship to other objects, you could say something about it. But when you've gotten it from the surface, it could come from just about anywhere."

"But just what is it?" Brady asked. "Can you tell?"

"Oh, well, that's not too hard," Griffin said. "It's a bell."

"A bell?"

"You know, jingle, jingle. The French used to trade them to the Indians, along with glass beads and pots. You go to the reservation today you'll see the dancers with bells on their costumes. But, of course, I don't know if this one was used for that. It doesn't look old and it's not valuable—looks to be nickel- or chrome-plated. And something flattened it pretty good, too."

"A bullet," Brady said. "I found it on a practice range."

The archaeologist laughed. "I guess some people will shoot at anything."

"Well, thanks a lot," Brady said, dropping the bell into his pocket. "I don't guess you know anything about lacrosse?"

"That game they play up north?" He laughed. "Not really. But if you find some potsherds or projectile points, give me a call."

"I'll do that," Brady promised. "Merry Christmas."

It was five-thirty, with twilight sliding toward darkness, as Brady pulled into Troy.

He needed to look up the land titles, but that would require getting into both the assessor's and the clerk's offices, and it was after hours. He reluctantly went home, throwing his windbreaker on a chair. His answering machine was blinking and he stood staring down at it for a long time, thinking as long as he did not play the message then nothing really bad could have happened.

Except he knew better, knew that he was just postponing the inevitable. He reached out to flick the switch that would play the tape but before he reached it the phone rang.

He drew his hand back in surprise, then picked up the receiver.

"Brady? Is that you?" It was Kelly's voice.

"It's me," he said, relaxing.

"Where have you been, you idiot? I've been calling and calling. I talked to Dad and he told me about that woman. You may be in danger."

"Sorry," he managed. "I was going to call you later on."

"Sure. Look, I know what was going on. You're mad at me, and

127

you wanted to let me suffer. Okay, okay, but I'm coming up tomorrow. I can't stand any more of this. I can't have you getting killed without me."

Brady smiled in spite of himself. "That *would* be pretty bad."

"And you need my help, too, admit it. Besides . . ." her voice softened. "I'm tired of this long distance, too. I'd rather fight with you up close."

"That would be nice," he said.

He flopped down into his chair. He should have felt better, because Kelly was coming, but something was nagging him, had been for hours.

Then, at last, he remembered what it was. It was what the archaeologist had said earlier, during their conversation: "I guess some people will shoot at anything."

Was that how it was going to turn out?

18

THE next morning Brady pored over the conveyance ledgers under the laconic eye of the clerk of court, Wilson Creswell.

"Maybe if you told me what you was looking for I could help," Creswell said, watching Brady bend over the long table to flip through the book. Under the table, on rollers that allowed them to be slid out and removed, were the other books for every property transfer that had occurred in the parish since records had been kept. Across the room, two landmen for oil companies were at work, expertly tracing the transfer histories of various parcels. Creswell was used to them; it was only the editor who was a relative novelty. And because when a newspaper person searched land titles, it was likely to mean problems for someone, he asked his question.

Brady, looking up from a handwritten entry whose faded ink was playing tricks with his eyes, debated for a second and then answered.

"I was checking the title of the land where the prison is going to be located."

"Ah," said the clerk. "There some problem with it?"

"Not that I know of," Brady said. "Matter of fact, I can't find

129

anything much about it at all. Forest Service bought it from Troy Lumber in 1935. Troy got it from a man named Conway in 1902. Conway's address is given as Chicago. Conway got it at a sheriff's sale from a Waldo Dinkens in 1896, and Dinkens got it from a"—Brady referred to his notes—"from a Matthew Canaday in ninety-five, and he got it from a Smith in ninety-four, and Smith had the land patented to him from the government in 1860."

Creswell nodded under his white thatch.

"Could of told you that, you'd asked. They did a pretty good title search when the Forest Service decided to turn it over to the state." He squinted and lodged a thumb under each strip of his galluses. "Don't tell me somebody from one of them families is laying claim."

"No," Brady said. "Nothing like that. I was just wondering if anybody had an emotional claim."

"Oh." Creswell sat down in one of the chairs. He had small, blue veins in his nose and the ruddy complexion that came from too much drink. "Well, who can say about that? But I doubt it. This Conway or whoever probably never *saw* the land; he was a land speculator, if he was from Chicago. Lots of 'em around the turn of the century. That's when they had the big lumber boom, built the railroad. People bought thousands of acres and sold the timber. Or held onto it till the price of timber went sky high and *then* sold out. 'Course, it all collapsed eventually. No more timber left. But it's been government land for the last fifty years or so. All those timber speculators are long since dead."

"Thanks," Brady said. He decided to leave the marriage records until later. He had a ten o'clock prepub meeting and Kelly was supposed to be in by noon.

After the meeting, he walked back out into the parking lot, hands in his pockets.

The Forest Service archaeologists had done a survey and hadn't found anything significant. The land titles were clear and seemed to descend in an unbroken chain to the current owners, and there were no notations about lawsuits regarding ownership.

But Miller Purdy was willing to fight the government over it, and there were two people dead, though for apparently unrelated reasons. There had to be some way to make sense of it all.

He went back inside and called Phil Griffin in Pineville. The other man listened patiently and when Brady was finished he heard a sigh at the other end of the phone.

"Well, there is a way, at least theoretically. It's called phosphate analysis. I've never done it, you understand."

"Does it work?"

"It's worked for others. But we're talking about an awfully big area: eighty acres. Frankly, Mr. Brady, this is a small office and I just don't have time to carry out the kind of project that would require. Plus, there are some expenses involved."

"I'll pay the expenses," Brady said. "All I ask is that you give me what time you can. If nothing shows, I'll leave you alone."

"It might not be a representative sampling," the archaeologist warned.

"It'll have to do," Brady said.

"Okay," Griffin agreed. "We'll give it a try."

Brady sat at his desk for a long time after hanging up the phone. He was going to look like a hell of a fool. After all, he didn't even know what he was looking for.

He tried to put it out of his mind and dialed Kelly's number. When he got no answer he tried Emmett.

"Easy, boy. She'll be along in her good time. Probably just got up late."

Brady had a vision of twisted wreckage on the highway.

"Probably," he said and replaced the receiver.

He turned to his assistant, making sure, before he spoke, that Mrs. R. had already left for lunch.

"Ripley, I've got a job for you."

The younger man listened, but after the first few sentences his enthusiasm turned to chagrin.

"Damn, Mr. B., that'll take forever. I mean, don't you even know the year?"

"I told you the approximate year," Brady said. "That's the best I can do."

131

"Well, look, not that I don't want to help, but why can't I just ask around? I mean, there're people who'll know."

"And who'll talk. And I've already taken a big enough chance. Let *me* be the one to screw things up."

"How do you know it isn't another parish?" Ripley demanded. "Say, Catahoula, or Winn, or—"

"I don't. But we have to start somewhere and this is the logical place."

"You don't need it today or tomorrow, do you?" Ripley asked hopelessly.

"Today would be best," Brady said. "Work overtime if you have to on the layout for tomorrow. I'll pay."

"Sure," Ripley muttered, dejected. "Look, what do I do if somebody asks questions?"

"Tell them you're doing a class project for a sociology course you're taking."

"Right," Ripley said, sighing. He picked up his yellow pad and headed for the door. "When last seen alive, Dillon was observed treading water in a sea of papers."

The editor went back inside, waited another half hour, and then left. He drove back to his house, left a note on the door, and then set out west again, the same way he had gone yesterday.

He reached the turn off to the prison site and went left, once more following the line of orange flags. He could tell from Griffin's voice that the archaeologist was humoring him. And maybe Brady *was* crazy. Maybe he should just drop this and let things take their course. Maybe . . .

Ten miles later he pulled to the side of the road. It was the same place he'd been yesterday but something about the site had changed.

The big sign was gone. Someone had pulled it down and now it was lying by the side of the road.

Brady got out and went over to look down at it. The pair of uprights to which it had been nailed were snapped off and he wondered how it had been done. Probably, he decided, by someone's tying a rope around the posts and then pulling with his car. Or truck.

Because it was probably Miller Purdy who had done it. Anyone

132

else in the parish would just have shot the sign full of holes, or maybe pulled the signboard itself down. But that way it would have been easy to put back up. Purdy had fixed it so new posts would have to be sunk. A thorough man.

Brady started down the path again, wondering what he hoped to see.

For some reason he heard himself humming "Jingle Bells" and halted.

No time to be scatterbrained. *Keep your mind on where you are.*

The Forest Service man said he knew of nothing out here.

What the hell did Brady expect to find? The topsoil was thin and acidic. There was no gold, no silver, no uranium reported for this parish or for the region, for that matter.

He stepped over the same log as yesterday and halted. There was the sound of a vehicle coming down the road, headed in his direction. He walked back out down the trail, reaching the gravel as the green Forest Service truck skidded to a halt just behind his own car. A few seconds later Phil Griffin climbed out, giving Brady a desultory wave. The archaeologist reached into the bed of the truck and took out some equipment. Brady hurried forward to help him.

"Soil probe," Griffin explained, nodding at a metal tube about two yards long with a handle at one end. "You can carry the sample bags."

Brady picked up several packages of polyethylene bags and started after the other man.

"You got any idea where to start?" Griffin asked as they made their way down the trail.

"Not really," Brady said helplessly. "I guess it's going to be pretty hit and miss."

"Yeah," Griffin agreed, his skepticism evident. "You know, we need some control borings, too." They stopped at the edge of the field and the archaeologist shook his head. "We could be out here a long time."

Griffin set down the probe and spread his map out onto the ground. He made a few preliminary calculations and took a reading with a pocket compass.

"I guess," he said hopelessly, "we might as well traverse the field."

He rolled up the map and Brady followed him to an area of burned soil and watched him stab the blunt nose of the instrument into the ground and twist. With each turn of the handle the probe bit deeper into the ground until, thirty seconds later, it was implanted approximately a foot into the earth.

"Let's see what we've got," Griffin said. He began to twist the handle in the opposite direction, freeing the drill. He lifted the bit end of the probe and Brady saw a narrow column of earth trapped in its hollow screw-end. The archaeologist took out a pocket knife and scraped some of the soil into a plastic bag, which he labeled with a felt pen. Then he made a notation of the approximate place on his map. "I'll just have to go by pacing," he explained. "It would take forever to try to measure accurately. One more now." He put the business end of the probe back into the same hole and removed another sample of dirt, this time a foot lower than the first. This, too, he dug into with his knife, saving a portion.

"Test Number Two," Griffin said and started pacing across the burned field. Brady counted forty steps before the other man stopped. "We'll call that a hundred feet."

In an hour they had punched holes in a line from east to west across the charred field and come out on the other side.

Griffin checked his watch. "Three-thirty. I say we make a line from north to south and then see what we have."

Brady nodded, realizing he was in no position to argue.

"If there's anything promising, we can always come back and do more, in a smaller area," Griffin added, as if to mollify the other man.

They had reached the center of the field when it happened—a gunshot exploded out of nowhere and something kissed Brady's face like a deadly serpent. Griffin dropped the probe and fell to the earth, Brady following only a millisecond later.

He heard the archaeologist swear and raised his head slightly.

"Are you okay?"

"Yeah," Griffin answered. "If there's some deer hunter out here shooting at anything that moves . . ."

134

The second shot gouged the earth two feet from Brady's face and he tasted charcoal dust in his mouth.

"That wasn't an accident," he heard himself say. "Somebody's shooting at us."

"Son of a bitch," Griffin swore. He lifted his head slightly. "I think I see movement over at the edge of the trees, on the trail." He lifted himself a few inches farther and yelled:

"Purdy, is that you? Damn it, you'd better quit while you still can!"

A flash of light blinked in the trees and both men threw themselves back flat on the ground as another shot flew over them.

Purdy, Brady thought. *The other man was right. And they were completely at his mercy.*

He started to crawl toward a fallen tree, for cover, and another shot sprayed dirt in his eyes.

"Are you okay?" Griffin called.

"For now," Brady answered.

A fifth shot whipped at the arm of his jacket and his eyes shut, involuntarily.

He wouldn't feel the next shot because it would be the one that killed him.

But the next shot never came. Instead, in the distance, he heard a motor start and realized, dully, that their assailant was leaving. He shoved himself to his feet and brushed off his clothes, aware that he was trembling.

"I've had it," Griffin swore, rubbing dirt off his cheek. "Making an asshole out of yourself at meetings is one thing, but shooting at government personnel on federal land is a little too much. I'll have his ass for this."

"I think he was warning us," Brady said. "Not shooting to kill."

"Yeah, well, let his lawyer bring it up at the trial," the archaeologist mumbled, picking up the probe. They walked back across the field to the trail, and then to the road.

Brady nodded at their vehicles.

"He doesn't seem to have cut the tires. He could have."

Griffin tossed the probe into the back of the truck.

"He was a real gentleman. Ought to get him about a year off his sentence."

Brady managed a smile. "I'm sorry I got you into this."

Griffin grinned back. "Hey, that's why I get paid big bucks. Look, I'm going back to make a report on this to our enforcement people."

Brady nodded. "I'll come with you." He almost added that he could use a stiff drink.

Griffin halted. "Are you okay?"

"Yeah." Brady smiled crookedly. "I'm just not used to being shot at."

"Who is?" The archaeologist opened the door of his truck. "You said something on the phone about heading toward Natchitoches."

"Well, that was my intention. But I'm sure your people will want me to sign something—"

"Were you going to Natchitoches on this investigation?"

"Yep."

Griffin folded his arms. "Then our paperwork can wait. Do what you have to do and I'll catch up with you later."

Brady took a few deep breaths and realized his trembling was subsiding.

"Okay. I should be back in a couple of hours."

The archaeologist shrugged. "Doesn't matter. I'll start the ball rolling. And I'll analyze these samples and let you know what I found."

"Thanks," Brady said, holding out his hand. "I appreciate it, Phil."

Phil Griffin shrugged. "All in a day's work for the Men in Green."

Brady watched the other man drive away.

Miller Purdy. It had to be Miller Purdy. But what was there about this land worth going to federal prison for?

19

BRADY'S tires bumped on the brick street as he passed through the Natchitoches business district. It was nearly four-thirty and traffic in the old colonial town was beginning to clot the narrow main street as people left their offices for home. On his left was the lake and on the right the restored buildings of downtown. Memories flooded over him of the times he and Kelly had come here, to soak up the atmosphere of the old French settlement, visit the museums, and watch the lighting of the Christmas lights. He looked overhead at the strings of cables. Had they already done it this year? Somehow, he couldn't remember.

He came to one of the traffic lights and stopped. As he waited, his eyes wandered over to the grass embankment that led from the street to the water's edge. One Christmas he and Kelly had come to watch the fireworks display. They had lain on the grass among the other thousands of visitors and eaten meat pies, for which the town was famous, and drunk Cokes from a cooler, and he had complained about the crush of bodies. But afterward he'd realized he had enjoyed it—enjoyed overhearing the snatches of conversation from those camped out around them, enjoyed wandering through the venders' stands, enjoyed the breathtaking patterns of the red, blue, green, and yellow explosions against the night sky. Enjoyed, most of all, having her with him to share it.

When had that been? This past year or the year before? His mind refused to cooperate.

He recalled her furtive conversation on the phone last week: What if she had decided to go back north? She had never said much about her ex-husband, and he gathered that it had been a painful episode. But people did get back together sometimes . . .

A horn honked behind him and he realized the light had changed. So much for daydreaming at traffic signals. He was being irrational again. The things that had been happening lately were interfering with his equilibrium.

What equilibrium? He was just a lonely, middle-aged, ex-alcoholic (if there was such a thing) who had escaped the pressures of the big city for the anonymity of a small town. He had fled his own success because the price of it had been the murder of his source. Now, in love with a beautiful woman nearly twenty years his junior, he was afraid what price success would exact this time.

He found a parking place and got out, a tired man with unkempt, dark hair and glasses falling down on his nose. A Santa Claus on the corner saw Brady and turned toward some more likely prospects coming from the other direction. Chagrined, the editor fished out a handful of change and dropped it into the cup.

"Thank you, sir," said the surprised Santa. "Merry Christmas."

"Ho, ho, ho," said Brady, crossing the street.

He went through a glass door, grateful for the warmth inside the office. The young woman at the front desk smiled, but her eyes took in his mussed clothes and scraped cheek.

"Is Mr. Hornbaugh around?" Brady asked, handing her his card.

"I'll see." She got up and went into the back.

It was a new office, with fresh paint and new filing cabinets. On the walls were framed issues of newspapers, chosen apparently, for their significance. Brady looked around, envious. One day, he thought—

A movement behind him interrupted his musings.

He turned to see a man pushing his way forward with the help of assorted wheezes and coughs. The man, who was immensely fat, halted at the receptionist's desk to catch his breath and gave Brady a flabby paw, meanwhile eying the other's disheveled appearance.

"Peter, how good to see you. What brings you over this way? Not deciding to sell out, are you?"

Brady smiled. "Your last offer was too good to accept," he told the fat man. "But keep trying."

"Too bad," Hornbaugh said, shaking his head. "I tried to get it when Emmett stepped down, you know, but you beat me to it. I haven't forgotten."

"Well, your time may come," Brady laughed.

"Come in the back," Hornbaugh invited him, heaving himself around before Brady could answer. "When you pass the ice box there, get yourself a pop and give me a Dr. Pepper." The fat man stumped into an office at the rear but Brady halted at the small kitchen, where there was a microwave, sink, and refrigerator. He took out a Dr. Pepper for Hornbaugh and a Seven-Up for himself.

"Sit," Hornbaugh ordered as Brady walked into the room.

Brady looked around him, bewildered. Unlike the front office, Hornbaugh's lair was crowded with everything imaginable, from baseball mitts to a Stop sign that had evidently been pried from its metal upright and now leaned lazily against one wall.

Documents lay scattered about the floor, having apparently fallen from the card table that sat in the center. This table was stacked high with papers, some of which were anchored by rocks, some by empty glasses, and some by books. Hornbaugh lowered himself into a wooden-backed chair and peered at Brady over the mess.

"Now, what really brings you here?" he wheezed, sipping his Dr. Pepper the way an oenophile might taste a rare wine. "It wasn't my company, was it?"

Brady smiled. He knew Horace Hornbaugh only well enough to recognize an eccentric when he saw one. This was the first time Hornbaugh had invited him back to his office.

"I need your business knowledge," Brady told him. "One publisher to another."

"Ah. Professional courtesy requested. This sounds serious. So what is it?"

"There's a contractor here, Laverne Penniman. I need to know as much about him as possible."

"Penniman," Hornbaugh echoed, his double chins vibrating. "Of the Troy-Penniman Motors Pennimans. I know him." The fat man closed his eyes and leaned back with his hands together in a praying position.

"He's almost bankrupt, if that's what you're asking," Hornbaugh breathed, as if reading the words from inside his mind. "Had to let most of his people go. He underbid eight other companies to get the Troy Prison contract. From what I've heard, the other bidders don't know how he can do the work for that price."

"How *will* he do it?" Brady asked, already knowing the answer, but wanting to hear it anyway.

Horace Hornbaugh sucked in air for a few seconds and then blew it out again noisily, reminding Brady of a beached whale.

"The usual ways," Hornbaugh pronounced. "Claim something they want is an extra, not included in the contract. The roof, for instance. Some little thing like that. Threaten to hold up work. Write his congressman that they're persecuting small business if they try to hold him to the terms."

"Use inferior materials," suggested Brady.

"That goes without saying. After all, you're dealing with convicts. Who gives a damn if a wall falls on *them*?"

Hornbaugh's eyes came partly open, making him appear half asleep. "And he'll probably make off with some of the materials from the job site for some other project."

"But the prison project may never get done," Brady said.

Hornbaugh snorted. "Says who? A bunch of crazy environmentalists? That hearing they held was just to be able to say they'd been fair to everybody. It's a done deal."

Brady nodded, thoughtful. "You know where his office is?"

The fat man blew out again. "You planning to go there?"

"I thought I might."

"It's four-thirty. Won't be open."

"Maybe I'll be lucky."

Hornbaugh shrugged and told him.

Of course, Brady told himself, as he headed through town and past the gates of Northwestern State University, *Hornbaugh was probably right.* The office would be closed and even if it weren't he wasn't sure what he expected to find. But he was a firm believer in chaos: that even the best plans went awry when put into the hands of fallible humans and that often investigative success consisted of the exceptional good fortune of being in the right place at the right time. At least, it had worked that way in New Orleans and he couldn't see why it wouldn't work here. Just his *being* where he was unexpected might surprise someone into a lie or some other act of relevation.

Like going to the prison site, he told himself wryly.

Right on.

He slowed as he came on the gas station Hornbaugh had told him to watch for and then saw the building itself, a tin shed set back from the highway by a gravel parking lot. He drove past, noting the chain-link fence in the back and behind it a couple of bulldozers waiting like sleeping dinosaurs.

There was a light in the front office window and a black company carryall in front. He turned around at the first chance and came back, parking beside the filling station then walking diagonally across the gravel toward the front door.

He got to the carryall and stopped, thoughtful. Then he walked over to the door and turned the handle.

The door was locked, so he walked over to the window and peered into the office.

The office seemed to be unoccupied but there was another light coming from a door to the rear and as he looked in Brady thought he heard voices. They seemed to be raised in argument, but the glass of the window and the sounds of the highway muffled them, so he walked around the side of the building to the chain-link fence. The fence was six feet high, but halfway down there was a hole where someone had cut through it, so, with a quick glance over his shoulder, he ducked under and into the equipment yard.

Threading his way past backhoes and front end loaders and a stack of galvanized piping, he got to the back of the building and peered around the corner. There was a red Mustang in the back lot, half-hidden by the bulldozers. He strode over to it, checked the license: Texas.

He turned back toward the rear of the structure and noticed the back door was cracked open. Grateful for the gathering dusk, he pulled the door wider, careful lest the hinges betray him, and when it was open enough, he slipped in.

He found himself in a shop area, heavy with the smell of machine oil and exhausts. A safety light over the door glowed a sickly green, while to the front light spilled out of the big window that looked into the shop.

There was a lathe and a welding rig on the left and he slipped behind them. The men who were arguing were up front, in the foreman's office, behind the big window, and as he made his way forward he could see one of them pacing back and forth, waving his hand. It was only when he was ten feet away that he recognized the pacing figure as Laverne Penniman.

"That just wasn't the deal at all," Laverne was complaining.

Brady edged his way to the wall, where he could hear better.

"It's the best I can do," another voice said. It had a faint accent and when Brady snuck a look around the edge of the window he saw a short, heavy man with a dark moustache seated at a desk, and another man, younger and thinner, standing behind him. There was an attaché case on top of the desk and the thin man's eyes seemed fastened to it.

"Well, try again," Laverne ordered. "We made a deal. You bring it here, I pay. I don't send you back with the money to buy shit. That's your problem. I'm not front-ending this deal, I'm just a buyer."

"I got what I could for the money there was," the man in the chair said. His voice was calm, matter of fact, against Laverne's excited protests, and for that reason made Brady uneasy.

Laverne opened the attaché case then and Brady glimpsed rows of treasury notes.

"Here." Laverne took out several of the bundles and tossed them onto the table. "Here's for what you brought. The rest stays with me until you make another run."

For the first time the thin man spoke. "I don't think he trusts us, Baldo."

"No," Baldo agreed. "Look, Penniman, we run the stuff up from Brownsville to Natchitoches, that's a long day and then some. We got Texas plates, and Mexican faces. The cops in two states pull us over just for our profile. We get stopped with the goods, it's our ass, not yours. We'd kind of like to be paid beforehand, so we could hire a lawyer."

"No goods, no money," Laverne said, snapping shut the lid of the attaché case.

"That's final?" Baldo asked.

Brady didn't catch all of what happened next, just a movement of hands as Baldo and his friend reached for their belts, but before anything more happened Laverne had a pistol pointed at them and suddenly the hysteric note was gone from his voice: "You two greasers get the hell out of here," he said, "and don't come back until you know how to behave. I don't pay for what I don't get and you can spread that around to your friends. And if there's any idea about coming here and arguing with me, just remember, I've got friends in this parish and in two hours your description and plate number'll be on every sheriff's computer in the state. Now go."

Brady faded back into the cover of the machinery and watched the two men back slowly out of the office and into the shop area, Laverne following. As they neared the rear door, Brady slipped through the open doorway into the foreman's office. The attaché case sat unprotected on the table, and on the floor, out of sight of the window, was a suitcase. He lifted the top of the attaché case and made a quick survey of the contents: at least forty thousand in twenty dollar bills, with a space where Laverne had taken out the money to pay Baldo and his friend. A quick estimate was that the two men had received about twenty thousand. Brady bent down and opened the suitcase. It was half-filled with packets of white powder. He closed it quickly and started for the door, but at that moment he heard footsteps approaching.

Laverne was coming back.

Brady looked around quickly. There was a door that led into the front office and he went through it, careful to ease it shut so that no sound would be heard. Through it he heard the muffled sounds of something being dragged—probably the suitcase, he decided. Then something clicked and he realized the door to the shop area was being closed. He eased his own door open. Through the open doorway into the shop he could see Laverne walking into the gloom at the rear of the building, a case in either hand. The other man vanished for a moment and Brady closed his door and went across the front office to the front door and tried to open it.

It was locked. He bent over to examine it in the dim light from the front window and then straightened up again, defeated.

The lock was the kind that required a key to open from both sides. He would have to try make his way out the back.

He waited for two minutes, then lights flashed on in the parking lot outside. The pickup truck backed out on the gravel and drove up onto the highway and away.

Why had Laverne gone out the back, when it meant carrying the two cases all the way around the building?

Brady went into the foreman's office and looked out the big window into the shop area. Nothing seemed changed. *Except,* he told himself, *that Penniman had probably locked the back door on his way out,* which meant Brady was trapped inside. But it was worth checking.

He nudged open the door and started into the cavernous shop. Ahead of him, like a hangman's rope, hung a chain hoist for lifting out engines, and he ducked around it, then froze, the hairs on his neck bristling.

Some heightened sense of hearing or smell told him he was not alone in the room.

He turned around, fearful in a way he had never been before in his life. Somewhere in the shadows there was a sound, deadly soft, of velvet against the cement floor.

The door was only thirty feet away but it might have been infinity. Brady recognized the fear now: the draining, paralyzing terror of a hunted animal, knowing the hunter is at hand.

His brain fought for control, telling him to turn back around, slowly, but his muscles refused to obey. Only his eyes worked and when he let them roam right he caught a shade of movement in the shadows along the wall.

Now, he thought, *I know what the deer feels like.*

He took several deep breaths and broke the trance.

Standing here was suicide. He had to get back to the office. He started to turn around, alert to any change in the texture of the darkness, of any unusual sound.

Nothing.

He took one step toward the door, then another.

He was going to make it. The whole thing had been an illusion, the result of his overwrought imagination.

A third step and a fourth.

The door was just ahead. He reached out.

And then the beast leaped.

20

IT flew out of the darkness like a demon, jaws open and teeth pearl-white, and Brady, without thinking, grabbed the chain hoist and swung as the huge, furry body pummeled him and then, surprised that he did not go down, fell itself, snarling.

A Doberman. That's what had taken Laverne so long. He had probably unchained it from somewhere in the back and set it loose inside the shop to roam free as protection against intruders.

The dog launched itself again and Brady kicked out, connecting with its muzzle and eliciting an angry yelp.

Before it could leap again, he swung the chain in its direction and ran for the open door. Behind him he heard the chain connect with something soft. It knocked the dog off its stride, giving Brady just enough time to slam the door after himself before the Doberman crashed against it.

Brady took a few deep breaths, to let his heartbeat smooth out. It was going to be the front door or nothing, unless he wanted to knock out the front window.

He went into the front office and hunted through the desk

drawers. In the one that must belong to the secretary he found a key ring and carried it to the door. The third key was the right one; he turned it with a click and a second later stepped out into the comforting coolness of the night. He walked quickly to his car and drove away, tossing the keys in a nearby culvert as he passed. An hour later he was back in Troy.

For the first time in hours it occurred to him that it was Wednesday; he had a paper to take to press.

He skidded to a halt in the lot in front of the darkened *Express* office and went inside. Where was the dummy? Hadn't they left it for him?

He looked down at his desk and found a scrawled note:

Mr. B:
Finished the dummy but please don't do this to me again (make me work by myself with Mrs. Ripper). And I found what you needed in the Clerk's Office. Elmer Purdy married Anna Castete in this parish in 1952. Judging from the name, she was probably one of those Frenchies from Natchitoches. Enough. Am running dummy down to Alec since I assume you want an issue for tomorrow.

R. Dillon

P.S. Some man named Gillespie from the Forest Service Enforcement Section called you and wanted to talk. Am I missing a story?

He read the note a second time, then folded it and put it into his pocket. Still no word from Kelly. He tried her number but got no answer. Well, there was nothing to be done but make his report to Matt.

Except that when he called, a worried Mitzi told him that Garitty was not at home.

"He had a call, something about Miller Purdy. He went back to the office and told me not to wait up."

"I see. And Scotty? How is he?"

"I don't know." Her voice lowered conspiratorily. "We went to the psychologist today. But at this point all he did was take a family history and ask us what was wrong. He wants us to come back. Oh, Pete—"

"What is it?"

"Scotty said he wasn't going again. He said there wasn't anything he couldn't handle. But his teacher called today. She said some of the other boys had teased him, called him the deer slayer. She said he seemed to take it all right, but his work has fallen off. The last few days it's been all I could do to even get him to go." Her voice changed to a sob.

"I know it's tough. But I'm sure it'll work out. Scotty's a strong kid."

Brady hung up the phone, locked his office, and drove over to the courthouse, where the lights were on in all the offices of the Sheriff's Department.

The duty deputy greeted him with relief.

"Oh, it's just you, Mr. Brady. You know we've had people from the *Towntalk* in here already. They insisted on going out there, no matter what I said. I told them they might get shot but that didn't stop 'em."

"What's happening?" Brady asked.

"Big manhunt out to the Purdy place. Forest Service enforcement agent came in here with a warrant about an hour ago and Sheriff Garitty headed out there with him to make sure none of our people got shot, you know what I mean. It's a real circus." He made a face. "Forest Rangers, deputies from two parishes, FBI. They were asking about you and where you'd got to."

"I've been stirring up my own trouble," Brady said. "Look, are you in contact with Matt right now?"

"Last transmission I was. They were set up right outside Purdy's house, getting ready to call him out."

As he spoke the radio crackled and Brady heard a distant voice: "He's headed for the back. Hold your fire."

It was Matt, and Brady leaned toward the radio, trying to catch it all.

". . . got a gun," another voice called. "Don't take any chances . . . dangerous."

"That Purdy's a strange one," the deputy said, shaking his head. "They may not be able to take him alive."

". . . headed your way . . ." the radio advised.

". . . going for the woods . . . headed back this way . . ."

And then: ". . . down. Get over there quick. Say again, the subject is down. Converge on quadrant Delta."

Brady felt his stomach sink.

"Looks like they got him," the deputy commented. He went over to the radio and pressed the transmit button: "Troy One, this is Troy Central. Do you have a prisoner? Over."

Silence while the radio crackled with a voice too distant for Brady to make out.

The deputy repeated the transmission.

More silence.

Then Garitty's voice spoke in the room, as clear as if he were there with them.

"Central, this is Troy One. The subject is in custody. He's been slightly wounded. We're, ah, discussing where to take him right now."

"Ten four, Troy One." The deputy smiled. "Sounds like they're arguing over who gets to take him."

Five minutes later the radio spoke again: "Central, Troy One. Please alert Troy General Hospital that we're en route with the prisoner."

The deputy's smile broadened. "Sounds like the sheriff won."

Brady went back out to his car and drove over to the hospital to wait for the arrival.

Dr. McIntire came out from behind the emergency desk and shook Brady's hand.

"Sounds like a big one," he commented. "Half the cops in two parishes." He shook his head. "God, I hate to treat reluctant prisoners. And something tells me this one's going to be a pain in the ass."

Twenty minutes later they heard sirens and a few seconds later a circus of flashing lights and slamming doors broke the stillness outside.

"Wish me luck," McIntire said, heading out with the gurney crew.

The first thing Brady saw was a gaunt, blue-jeaned man with a cowboy hat and a badge on his belt, helping a blue-clad, manacled form out of a sheriff's cruiser. Matt came around the police car to take his place on the other side of the prisoner, as the cowboy hustled him forward. The hospital crew met them halfway and forced Miller Purdy down onto the gurney.

For a second, as the gurney was wheeled past, Brady's eyes met those of the prisoner and the publisher tried to read what the other man was thinking. But the group vanished inside, leaving Brady in the cold to ponder.

He followed, careful not to get in the way, and caught up with Matt outside the examination room.

"Will he be all right?"

The sheriff nodded. "Yeah." He gave the Forest Service agent a venemous look. "I think they'd have been happy enough to kill him but it came out all right." He pressed his fingers against the bridge of his nose and slumped against the wall. "God, it's been a long day."

Brady took a deep breath.

"It's not over yet," he said and told Garitty about Laverne Penniman.

When he had finished Garitty stared at the floor tiles for a long time before answering.

"Well, it sounds like Laverne's desperate to raise money to stay in business," he said finally. "I'll call the sheriff over in Natchitoches and have him look into it. I'll call it an anonymous tip."

"Thanks," Brady said.

"I can't see that it connects with anything over here, though."

Before Brady could reply he heard someone behind them and turned.

"Well," Joe Gant said, trying to sound cordial, "I understand Miller Purdy finally overstepped himself. Good work." He patted Garitty's shoulder and Brady thought he saw his friend flinch. "I'll call the U.S. Attorney in Alec tomorrow and see whether he wants to prosecute or turn him over to us. I think I can make a case that this is a state matter. After all, he did kill that girl, as a blood test will probably show. That's a little more serious than assault on a ranger. And Purdy's been kicking up his heels at the law for too long."

Which means, Brady thought, *you'll let everybody in two parishes know that Matt Garitty wouldn't do anything until the feds took over.*

"By the way, Matt"—the DA leaned toward the sheriff in a confidential posture—"the grand jury should be making a report pretty soon on that other matter. I wouldn't worry too much."

The prosecutor walked away to talk with some of the federal officials and Brady saw Matt's eyes follow him. It wasn't hard to read the loathing in them.

Emmett had been right: He was going to use the Grand Jury to show how fair he was, exonerating both Scotty and Matt at the same time he stamped the incident indelibly into the minds of everyone in the parish.

Brady went home and tried Kelly again. To his relief he got her this time but her voice was heavy with sleep.

"I thought you were on your way up," he said. "I've been worried to death."

"I'm sorry, darling. I . . . I just had some things to finish up down here."

"Kel, what's going on? Is everything all right?"

"Yes. I just . . . I need some time."

"Time for what? I don't understand." He hesitated and then said it: "Is there somebody else?"

"What? No. Of course not. Why would you think that?"

"I don't know. The fact is I don't know *what* to think."

When she spoke again the sleep had fallen away and it was like she was standing in the room with him, a ghost just out of reach.

"Brady, listen to what I'm saying: I haven't been myself lately, I know that. I've had so many things to sort out. It isn't your fault. It's connected to things that happened before I even knew you. But I have to resolve them before we go any further, does that make sense? I was on my way up and I got in the car and I just sat there with the motor running. I couldn't make myself go. Because you're so special to me, and if I can't respond to that without evading your every question, I'm cheating you, don't you see? I realized then that I'd been putting things off, not coming to grips. I could've done this thesis last semester. But I always found an excuse, something else that needed to be done."

"It's almost Christmas," Brady heard himself say. "Emmett and I would like to see you."

"And I want to be there. I will be. Just let me have another day or so to think. And just imagine . . ." she said, her voice full of the old buoyance he remembered, "we'll have a lot of time to make up."

"Right." He thought of the telephone conversation she'd had with someone about a job. What if she was hanging around, waiting to hear? What if the job was in New York? San Francisco? Or even Fargo, South Dakota?

"I love you, Brady. I really do."

"Come home," he said and wondered if it sounded like a plea.

"I will, darling. Soon."

He replaced the receiver and sat alone in his chair, feeling the emptiness of the house more than ever. He'd gotten a Christmas tree the day after Thanksgiving but now it looked forlorn in the corner, with its tinsel dripping like congealed tears and its pitiful few lights staring back unlit. Even the star at the top leaned at a ridiculous angle, as if it were too tired to stand up straight.

Much later, when he was in bed, staring at the ceiling, the phone rang and for a few seconds his heart started to throb with hope.

She had changed her mind. She was calling to say she was on her way.

But instead it was a voice he didn't recognize until it identified itself.

"Mr. Brady? This is Sergeant Collins at the Sheriff's Department. Sheriff Garitty asked me to call and tell you what happened."

Brady struggled upright in the bed.

"What? What happened where? To whom?"

"Over at the hospital, about a half hour ago: While Doc McIntire was trying to take a blood sample Miller Purdy plastered him and escaped."

21

"HE let Doc think he'd lost more blood than he had," Matt said the next morning. "Doc had him transferred to a room and there was just one guard outside. When Doc came in at eleven-thirty to take a blood sample and check on him, Purdy cold-cocked him and went through the window before the deputy outside knew what had happened."

Brady sat back in his chair, eyes gritty from lack of sleep.

"Any idea where he went?" Brady asked.

The sheriff ran a hand through unkempt hair. "Somewhere in the Forest. I have a posse out with dogs and I'll be headed out to check on them at noon. The Grant sheriff has his posse, and there are about ten FBI agents, along with twenty or thirty Forest Service personnel." He sighed. "Add the fact that there are deer hunters all through the damned place and it's a formula for disaster. Some of those guys would shoot Santa Claus."

"What about Purdy's wound? Is it bad enough to hinder him?"

"Who knows? Doc isn't sure what to believe anymore. Best bet is that the hole in his arm won't hold him up unless and until infection sets in. But he's already had antibiotic shots at the hospital."

"What about exposure?"

"I have a feeling our man knows how to handle himself. It would have to get a hell of a lot colder to make him come in."

Matt picked up his coffee cup and drained it.

"Anyway, I called Natchitoches on that other thing. They said they'd look into it. But I had the feeling there might be some kind of investigation already under way, so I didn't insist."

Garitty buried his head in his hands for a second, then sat back up straight.

"What a hell of a Christmas."

Brady wandered back to his office, feeling helpless. Mrs. Rickenbacker looked up from her desk.

"I've put today's edition on your desk," she sniffed. "It may be a little ragged. We didn't have as much help as we'd hoped for and then that boy had to take it to Alexandria himself, which is a caution right there."

"I'm sorry," Brady apologized. "Something came up."

"I told him I was sure you had a good reason. I told him, 'Mr. Brady wouldn't leave us to do the whole job of putting this issue to bed without there being some terrible emergency.'"

"Right." He scanned the front page. "Well, it looks like the two of you did an excellent job."

"We did our best, under the circumstances. But Mr. Brady, I will say one thing now, with no disrespect intended: I came here to work in good faith when Mr. Larson was publisher and I only asked to be treated with respect. That was twelve years ago now and for most of that time I was satisfied. But since that boy has come, well, I simply can't continue like this. His language is terrible, for one thing, and he has no respect. I know he gets a lot of advertisements for the paper, but that's no excuse; if I am ever asked to work with him again, as I was yesterday, I will hand in my resignation. Now. I've said it."

Brady suppressed a sigh. How many resignations had she handed him in the nearly three years since he had been here?

"I'm sorry, Mrs. Rickenbacker. We'd all hate to lose you. I'll talk to Ripley."

He opened the newspaper to the full-page ad that Laverne Penniman had inserted. *Well,* that *one was a moot matter,* he thought. Miller Purdy was running from a posse and Laverne would likely be in prison—the old one, not the new one he'd been going to build. Idly, he wondered who *would* build the prison. But there were plenty of hungry contractors out there.

The phone jangled him out of his thoughts and he lifted the receiver.

"Express."

"Pete Brady?" It was Phil Griffin's voice, tense with excitement.

"What is it?" Brady asked, suddenly alert. Had they found Purdy?

"Look, I wanted to talk to you about those samples we took. Some interesting things are coming up."

"Like what?"

The archaeologist laughed. "Well, everything's turning blue."

"I can be there in fifty minutes."

"I'll wait."

Actually, he was there in forty-five minutes, wheeling into the lot and braking to a halt in one of the visitors spaces. He found the archaeologist in his office at the end of the hall, studying a textbook in soil science.

"Ah, there you are; record time, I'd say," greeted Griffin, getting up. "Let's go into the lab and I'll show you what we've got."

Brady followed him into the next room where the plastic bags holding soil samples were laid out on a big table.

"Like I told you yesterday," Griffin said, "this isn't definitive, but it's pretty suggestive. The whole principle, like I explained, is that wherever you find human beings you find phosphorus in the soil. Excretion, burials, garbage—they all deposit phosphorus. Acid soils like these leach some of it out but enough stays to allow it to be detected." He opened one of the bags of earth and lifted out a small portion of dirt with a pocketknife. He carried it to a piece of filter paper and dropped it onto the clean surface. Then he did the same with dirt from a second bag, which he placed on a piece of filter paper beside the first.

"Now," he said, donning gloves and picking up a bottle marked *A.* "We apply Reagent A, so . . ." With a medicine dropper he dripped two drops from the bottle onto each soil sample, then looked down at his watch. "We wait thirty seconds. Now . . ." He picked up another jar and, using another dropper, deposited two more drops of liquid on each of the samples. "Give it another thirty seconds. The first sample is from the western edge of the field, the second is from the middle."

Brady stared down at the two fragments of earth, waiting. As he watched, their color started to change, going from brown to bluish. In the first sample, the color seemed to fix at a dull cobalt, but in the second dark-blue lines began to radiate out from the slice of earth.

"See?" the excited Griffin pointed. "A high phosphate content. All the samples from the center have a high level, but those at the edges have little or none." He shook his head. "I've got to admit, when you came to me with this, I didn't think it had a chance. I was just humoring you. I figured that to get any real results would take us the better part of the week. What we did yesterday was strictly hit-and-miss. That's what makes it such a long shot. But it looks like we managed to hit. *There were people living on that land sometime in the past.*"

The archaeologist stripped off the gloves and washed his hands at the sink.

"The job now is to go back out there and do an intensive survey. If there were people, odds are they left something besides phosphorous behind."

"But I thought you said a survey had been done," Brady reminded him.

"It has. But surveys are never a hundred percent, especially here on the Forest. The ground cover is so heavy that standard shovel tests every hundred feet or so tend to miss as much as they find. Trouble is, we have so damned much forest it's all we can do, unless we have special knowledge that a particular location is likely to have remains. In this case, though, there wasn't any reason to think that. If it hadn't been for you, there still wouldn't be."

"It still doesn't quite explain why Purdy was so protective," Brady said. "So people lived there. What's his stake? I looked up the land titles and there's no sign this was ever homesteaded. Purdy's father was a rich man, but he never held a title to that land. Nor did his mother, Anna Castete."

"Castete?" Griffin looked up sharply. "Oh, shit. Are you sure?"

"That's the name in the records," Brady said. "Why?"

"Because," Griffin said, throwing up his hands, "it may explain everything."

That afternoon, with the wind whipping rain clouds across the sky in gray sheets, Brady made another trip to the camp. Maybe there would be something he had overlooked. Because even if Purdy were caught and convicted of the murder of Jean McInnery, it would not explain his relationship to the killing of Dwayne Elkins.

And yet, if Purdy had killed Jean, there had to be some link. Had she seen Purdy come out here, argue with Dwayne? Set up some kind of trap to kill him?

But even the thought of a trap rang hollow. The verdict of the crime lab was clear: Elkins had been shot by Scott Garitty. What could be plainer than that?

Unless, in some incredible way, Scott had been set up. In which case, Purdy could have been set up, too. No one was unhappy to see Elkins out of the way but his wife. And no one would be sorry to see the troublesome Purdy gone.

The contradictions spun through his brain like Mobius strips, turning back on themselves everytime his mind managed to freeze one's motion.

Purdy and Elkins had had trouble over land, yet there was no valid land claim issue that would cause Elkins to inherit Purdy's land, with him out of the way.

Elkins was the manager of Troy-Penniman Motors, yet with him dead things would go on as before, because the law of succession at the time when Maud Penniman's parents died left her one-half and a quarter each to Debra and Laverne.

Laverne was desperate to stay in business, and had hated both Elkins and Miller Purdy, but he had found a way to meet his payroll until the problem of the prison was resolved.

Debra was still distraught with her husband's death; she seemed an unlikely suspect, to say the least.

And Maud seemed physically incapable of killing anyone, even given the motive.

But somewhere, he told himself as he bumped along the dirt road, there was a thread that held it together.

Somewhere . . .

A couple of trucks were parked in the place he and Matt had used when they'd come hunting, and there was the heavy smell of wood smoke in the air.

Not far away, maybe at the camp, something was on fire.

22

BRADY parked and hurried up the trail, toward the source of the smoke. As he drew near he heard the sound of the fire crackling and heard human voices, shouting and laughing. He came out into the clearing and halted. There were three ATVs parked in front of the Elkins trailer, and as he watched the door of the trailer opened and a man stumbled down the steps with a plastic cup in his hand.

He stopped when he saw Brady and pulled a long-barreled pistol from his belt.

"You madman Miller Purdy?" he demanded, waving the pistol generally in Brady's direction. He wore a checkered shirt and jeans, and though a heavy beard obscured his features, Brady could see that his eyes were bloodshot.

"No," Brady said. "I'm not Miller Purdy."

"Didn't think you was!" the man laughed. "You want a drink?"

"No, thank you," Brady said.

"That's cool, man. That just means there's more for us!"

The bearded man swayed and for a second Brady thought he was going to fall, but at last he steadied himself.

"Hey," he said. "You ain't a game warden?"

"No, not me," Brady said. "You renting this camp now?"

"Renting hell. Hey, Gopher, this feller over here wants to know are we renting this place."

A short man with a beer belly and red suspenders came around the side of the trailer.

"Who's that?" Gopher asked, then frowned over at Brady. "Oh, I know you. You're from the bank."

"No," Brady said. "The *Express.*"

"*Express?*" Gopher wrinkled his nose under the bill of his baseball cap. "You mean that thing they publish in Troy."

"That thing," Brady agreed.

"Shee-it, what they want to publish *that* for?" Gopher asked, spewing out a stream of dark-brown tobacco juice.

"Where's Twenty-Five?" the first man asked. "He ain't fell in the fire, has he?"

"Hell no," Gopher pronounced. "If he did he'd blow up." He squinted over at Brady. "You wanna stand there and freeze your ass, or you wanna come around back to the fire and get warm?"

"Thank you," Brady said, following.

It was when he rounded the corner of the trailer that he saw the fire. It was a conflagration, filling part of the area between the rear of the camp building and the targets Elkins had shot at. Huge flames jumped skyward, and orange cinders rose up through the air toward the gray overcast. But it was not only the fire that caught Brady's attention; for seated in a lawn chair beside it, head slumped onto his chest and empty whiskey bottle on the ground under his limp hand, was a third man. And while his eyes were open, it was clear that he was dead to the world.

"Look a there," Gopher said, shaking his head. "Ain't that plumb pitiful."

"Twenty-Five never could hold his liquor," the first man laughed. He turned to Brady: "His name's Elmo, but we call him Twenty-Five. Know why?"

"If he don't, Buford, you're gonna tell him," Gopher said.

"Why?" Brady asked.

"Cause," said Buford, "that's how many times he punched his

160

old lady on their honeymoon." He slapped Brady on the back and let out a howl of delight. "How you like that?"

"Unique," Brady said.

"Yeah, he's a real individual," Buford chortled. "But you know what? I think he lied. I think he probably oughta be named more like A Half or A Quarter!" He guffawed. "You sure you don't want some blood-warmer?"

"I'll pass," Brady said.

"Suit yourself," said Gopher. He turned to warm himself at the flames and Brady saw that his hair was gathered up at the neck and tied with a rubber band. "You not thinking about buying this place, are you?"

"Didn't know it was for sale," Brady countered.

"Ain't. At least, not for now. We went and seen Deb and asked could we keep using it. We was real close to Possum."

"Possum?"

"The late deceased," Buford explained. "Our friend and her husband."

"Oh."

"It was a hell of a thing what happened to him," said Gopher. "But he never was much of a hunter. Never mix hunting and nookie, I always say."

Buford nodded sagely. "Right on." He bent down and picked up a rifle that was lying on the ground. "Looka there: Twenty-Five done let his assault rifle fall over. No way to treat a fine piece."

Brady suddenly had an image of the .22 in the gun rack inside the camp, the .22 its owner hadn't bothered to clean.

Buford wiped the barrel lovingly with a handkerchief.

"He hunts with *that*?" Brady asked.

"Sure," said Buford. "It's his constitutional right." He jacked back the slide and raised the weapon. "This baby fires forty rounds fast as you pull the trigger. Course you ain't supposed to use a forty-round magazine, but what the hell?" He winked at Brady. "And this little old bullet, it ain't hardly bigger around than a .22, but when it finishes with a piece of flesh, you got goulash." He swung suddenly and fired into the flames, making Brady jump and sending a new flurry of sparks toward the heavens. "Gotcha!"

Brady looked into the fire and saw a ghostly deer staring out at him.

"Nice fire," he said. "You get the wood around here?"

Buford cocked his head, trying to make sense of the change of subject.

"Got it from back there," he said, pointing to the weeds behind what used to be Elkins's shooting range. "Possum had all kinds of shit back there, a regular trash pile. Old tires, plywood, sign boards, you name it."

"It makes a good fire," Brady said.

"It sure as hell does," Buford said. "Damn, I'm gonna miss old Possum."

Gopher took off his cap. "Amen to that."

Brady slipped quietly away, leaving them to stare into the flames.

When he got back to Troy it was midafternoon. Despite the heater in his car he found himself shivering as he drove down the main street, headed for his house. Ahead he saw the courthouse and as he passed he noticed a cluster of official vehicles.

His chill increased.

They've got Miller Purdy, he thought, turning into one of the parking places in front of the statue of the Civil War veteran.

A small group of men in quilted jackets and padded windbreakers was gathered by the vehicle garage and Brady recognized several of them as members of the Troy Posse, the reservists who mobilized for emergencies. He went up the walk quickly and down the hallway to the Sheriff's Department and stopped short.

There was something wrong, something that went beyond the Purdy business—he could see it in the faces and the hushed tones of the deputies.

One of them greeted him and looked away quickly.

"Sheriff's in there, Mr. Brady," he said, gesturing to Matt's private office.

Brady went through the gate, aware of their eyes on him, and gave a perfunctory knock on Matt's door.

162

The person who opened it was Mitzi and Brady's blood went cold.

Matt was seated behind his desk, his face only a mask of the face Brady had known. Mitzi gave Brady a quick hug and went back to stand beside her husband, whom she had evidently been comforting when Brady knocked.

The publisher looked from one face to the other.

"Matt? Mitzi? What's happening? For God's sake, tell me. What's going on here? What's wrong?"

When Matt finally spoke his voice was a croak. "It's Scotty," he said. "He's run away."

"What?"

"Yeah. Only this time he took my rifle with him."

23

FOR a long time Brady was speechless. Finally he managed to wander over to one of the chairs and sit down.

"How long has he been gone?" he asked.

"Since noon," Mitzi said. "He left school at lunch and never went back. I was shopping and didn't see him come home but when they called to say he hadn't come back to class I went to his room and saw his bed was mussed, like he'd been sitting on it. And I'd made it this morning after he left for school. Then I looked at the gun cabinet and noticed it was open and the lock was broken."

"Does anybody know where he went?" Brady asked.

Matt pointed to the parish map on his wall.

"Ward Connolly claims he saw him on 167 south of town, near Fuller's Creek. He recognized him and wondered why he wasn't in school. But when he stopped his car Scotty was gone. Into the woods, probably. I sent some people out but they lost his trail. We're fixing to head out that way again, and I've sent out a call to the Forest Service—those that aren't hunting up Purdy."

"They'll find him," Brady promised.

"That's what I keep thinking," Mitzi said hopefully. "It hasn't been so long, just a few hours." She stared down at the floor. "I should have known this morning. He was so quiet."

"It's my fault," Matt said in a hollow voice. "I was so damned tied up with this manhunt for Miller Purdy I wasn't paying Scotty the attention he deserved."

Mitzi leaned her face against his arm. "It wasn't your fault. There wasn't any way you could know."

"I should have seen from the way he's been acting, the way he tried to run away the other day. But all I was thinking about was Gant and the things he was saying, about how I couldn't hold onto my prisoners . . ." He regarded Brady from sunken eyes.

"Pete, I'm glad you're here. There's something I have to say. I've thought about this a lot and I've made up my mind. I've told my chief deputy and a few others and I might as well tell you." He reached down, pulled the credential case from his top pocket, and laid it onto the desk. "Gant's been pushing for a new face in this office next election. Well, he won't have to wait that long. When this is over, I'm stepping down. My family's worth more than any job."

Brady shook his head. "That's nonsense, Matt. You said yourself Gant wanted to put an insurance salesman in. Is that who you want to turn this job over to?"

Garitty reached for his hat. "Don't try to argue me out of it. I've made up my mind. Now I'm going to find my son."

"I want to go, too," Brady declared.

The sheriff shook his head and patted his friend on the shoulder.

"Better leave that to us, Pete. Thanks anyway. But I've got a posse of good old boys that know these woods backward and forward. If they can't find him, nobody can."

Brady thought about the trio he had met at the camp, but decided it was best to hold his tongue.

"Good luck," he said.

When Garitty was gone Brady held out his arm and Mitzi folded herself into it. He felt her tears, wet on his jacket.

"God, Pete, I'm so scared. He's out there alone and there's that crazy man, and men with guns that shoot at anything."

Brady thought of his own long trek to the hunting stand.

"Yeah." Then he added, "Tell me, Mitzi, do you have any feeling for what's going on in his head?"

She sighed and drew away to dab at her eyes.

"It's hard to say. When I saw the gun was gone my first thought was the worst. But when I called Matt he said the boy had more grit than that, that if he took the gun it was to try and prove something. But Matt, bless his heart, has been trying to believe the best from the first." She went to stand by the window. "Maybe it's time we all started to face reality."

Brady went to stand beside her. From his place at the window he could see the Christmas lights strung out across the street, and the back of the plywood snowman that dominated the front lawn. *Odd,* he thought irrelevantly, *how the back of the snowman is unpainted, as if all that matters is the side facing the street. The side with the jolly eyes and smile.*

"Matt's no fool," he soothed her. "If he believes something, it's for a reason. He's seen too much to give in to wishful thinking."

Now, he thought, *if I could only believe it myself.*

Mitzi turned her face up to him. "Thanks, Pete. I hope you're right. But it's been so hard for Scotty. And I don't mean just the last couple of weeks."

The publisher frowned. "Oh?"

"You see," Mitzi went on, "it's hard when your father is a man everybody looks up to, a man who wears a badge, a man like the hero in all the old cowboy movies. What can a little boy do to live up to that image?"

Brady nodded, beginning to understand. "And if he feels he's let his father down—" he began.

"You see how it is. He must feel that he's fallen to an incredible low." Her hand fastened on Brady's arm like a talon.

"Pete, they have to find him! They have to find him out there before—"

"They will," Brady assured her. "I promise they will."

He left her there, looking small and vulnerable, and went home. He was tired, his body told him that, but somehow his mind denied

166

this. There was a boy out there, in a forest teeming with armed men and an escaped prisoner. It was already weather for coats and gloves and tonight the temperature would drop to below freezing. There was no mention of the boy's having taken any camping gear, so it was prudent to assume he hadn't.

Brady bathed and changed clothes, donning a pair of corduroy pants he had been resolving to throw away for years. Then he found a long-sleeved, flannel shirt, and slipped a sweater over it. He dug out his heavy jacket, not the old, threadbare trenchcoat he'd worn during his years on the *Picayune,* but the padded jacket he'd worn on the deer hunt. The stocking cap would keep his head warm. For his feet he selected two pairs of cotton socks and the boots he'd bought a few years back as a token of his move to the country. They still had not been completely broken in, but they would do.

He went out to his car and dug the flashlight out of the glove compartment. Satisfied that the batteries were good, he drove back to his office, where he raided the storage room for topographic maps. Thus equipped, he drove back out the way he had come earlier.

Maybe, just maybe, he thought, *I can guess where the boy is headed.*

The woods seemed darker, more menacing now, but he knew it was merely because the shadows were longer and the cold more intense. The pickups belonging to Elkins's friends were gone, a couple of empty beer cans the only reminder of their having been there. Smoke still clung to the air, but the smell was faint now, as if the fire had burned itself out. He took the path toward the deer stands, hurrying now, not thinking of Elkins, but only of the boy.

Because that was where he would have gone. Not the first time, of course; the first time, when Brady had seen him thumbing a ride, he had only been trying to escape. But frustrated in that, he had reacted in the opposite fashion, going directly to the source of his fear. He would have headed south on 167, where he was seen, but that would only have been to lead people astray: From 167 to the deer stand was a good five miles cross-country, but there were roads he could follow, ducking into the woods when he heard a car. Yes, it had to be the deer stand.

At least, Brady thought, *that's what Matt would have done.*

And if it was true, then the boy was there now, in the stand, running it all back over and over in his mind, sighting through the rifle, trying to summon up the conflicting images, deer and man, comparing, and attempting to convince himself which had been the one he had really seen.

Which was the danger, of course. Because unless he were able to convince himself he had acted rationally and the way he had been trained to act, then he would have to admit finally and unequivocally to himself that he had made a mistake and taken a life. And in the primitive world in which the boy now functioned, who was to say that the only logical restorative would not be to give a life for the one that was snatched away?

A branch poked at Brady's face and he flinched. It was getting too dark to see his way. But he had to push forward, not stop. Even if he was wrong he could spend the night huddled in the deer stand, safe enough until morning. But if he was right, he might find Scott in time to convince him what had happened and avoid another catastrophe.

The problem was the woods and even the path looked different now, transformed by the impending night. He flicked on the flashlight but it neutralized what little daylight was left, so he cut it off again.

He thought of yelling the boy's name. But that might only drive him deeper into the woods and if that happened Brady would never find him.

He increased his pace, blundering into briars and branches. The last light fled and the wind lashed out to punish him for his audacity.

Once, in New Orleans, he had spent the night on the Algiers levee with some dopers, trying to get the goods on a big-time dealer. He remembered the swaying willows and the oil-heavy smell of the wind off the Mississippi, and the clank of chains on the ships anchored midstream. It had seemed a big chance to take then, but now, another world away, he recalled it as little more than an adventure in slumming. What was it Matt had told him once? That hunting took man to his most elemental self? He felt pretty elemental now, he had to admit.

His boots came down in a standing puddle and he slipped, reaching out in the darkness to keep from falling. His hand grabbed a briar and he let go as the thorn bit into his flesh.

What if he missed the stand altogether? What if he ended up blundering around in the dark all night? He had no compass, because he had been so sure he could find his way. Now he understood why Matt said he never left his compass, even if he was going into the woods for only a couple of hundred yards. You could get turned around, mistake the path, wander on a false bearing.

Something smashed him in the midsection and he lost his balance, falling in the middle of the trail, the flashlight rolling out of his hand to lie still ten feet away, a pale white stripe on the darkness.

Chest throbbing, Brady sat up and waited for the pain to subside. Whatever had hit him was dangling beside the trail, suspended from a branch. As Brady sat in the trail, fighting for breath, he watched it swing backward and forward, barely perceptible against the darkness as a slight change in the texture of the forest.

He reached out for the flashlight and brought it to play on the hanging object.

What he saw was a five gallon can twisting slowly in the darkness on a thin cord.

Brady got slowly to his feet and shone the light on the object up close. Jabbed into the bottom of the can was a thin tongue of wood and suddenly Brady knew what the thing was. He flashed the light along the ground and it stopped on a small stone the size of a bar of soap.

A molasses block.

He had stumbled on a deer-feeding station. Matt had showed him how the gas cans were filled with grain and suspended with a sharp stick thrust into the bottom. The deer, Matt had explained, would nudge against the stick, causing grain to spill onto the ground from the can. The molasses bar was a freebie, a sweet for when the animals were tired of the grain.

It had struck Brady at the time as unfair, but now he was glad to see it. Because Scotty's stand was only a few yards away.

Brady flicked out the light. If the boy was here, Brady might already have alerted him. He waited, listening for sound, but the only noise he heard was the swaying of trees and the occasional soft clang of the can against a branch. He turned on the light again and searched the darkness.

The beam picked out leaves, branches, trunks, and there, just ahead, overlooking the trail like a guard post—its ladder a pattern of sidewise jail bars—was the stand.

Brady started forward, alert to any sounds, but the only noises he heard were the wind and his own boots, crushing the pine needles. He reached the ladder and looked up, but all he could see was the square hole in the bottom of the wooden platform. He put his hand on one of the rungs and started to climb, feeling the tree sway slightly as he went.

He was vulnerable now, halfway up—the hole yawning above him, the hard ground below. But why should he be afraid? The boy, if he was here, was no menace.

His head was only a foot below the floorboards now and he stopped.

"Scotty?" he called softly. "Scotty, it's me, Pete Brady. Are you there?"

The only answer was a creak of a board as the stand moved in the breeze.

The boy wasn't there. He couldn't be or he would have answered. Unless he had fallen asleep. But who could sleep in this cold?

Brady shone the light through the hole and then went motionless.

The beam played off something red, a piece of cloth.

It was Scotty's scarf, the same one he had been wearing that day.

"Oh, my God," Brady muttered. For a long time he hung suspended, not daring to go farther up, refusing to go back down. Finally he took a breath and raised himself through the hole.

If Scotty wasn't asleep then . . .

He jabbed his hand, with the flashlight, into the opening and played it around the little room.

The stand was empty.

Not knowing whether to be relieved or not, Brady pulled himself the rest of the way up and squatted, back to one wall, staring down at the scarf.

Scotty had been here, that much was clear. But why leave his scarf? What had made him go back down, and where was he now?

He was still staring at the red cloth when he heard a branch crack somewhere below and he flicked off the light. He turned his body so that he could look out through the vantage slit and tried to decipher the patterns of darkness.

The crackling branch came again and his eyes shot to the area slightly to the right in his field of view.

As he watched a body slowly materialized in the gloom. A body and then, as it moved out of the shadow, a face.

The face of Miller Purdy.

24

AS Brady watched, the figure faded back into the darkness.

My God, did he have Scotty?

Brady started back down the ladder, slipping halfway to the bottom, and skinning a knee. He got back to his feet and stabbed his light in Purdy's direction. The man was gone now, but Brady heard a crashing in the undergrowth ahead of him.

He plunged forward without thinking.

"Purdy, come back. It's me, Brady."

The steps stopped and Brady, panting, stumbled toward the last sound. But in the darkness, without sounds to guide him, he was lost.

What if Purdy didn't have the boy? What if Scotty was somewhere else? What if Purdy had killed him?

But everything was a *what if?* He didn't know where Scotty was, only where he had been. That Purdy was here seemed to indicate he was in some way involved, so that finding him was the only chance Brady had.

"Purdy?"

Silence.

"Purdy, I don't have a gun."

More silence, and then, somewhere ahead of him, cloth brushed against tree bark.

Brady started forward again at the sound, crying out as a low limb caught him on the forehead and sent him seeing stars.

He shook his head to clear it.

"Purdy, do you have the boy?"

A twig crackled.

Brady raised a hand to guard his face and blundered on.

After twenty more steps he halted. There was no more sound but the panting of his own breath and the sigh of the wind.

Damn it, he thought, *had the man escaped?*

"Purdy, for God's sake, I know the truth. Come out, wherever you are. We need to talk."

No answer.

He took a few experimental paces.

"Purdy?"

This time the footstep was to his right, but even farther away.

Brady started toward it, collided with a tree, fell to his hands and knees. Now he could hear the sounds, footsteps growing gradually more distant.

My God, could the man see in the dark?

"Come back. I don't care about anything but the boy. You can go free."

Which is ridiculous, a voice in Brady's mind told him, *because he already is free.*

"Purdy!"

The only answer was wetness on Brady's face, as a raindrop landed, ran slowly down his cheek. He wiped it away with one hand, leaving a cold smear.

Now he heard them, almost too soft to detect: other raindrops pattering softly through the branches.

He looked around him. It was impossible to know how far he had come from the deer stand, or in what direction. His intuition told him it was back to his left and behind him, but Matt had told him many times never to trust intuition in the woods.

The mist was becoming a drizzle. Water soaked his cap then

rolled down his face like tears. A branch crashed down ahead of him and he jerked to attention.

"Purdy?"

But it was just a piece of rotten wood, made heavy by water.

He plunged forward again, toward the last sound of footsteps. The ozone smell was permeated now with the fresh odor of earth, carried on the rain. But now, as he walked, hand outstretched and light dancing ahead like a pale eye, the smell grew stronger.

The dripping was louder and his feet slipped on a slick surface. He reached out—there was nothing but space. The dripping had become a rushing now, somewhere below him in the darkness, and as he tried to turn away from it his feet went out from under him and he felt himself sliding downhill, twisting and turning, his elbows banging into rocks and limbs as he went, the flashlight flying from his hand.

He landed face-up in the stream, the water coursing around him, its coldness seeping in like a slow death. He raised himself, found a log to grasp, and fished out the flashlight, which shined from the bottom like some kind of strange electric fish. His bones ached from the fall and water flooded down into his boots.

He tried to gather his wits. He was in a creek bottom, almost dry now, but with a shallow residue from last week's rain, and being fed now by the drizzle that was pattering through the trees.

Brady reached out in front of him for a handhold. He had to climb out of here, find someplace to get dry. He could survive the night dry, but not wet, not with temperatures set to go below freezing.

He hauled himself upward, his fingers already beginning to go numb. With each foot his knees slid from under him on the slick clay sides, and when he was nearly to the top a piece of the bank crumbled and he felt himself start downward again. But somehow his foot lodged against a tree root and he stopped, drew a few deep breaths, and pulled himself the rest of the way.

For a long time he lay on the ground, face down, trying to get his breath. Purdy was long gone now. All Brady could hope for at this point was to survive.

He had failed. He had come so close to finding the boy, but in the end it wouldn't matter.

He found himself thinking of Dockerty, remembering that day two decades ago when he'd been a fresh young reporter on the *Picayune,* breathlessly telling the old editor how close he had come to finding the evidence that would indict a city official.

Dockerty had blown out a cloud of pungent cigarette smoke and shaken his head: "Close counts in horseshoes. That what we're playing here, Son?"

What would Dockerty say now? Had Dockerty ever been in these woods? He would have to take Dockerty out here sometime, hand him a hunting rifle and canteen, and point him into the forest . . .

Except that he wouldn't be able to, because he would be dead. It was something he needed to keep in mind, he told himself, chuckling even more.

He blinked the water away from his eyes and tried to control himself. He was becoming hysterical, already giving up.

Damn it, he told himself, *I'm still alive. So get up, put one foot in front of the other, make noise, and most of all, keep moving, even if it means walking in my sleep.*

He staggered forward once more, unsure of his direction, his face now numb to the thorns and twigs that scraped it. And before he had gone ten steps he tripped again and fell headlong.

For a long time he lay without moving and then realized dully that what lay under him was too soft to be a log, too warm to be an upturned stone. He felt under him with one hand, found a fabric surface, probed, touched skin and stopped.

He had tripped on a body that was lying across his path.

Purdy. It had to be Purdy. He rolled away and his hand went out, touched the jacket, then went up the chest to the face, touched it, probing . . .

There was no beard.

He had found Scott Garitty.

* * *

He put his face close to the boy's but it was impossible to tell if there was any breath. Then he remembered the first aid course he had taken years ago and felt for the carotid pulse.

It was there, regular and strong.

Then why was the boy unconscious?

He shined the flashlight on the wet jacket, looking for blood, but there was none. As the light hit the boy's closed eyes a groan escaped the pale lips.

"Scotty?" Brady shook him gently but the boy didn't move.

The publisher tried to think: He couldn't be far from the deer stand, not more than a half mile. But there was no way of telling the direction in the dark. And the creek made any attempt at carrying the boy back impossible. They would have to wait here until tomorrow and hope that a search party stumbled across them.

What they both needed now was heat.

Brady hunted inside his coat and found the packet of matches he had brought. But what could he use to start a fire? He forced himself up, shined the light around, looking for some kind of kindling. But the wood he found was all damp and when he tried to light it the match went out.

Scott groaned again and Brady tried to soothe him.

Then an idea came to him: If the boy had taken his rifle with him, maybe the weapon was nearby, where he had dropped it. If Brady could find it he could use it to fire a shot and signal the rescuers . . .

As quickly as it came the idea evaporated: The boy hadn't gotten here on his own. He had almost certainly been brought here by Miller Purdy. Which meant Purdy had the weapon, which might even now be leveled on Brady's chest.

If Purdy was even still around, which seemed unlikely. After all, he wouldn't have left the boy if he'd intended to stay.

Brady rubbed his hands together and glanced at the luminous dial of his watch: seven-thirty. It was only seven-thirty, for Christ's sakes. He had the whole night in front of him.

The only thing he could hope to do was shelter the boy from the cold. He lay down across Scott, trying to cover as much of his body as possible. Strange images fluttered through his mind, of the city room at the *Picayune,* and the days when he had been a mainstay of *Frankie and Johnny's* down by the river. People had said he was a lot of fun, but the fun had come from the whiskey he was drinking more and more of. Finally, he had made himself stop, because he had seen too many bums lying in the doorways on Camp Street, between Lee Circle and Canal. Now he thought of the irony of it all: Here he was, mud spattered and soaked to the marrow, every bit as derelict as one of the winos, and he was totally sober.

The tempo of the rain increased until the patter was a steady torrent, crashing down through limbs and undergrowth, almost like footsteps against the wet earth.

He raised his head.

My God, it *was* steps.

He sensed, rather than saw, the figure looming over him, felt the eyes probing the scene, and then at last heard the heavy exhalation of breath and the words: "You've got to cover up the head," Miller Purdy said. "That's where most of the heat gets out, you know."

25

THE two men stared at each other and then Purdy nodded over at the boy.

"He fell out of the stand. I was up there, trying to keep warm, and when he came up the ladder and saw me, he lost his grip. When I heard you coming I didn't know what to do. I was scared to leave him there. I figured whoever it was would think I'd hurt him. I figured if I just carried him with me he'd wake up and come out of it."

Brady put a hand on Scott's forehead. It was cold, as cold as the falling raindrops.

"We need to get medical help," Brady said.

"Don't know how to do that," Purdy said. "I'm as lost as you are. We could wander around in circles all night. And I left the rifle back there by the deer stand, so we can't fire off any shots. Besides, it probably doesn't do any good to carry him." He moved a few steps closer, rubbing his hands. "Look, I went off to get some dry wood. I didn't know you'd find him here. But you did, so we might as well make the most of it. The rain's letting up a little. I'll build a fire if these matches the boy had aren't too wet."

"I have some," Brady said, handing over his own. "What about your arm?"

"A scratch is all. Damn Forest Service people can't shoot."

Scott moved then and tried to say something. Purdy bent down and felt his limbs.

"Can't find any compound fractures. Probably a concussion. He'll need X rays, but it looks like he may be coming out of it if we can keep him warm enough."

He stood back up, water dripping from his beard.

"I didn't kill that woman," he said. "I didn't even know who she was."

"No," Brady said. "I didn't think you did."

"I'll be back," Purdy said. He vanished into the forest, leaving Brady with the boy. Scott's breathing had evened out now and he seemed restless, moving his limbs. What did the first aid book say about concussions? Brady seemed to remember that if the vital signs were stable there was no immediate danger. On the other hand, the book had warned that injuries to the head were unpredictable.

Brady stared down at the boy, suddenly thoughtful.

A crash brought the editor back to the present and he looked up to see a load of wood on the ground a few feet away. Miller Purdy brushed off his hands and squatted down.

"A little tinder and I think we'll be in business. Only the outside was wet. You'll have to strip off the bark with your fingers. Put the sticks under your coat until I'm ready. Then aim the flashlight where I tell you."

Brady struggled to comply, but his hands shook from the cold and his numb fingers began to bleed. A few feet away, Purdy used a hunting knife Brady recognized as Scotty's to fuzz the ends of sticks for tinder.

"Now give me your sticks," Purdy ordered and Brady handed them over. He watched the other man clear a small space on the damp ground and, leaning over so his body sheltered the spot, make a teepee of sticks with the tinder at the center.

Purdy struck one of the matches, keeping his other hand over it to fend off dripping water, and thrust the flame under his kindling. The little structure glowed, dimmed, then sprang into life.

"Quick," Purdy said. "Make me some more sticks."

Brady hastened to strip off more bark and handed the pieces to Purdy, who laid them around the others in careful, geometric patterns.

"Once it gets going enough, the wet wood will dry out," Purdy explained.

Brady shifted his weight, realizing dully that his legs were asleep. He stretched his hands over the little fire and felt a comforting warmth.

"You know this might bring a search party," he said.

Purdy nodded, adding some more wood. "Chance I'll have to take. If it happens, though, I'll be gone before they get here. Unless they've got dogs, I can lose 'em at night."

He got up. "More wood," he said over his shoulder.

Brady looked over at Scott and realized with a shock that the boy's eyes were open.

"Hey, Trooper, you're awake!"

"Mr. Brady?" Scott moved his head and frowned in pain. "Where are we? What happened?"

"You had a fall. But you're all right now. It's just a matter of getting you out of the woods. But we'll manage. First things first, okay? Right now we have to keep warm by the fire."

Scotty frowned and turned onto his side, facing the flames.

"I remember, I was going to the stand. I was climbing the ladder and I heard a noise."

"That's right," Brady agreed. "You slipped and took a whack on the head."

"Yeah, I guess so. Mom and Dad'll be mad."

"I doubt it," Brady said, grateful for the spreading warmth. "But they're curious about why you left. You worried them."

"I guess so." Scotty took a deep breath. "I just didn't think they'd understand."

Brady smiled. "Then try me. Maybe I'd understand better."

The boy shook his head. "No. Nobody can. I mean, not after . . . Mr. Brady, I wasn't lying about the deer . . ."

Brady patted Scott. "I know that," he said gently.

"But they'll think so. They'll think I was lying to get out of trouble."

"No," Brady said. He squeezed the boy's arm. "They know some problems are too big for one person to solve. Sometimes we all need help."

Scotty stared into the fire. When he spoke again his words took Brady by surprise. "Dad says you solved *your* problem."

Brady looked into the flames. "Yeah, I guess I did. But I don't know if it was by myself. You see, Scotty, when I came here to Troy I was still pretty messed-up."

"*You?*"

" 'Fraid so. But I was lucky enough to meet people like Emmett Larson, and Kelly, and your parents, and they helped me. Everybody needs friends."

Scotty licked his lips nervously and a tear crept out of the corner of one eye. "Mr. Brady, the fact is I thought I saw a deer but now—"

"I know," Brady said, as footsteps announced the return of Miller Purdy.

"Well," Purdy said, tossing down another armload of wood. "I see you got tired of sleeping. You reckon you're ready to help us build up this fire? It's going to be a cold night."

Much later, as Scott slept in the lean-to Purdy had constructed, Brady and the other man huddled around the fire. The cold had begun to retreat from Brady's bones and now he luxuriated in the comforting crackle of the flames. He was even beginning to think about food when Purdy broke the silence with his question. "So how did you find out about me?" he asked. "I didn't tell a lot of people."

Brady held his hands out over the flames.

"It was the racket," he said finally. "I wondered why you were lying about it. It got me to thinking. Phil Griffin, the archaeologist, told me what it really was. But the phosphate analysis he did was the clincher."

Purdy nodded. "Phosphate, eh? I wondered what you two were doing out there."

"If you'd told the truth it wouldn't have come to that."

"I guess so." He shrugged. "It was just a reaction. I'm so used to not telling the truth about that."

It was Brady's turn to nod. He leaned back against the tree that served as a backrest.

"It'll come out now, you know."

"Yeah. You'll tell folks."

"I don't need to. Some people know already. My bookkeeper, for instance. She was about to tell me the other day but she got distracted. I didn't figure out that was what she was going to say. But the point is that some of the older families remember and, besides, it's public record and you've made yourself pretty public these last few days." Brady looked over at the boy, who seemed to be sleeping peacefully now. "You know, it might be the best card you hold."

"My mother's people lived on that land," Purdy said. "They moved away to work at a sawmill in Texas, but she came back. That's when she married my father. She talked about the old place. Hell, they didn't have any land titles, it was all just tradition. The owners lived somewhere else and nobody bothered 'em. I guess you'd call 'em squatters these days, but I think they've got a better claim than any millionaire in Chicago or New York." He looked Brady in the eye over the fire. "My mother's family is buried on that land."

"The Castetes," Brady said.

Purdy nodded. "Among others. And when I saw you all out there the other day, digging holes in the ground, I just went kind of crazy. I didn't want to hurt anybody, but, by God, they're *buried* in that earth. And those bastards want to turn it into a prison."

"I think I understand," Brady said. "Tell me, did you get the racket from your mother?"

"Naw, just from one of the old people over at Marksville. They explained how it worked and I thought it was neat, so I kept it, sort of to remind me. It really was the origin of lacrosse, so I wasn't lying totally. And they still play the game in Mississippi, you know. Once it was played by every group in the Southeast."

"Yeah, I understand it's quite a celebration."

Purdy poked the fire. "It is. Drums, dancing, music, betting, the whole nine yards. People took it pretty seriously in the old days. Now it's just for fun."

Brady turned slightly, to catch more of the fire's warmth.

"I hear people sometimes got killed in the old days."

Purdy smiled. "That's what they say. Well, you've seen what's used for a racket; it can throw one of those little balls pretty hard. And the stick is made of hickory. I wouldn't want to get hit in the head with it. By the way, who told you about Indian stickball?"

It was Brady's turn to smile. "Well, I knew I'd read about it somewhere, but I couldn't remember the place. So I asked the Forest Service archaeologist. Same person that told me your mother's name, Castete, means *tomahawk* in Choctaw."

"Tunica," Purdy said. "But that's close enough, I guess." He sighed. "Her folks were part Choctaw, anyway. A lot of the tribes who fought each other before the whites came joined up afterward, for self-protection. The Tunicas were nearly wiped out. The main contingent now is at Marksville, on the reservation, but there are stragglers all over the place."

Brady searched carefully for his next words. "If you'd told them the prison site was a burial ground they'd have changed the location."

"Sure. Let 'em call me a professional Indian. Or worse, a half-breed. You know the kind of prejudice there is in that town."

"Yeah," Brady agreed, recalling Mrs. R.'s comment about redbones.

Purdy shook his head bitterly. "I'd rather be looked at as a nut than some kind of curiosity."

Brady made himself get up, to shake out the stiffness, and went to the edge of the camp circle to pick up another stick of wood. The rain had stopped, but the wind was still a whipsaw, ripping at his clothes and face.

"Ever see one of these?" he asked, holding out the little bell with the bullet dent.

Purdy took it and held it to the fire light.

"Yeah, I've seen 'em," he said. "Why?"

"I found it in the woods," Brady told him. "Somebody put a bullet in it."

"Crazy bastards will shoot at anything."

"Yeah."

Brady lay back down, grateful for the warmth. For a long time, as he stared into the flames, he thought he saw a herd of deer, racing across the embers, their white flags high in alarm. Then he saw one with a red nose and realized they were really reindeer. And when he at last drifted into sleep, there was no rest, for once again he was pursued by the demonic Santa Claus on an ATV, except that this time the red-clad figure was wearing the head of a deer.

When Brady awoke a chill mist was sucking at his body and the fire had burned to embers. He sat up, shivering in the cold, and looked over at the body. Scott was turning and even as Brady watched the boy's eyes opened.

"I'm cold," Scotty said.

"I'll build up the fire," said the publisher, getting to his feet.

And that was when he looked around and realized that Miller Purdy was gone.

Two hours later a pair of deputies, warming themselves in their jeep on a logging road, saw the bushes move twenty yards away and watched, incredulously, as two scarecrow figures emerged from the forest. One was a man, whose clothes, spattered with dried mud and leaves, appeared at first to be standard hunter's camouflage. But the other was a boy, and it only took them a second to realize who it was. Ten minutes after that the jeep with the deputies and their charges bounced off the logging track and onto a gravel Forest Service road, where six other vehicles from the Forest Service and the Sheriff's Department waited.

One of the car doors opened immediately and Matt Garitty jumped out. He started across the gravel before the jeep had stopped and a second later was hugging the boy who had just opened his door. Brady hoisted himself out of the jeep, feeling lightheaded. Everything had come out right, or so it seemed.

He looked up at the low, gray clouds and for some reason thought about the deer-headed Santa Claus of his dreams. He wanted to laugh and cry at the same time and realized it was fatigue and lack of food. People were talking to him, and hands were slapping him on the back, but all he knew how to do was lean on the vehicle and grin stupidly. Finally someone handed him a jelly doughnut and he wolfed it down, feeling the energy surge into his bloodstream. He watched Matt, arm still around his son's shoulders, lead the boy to the sheriff's white cruiser, and tenderly guide him inside for the trip to the hospital, where he would be checked out. Then the sheriff walked back to Brady and started to say something but no words came. Finally, he just turned on his heel, rubbing a hand across his eye, and walked back to his car.

Another car door slammed then, as one more vehicle joined the little roadblock, but Brady paid no attention until he felt arms around him and smelled her special perfume and heard her calling his name.

"You crazy, wonderful guy, I can't believe you did it."

Brady turned his head slowly and saw her jade-green eyes fastened on him in a way he would never forget.

"Luck," he managed. "I had a lot of luck."

"Sure." She held him around the waist and sank her head against his body, oblivious to the mud and dampness. His hand reached down and found her hair and for the first time it sank in that he was back.

"I've never seen Matt so emotional," she said. "If there hadn't been all these people around I think he would have kissed you, but since he's not here anymore, I will."

He touched his lips to hers and closed his eyes.

"Oh, Christ," he mumbled, pulling away and trying to rouse himself to the rest of the task. "It's not over, you know."

"They'll catch Purdy," she said. "*If* he did it." Her eyes narrowed slightly. "You know something, don't you, Brady? You know something you didn't tell. Is it about Purdy? Is that it? Or is it about Scotty? Come on, let me in on it. I can see you're holding something back."

"I need a bath," Brady said, moving through the crowd of well-wishers and toward her car. "I can't think straight right now. I need a bath and some food."

He put his hand on the car door and then, with an effort of will, jerked the door open, bent down, and forced himself inside.

It was warm and comforting and despite his excitement, a drowsiness overcame him and he started to drift toward sleep.

Kelly opened the driver's door and got in.

"Come on, Brady, out with it. You know what happened, don't you?"

Slowly, like a dreamer, Brady nodded. "I know."

"But you won't tell, either."

"Iffy," Brady slurred. ". . . needs a test . . . few things to find out . . ."

"You know who killed that girl."

Brady's head bobbed.

"And you know what happened out in the woods, with Scotty." Another nod.

She reached over and squeezed his hand.

"Matt and Mitzi are going to be very grateful," she said.

Brady's eyes opened and he gave her a curious look. "Will they?" he asked.

26

BRADY let the warm shower run down over him, basking in the comfort. He had lost track of time, standing in the shower seemingly forever, which was fine, because if he could stop time, he would never have to leave and do what he had to do. Outside the shower, he heard the dim sounds of the stereo, or was it Kelly humming? She had stripped off his clothes and checked him herself for injuries, then sent him into the shower while she went to prepare breakfast. He had refused to sleep, somehow waking up by the time they reached home. Now, in the warmth of the shower, he felt suspended between consciousness and delicious sleep.

Except that he couldn't sleep; there was too much to do.

The shower curtain moved finally and he watched a disembodied hand reach in and turn one of the knobs. For a second the wonderful warmth continued and then a shock of cold water blasted him. He stepped out, into the towel Kelly was holding.

"Breakfast is ready," she said. "Matt called and asked you to go over to the hospital so Doc McIntire could check you out, but I told him you were all right, that all you needed was rest—and me."

Brady let the towel enfold him and when he was dry stumbled into the bedroom, looking for his clothes.

"On the bed," Kelly said. "I laid out your flannel pajamas."

"No pajamas," he said, going to his chest of drawers and pulling out some underwear. "I've got to go out."

"Brady, you're crazy. Whatever it is will wait."

"No, it won't."

She gave him a quick, assessing glance, and then went into the kitchen. She came back a few seconds later with a tray.

"I know when you've got something in that hard head," she said, "so you might as well eat first."

Fifteen minutes later a worn but clean Brady drove to his office and called Tulane Medical School in New Orleans. It took him fifteen minutes of cajoling, but at last he was connected with Dr. Edmund LeFevre.

"Pete Brady! Where have you been? Ever since you did that piece on that hospital dope ring people have been scared to take an aspirin around here without a prescription!" The physician chuckled. "Then I called for you one day and they told me you weren't working there anymore."

"It's a long story, doctor. Right now I'm running the Troy Parish *Express* and I need your help."

"Troy Parish?" the surgeon snorted. "Is that in America?"

"Just barely," Brady said, playing along. "Look, Doc, I have to ask you a question."

"Sure. You helped me. They'd have charged *me* for that dope business, if you hadn't investigated."

"Right. Well, look, Doc, you've supervised the Emergency Room at Charity for a long time. I was in the woods with a boy who had a head injury, a concussion, and I've got to ask you some things."

"Go ahead, Pete. I'm all ears."

A few minutes later Brady drove to the hospital and found Matt Garitty in the hallway outside his son's room.

"I'm going to bring Miller Purdy in," he said. "But I need you to help me."

Garitty gave him a curious look. "What are you talking about? Haven't you done enough for one year?" He gave a little shrug. "Oh, what the hell. Doc said Scotty's fine, just wants to keep him a day or two, so I don't guess I've got any right to deny you, after what you've done." He held the door open. "Mitzi wants to thank you."

Mitzi looked up from Scott's bed and when she saw Brady she came forward to hug him.

"Pete—"

"Forget it," Brady said, embarrassed. "There's more to do."

He went over and gave Scotty a fake uppercut and the boy smiled.

"Why aren't *you* in here, Mr. Brady?"

"Too stupid to take the doctor's advice, Trooper," the publisher joked.

Garitty followed Brady into the hallway and grabbed his friend's arm.

"Look, I talked to Kelly while you were in the shower. Is it true? Do you really have an idea how it was done? Was the girl's death connected somehow to Elkins's?"

"They were connected," Brady confirmed. "But Matt—"

The lawman's eyes burned into his own.

"Then the boy . . . Somehow, if the two were connected . . ."

Brady shook his head:

"I haven't finished yet. I don't want to say things I can't prove—"

"But damn it, Pete, if Scotty didn't shoot him, if there's the slightest chance he was set-up somehow . . ."

Brady looked back into the other man's eyes.

"Matt, trust me."

When Brady reached Maud Penniman's house there were two other cars in the drive besides Maud's. One he recognized as Debra's and the other was the black carryall with the logo of Laverne's company.

Brady got out slowly and walked up to the door. He stood outside in the cold for a minute or two, turning over his words in his mind, making sure he had the right ones. Finally, he reached up and tapped with his knuckles.

A curtain inside moved, then the door swung open.

"Mr. Brady," Debra Penniman said, surprised. "Are you here to see Aunt Maud?"

"Yes," Brady said.

Laverne Penniman moved toward him from the other side of the room.

"She's not feeling very well today, Mr. Brady. Is it that important?"

"It's that important," Brady told them. "It has to do with the death of the McInnery girl and the burglary of your house."

Brother and sister exchanged glances.

"I'll go see if she can talk," Debra said and padded into the rear of the house.

Laverne closed the door and suddenly Brady felt confined, as if a prison gate had locked behind him.

"I hear the killer's loose in the Forest," Laverne said.

Brady nodded. "It won't be for long."

"No, I don't guess so." He shook his head. "Crazy bastard's caused me enough trouble. I hope they haul him in feet first."

The publisher pursed his lips. "What would happen to your contract if they moved the site of the prison?" he asked.

"Moved it? What do you mean?"

"I mean, if they put it in the next section, say a mile away, instead of where it's supposed to be now."

Laverne Penniman gave a crooked smile.

"Well, nothing, I guess. Wouldn't affect my costs any. But it might have to be rebid. Hell, if they changed the specs that much, there'd be all sorts of cries of 'foul.' And if they rebid it, I might not get it again."

"No," Brady agreed as Debra came back out. "I can see that."

"You can go back to Aunt Maud's room," she said, but caught his arm before he could start down the hallway. "Please, though: She's weak."

"I understand," Brady said. "It won't take but a minute or two."

He left the pair up front and went into a hallway heavy with the

190

smell of mothballs, emerging into a lavendar room scented with sachet. On one side of the room was an antique bureau of the kind Brady remembered from his grandmother's room, in the years of his childhood; on the side nearest him was a small bedside table with a lamp, old-fashioned black dial telephone, and a single glass on a tray. But it was the object between the bureau and the table that took his attention—an ancient four-poster bed, with cupola carvings for each upright, and a fancy curlicue design for the headboard. In the center of the bed, propped up on pillows like a doll in a frilly gown, lay Maud Penniman. She smiled and laid aside her magazine when she saw him.

"Mr. Brady, I'm so glad to see you," she said, giving him her hand. For the first time Brady noticed her slim, fine fingers, devoid of rings.

"You've got to excuse me; I just don't seem to be able to make this old heart work the way it used to. I'm not good for much, I think."

"I'm not so sure about that," Brady told her. "I came here because I thought you might be the one person who had the answer to some of the things that have been going on around here."

Maud frowned and pushed herself more erect.

"You've got me interested, I have to admit, but what an old woman like me can know that would make any difference is something beyond me." She shifted slightly. "Would you do me a favor and hand me that glass of water on the table?"

He gave her the glass and she opened a small pillbox that had evidently been on the pillow beside her. He watched her take a capsule and wash it down. She handed him back the glass.

"Now. What in the world is it I know that's so important?"

Brady sat down in the chair beside the bed.

"It's the property Dwayne Elkins has his camp on," he explained. "I understand his family owned it years ago, as part of a larger tract."

"Yes, that's what I remember. That was almost before my time. But what's that got to do with anything?"

"Suppose there was something buried on Purdy's land—the land that used to belong to Elkins. Suppose it was something valuable. Dwayne would have felt it was rightfully his."

"I guess so. But what is it you're talking about?"

"I don't know. But if that McInnery girl found out, say from Elkins, she'd be in danger, right?"

Maud's face screwed up. "Yes, that's probably so. But what is it that would be so valuable?"

"I was hoping maybe you could help me there," Brady said. "I thought maybe you could remember hearing of something."

Maud chuckled. "Well, I may be old and feeble, Mr. Brady, but I'm not *that* old. I really don't know what it might be. If there's anything at all."

Brady shrugged. "Well, I just thought I'd try."

There was movement in the hallway and Debra Penniman appeared with something in her hand.

"It's time for your medicine, Aunt Maud. I think you should rest now."

"Pshaw," Maud said. "I don't know what you've got there, but I already took my medicine. Mr. Brady can tell you that."

Debra gave Brady a stern look.

"She needs her sedative," she told him.

"Maybe I just need to go ahead out to Grady Grimes's Funeral Parlor," Maud said, "and get out of the way. My will's already made."

"Aunt Maud, don't even think such a thing." Debra flashed Brady a look of alarm. "We don't know what we'd do without you."

"You'd do the same as always," Maud said. "Nobody's indispensable. And so many things have changed. Sometimes I just don't think there's a place for me now." She looked over at Brady. "It's been so different these last years with Mom and Dad gone."

Debra flushed and Brady knew she was thinking of Dwayne's stewardship as manager.

"Well, I'm sorry to have bothered you, Miss Maud."

"No bother at all, Mr. Brady. You come back anytime, and if I'm still here . . ."

The ringing of the phone cut her short and she reached out, but Debra beat her to it.

"Hello?"

Brady watched Debra's expression go grim.

"It's for you, Mr. Brady. You can take it up front."

"Who is it?" Maud asked.

"I don't know," Debra said quickly, shepherding the publisher out into the hallway. Once the door to Maud's room was safely closed she leaned over. "I didn't want to excite her, but it's the *sheriff*. He says it's important."

Brady followed her toward the front but before they reached the living room she stopped.

"I couldn't help but hear some of what you were asking Aunt Maud. Is there something about Dwayne's land, then? That land he always claims old man Purdy stole from his folks?"

She must have had her ear against the door, Brady thought.

"I don't know," he said noncommittally. "It was just a thought."

"If Dwayne had a good claim to that land and there was something worth a lot buried there, I might . . . Well, I mean, I don't want to sound grabby. But I've got children with no father . . ."

"I understand," Brady said, looking around for the telephone.

"Up here," she said, pointing him toward the lamp table beside the big piano. Laverne got up as Brady entered, his eyes quickly questioning the publisher, and then falling away, and Brady wondered if he'd picked up on the phone when it had rung.

Brady lifted the receiver.

"Matt?"

"Pete, thank God I was able to get you. What's going on?"

"I had some questions to ask," Brady told him. "I think I know what happened now."

"You mean about the killing of the McInnery girl?"

"I mean about the death of Dwayne Elkins."

"Oh. Well, God man, don't keep it to yourself. Is it murder, then?"

"I'll explain about that later," Brady said, aware that the others were listening. "Look, what's up, though? You said you had something important."

"I do," Matt said. "You remember the personal things the McInnery girl had with her? The things Doc McIntire's keeping locked up in the examination room at the hospital?"

"Sure. But I didn't see anything worth a second look."

"Well, that's because we were holding some things back. Sorry, Pete, but it was necessary, even with you. We found some human hairs at the murder scene and Doc did some checking; he found there's a new test you can do on hair, that doesn't require it to be sent to the Crime Lab in Baton Rouge."

"Really." Brady glanced at the others, aware of their curiosity. "What's the bottom line?" he asked.

"The bottom line is that Doc's got the hairs soaking in a solution. Tomorrow morning he'll take them out and from that he'll get a complete chromosomal breakdown that will pinpoint the killer with ninety-eight percent probability."

Brady sucked in his breath slightly.

"Well, maybe so. I'm not so sure about some of these new tests—"

"Damn it, Pete, it will work. Doc talked to the head of the FBI Crime Lab in Washington. And it's admissable in court."

"What can I say?" Brady said. "Except good luck."

When Matt spoke again his tone had changed. "Pete, what are you up to?"

"Just a little test of my own," Brady said. "But since you asked me, I need you to help."

The room was dark, with its heavy door closed, and outside they could barely hear the passing of people in the hallway. Brady fidgeted in the hard-backed chair, too weary to relax, too on edge to allow himself to be comfortable.

What if he had misjudged? What if all his logic was wrong? What if he made a fool out of Matt? It could end up not only with his friend out of a job, but with the wrong person convicted.

"It's only seven o'clock," he said in an undertone. "Plenty of time."

Matt cracked the door and a shaft of light sprang up from the hallway outside. A second later, the sheriff slid the door shut again.

"So Scotty thought he saw a deer," Matt said. "But all he really saw was the bushes moving." He shook his head. "God, I thought I taught him better."

"Go easy on him," Brady soothed. "It was his first hunting trip.

He was excited. He thought it *had* to be a deer, and then, afterward, he convinced himself he'd really seen one. At least at the most conscious level. But deep down, of course, he knew he hadn't. That was what finally made him run away. He couldn't stand the thought that he'd disappointed you and Mitzi. He feels like he has a lot to live up to."

"Christ, I'm responsible, not him," the sheriff swore.

"Look," Brady said, "you did the best you could. You taught him to hold his fire until he was sure of his target. But he was excited. And he wanted to show you he was a good hunter . . ."

A noise outside cut off Garitty's answer and he went back to ease the door open. It was evidently a false alarm, for he closed it again in disgust.

"Another thing," he said. "Miller Purdy."

"He's a dangerous man," Brady said. "But as much to himself as to other people. He's a man caught in the worst kind of conflict: He doesn't know what world he falls into, the world of his father or of his mother. He's rejected his father and all he stood for, but he's scared to admit being a part of his mother's world. So he tries to justify his actions as environmentalism, as scientifically based."

Matt nodded. "He'd rather be looked at as a crazy environmentalist than a crazy half-breed. Says something about our society, I guess."

"Well, his position hasn't been comfortable in *any* society," Brady added.

Matt thought for a moment. "You know, if you're right, we're dealing with a pretty demented person."

"I know," Brady said. "It bothers me, too."

"I mean, to kill over *that.*"

"People have been killed for less. And, remember, the killing of the McInnery girl was cold-blooded murder, even if the death of Elkins wasn't."

The sheriff paced over to the other side of the room.

"It's still going to be hard on Scotty. It was my fault, putting him in that position. Making him think he had to say what I wanted him to."

195

"He'll need you both," Brady said. "But he's a strong kid, like his old man. He'll make it."

Matt's fists clenched and unclenched in anticipation and then, unable to restrain himself, he grabbed up the phone again and punched in his office's number.

"What's going on?" he hissed.

Even in the half-light Brady could see his expression change from one of haggard worry to excitement.

"It is? They did? Good. Follow through as planned."

He put the phone back and breathed out a sigh of relief.

"It's started," he said.

But it was fully two hours later that it happened.

Brady was half-asleep in his chair, fighting dreams of a tunnellike highway through the woods, when he felt Matt's hand shaking him.

"Over here," Matt whispered urgently. "It's going down."

The publisher roused himself and peered through the crack in the door as his friend held it for him.

Across the lit hallway the door on the other side was half open and as Brady listened he could hear movement in the other room. At first it was merely the sound of someone shifting things, but even as he moved silently across the corridor, with the sheriff behind him, there came the noise of glass breaking.

A nurse, coming from the other direction down the hallway, stopped when she saw the two men. Garitty motioned her away and her hand flew up to her mouth as she halted, surprised.

Matt stepped to the other side of the doorway and poised to go in, but Brady held up his hand.

There was the sound of more glass shattering. Then the steps inside moved quickly toward the door and Brady saw the sheriff tense.

A split-second later the door opened and the woman framed in the entrance stood frozen like a statue as she saw the two men.

Her mouth opened but no words came out. Finally she managed to speak.

"I must have gotten in the wrong room," Debra Penniman said.

27

THE hospital room was half-dark, but the old woman was awake, propped, as usual, in a half-sitting position, with pillows behind her.

"Debra? You mean she's been arrested?" Maud asked in a trembling voice, a hand to her throat as if the knowledge were too great to be tolerated. Her eyes went from the sheriff to the publisher, as if pleading to be told it was a mistake.

"I'm sorry," said Matt Garitty. "But it's true. We found her in Dr. McIntire's examination room, destroying what she thought was evidence."

"I can't believe it," Maud said again. "Not Debra. Has she admitted it?"

Matt nodded.

"She's given a full statement."

"It doesn't make any sense," Maud protested. She half-raised herself, then fell back onto the pillow. "My God, all this, in just a few days: her husband, then that young woman, and now . . . I just don't understand this world." She looked over at Matt. "And that poor young boy of yours. It makes me sick to think of it, having that on his conscience."

"Scotty will be all right," Matt said quietly. "He made a mistake, it's true. And he'll have to deal with that. But it could have been worse, a lot worse."

"Worse?" Maud croaked. "How?"

Brady leaned over the bed then. "What Matt means, Miss Maud, is that Scotty might have shot Dwayne Elkins."

"Might have? What do you mean?"

"I mean," Brady answered, "that he only heard Elkins in the brush. But he didn't shoot him. You see, his bullet missed."

Maud shook her head. "I don't understand. You mean there was somebody else out there?"

"No, not out there," Matt said. "What Pete means is that by the time Scotty fired—and missed—Elkins was a walking dead man."

"You're not making sense," Maud complained. "I talked to Doctor McIntire. A man with that kind of wound couldn't have lived more than five minutes."

The two men exchanged glances and then Brady spoke.

"It would seem like it. In fact, I wondered how he could have gotten as far as from where Scotty shot at him to where he fell. But Doc McIntire gave me the answer, though none of us recognized it then: He said it was possible, but not unheard of, for a man with that kind of wound, to stagger off. His term was 'running on empty.' But neither one of us pushed it any further, and Doctor McIntire isn't a trained forensic pathologist. When I talked to him again later, he admitted he hadn't thought to check for powder burns. It just seemed cut-and-dried. The kind of mistake a young doctor in a rural setting might make."

The old woman fixed the editor with a frown.

"A mistake? What do you mean? Talk sense."

Brady nodded. "I am. In fact, it's the only thing that did make sense. I've been to a lot of crime scenes and emergency rooms. But it took my being out in the woods with Scotty, seeing him lying there with a head injury, and remembering what a doctor had once told me about how unpredictable they were. So I called an old friend who supervises the emergency room at Charity Hospital in New Orleans. He confirmed what I was thinking. He even went to a textbook and quoted a case to me."

"What kind of case? What are you talking about?"

"A man in England, a few years back. He tried to commit suicide. Shot himself with a .45 caliber revolver. The bullet went in under the chin and came out the side of his head. He shot himself just before six in the morning and came back to his hotel after seven-thirty, spoke with the maid, went up to his room and died. And then there was the man who had the crowbar blown into one side of his head and out the other by an explosion and lived on for years. And finally, the woman who was shot and—"

"I . . . I still don't understand."

"Don't you, Miss Maud?" Brady asked. "After all, I found one of the sleigh bells at the camp, and I found the remains of the deer cutout, in the fire. That was the motive, wasn't it?"

"Motive?" Maud gasped, wringing the handkerchief in her hand. "I don't know about any deer cutout."

"Not just a deer," Brady said. "A *rein*deer."

The sheriff nodded. "We have a full statement from Debra, Maud. And when we searched your house an hour ago we found your revolver with an empty cartridge under the chamber, just like you left it. So you might as well tell us yourself. I'm going to read you your rights, but I've got to tell you we know exactly how Dwayne Elkins was killed and how you murdered Jean McInnery afterward."

It was a long time before the old woman spoke again, and then it was only to acknowledge that she understood her rights. Brady summoned the nurse with the call button, but Maud waved the other woman away.

"Well, it sounds like you've been very thorough," she said icily, her eyes fixed on the publisher. "But I still don't know how you decided."

"Various things," Brady said. "Mainly process of elimination. And logic. Why would Elkins be in the woods to begin with? Where was his rifle? It didn't make any sense unless he was drunk. Only a drunk man would stumble around in the middle of a hunting tract during deer season. And since he had alcohol on his breath and in his blood, I let that mislead me. I didn't realize he could have been wandering around *because he was already wounded.*"

"Very clever," Maud agreed, her lips fixed into a thin line.

"Matt asked me to look into it," Brady went on, "but at first I didn't have any luck. I went to the camp and I didn't find anything much except a dirty .22 rifle and evidence that Elkins was having an affair with a woman who was pressing him for money."

"A little tart," Maud hissed. "A piece of trash no better than he was."

"But one thing I did find was this." Brady pulled out the tiny bell with the bullet dent. "It looked like Elkins had been having target practice, but why shoot at a bell? I didn't even know what it was until somebody else told me. Then it took a while to put it together along with the colored glass from the Christmas lights."

He went over to the other side of the room, wishing he could hurry and get this over with.

"You still don't have any proof," she said scornfully. "Maybe you can explain how an old woman with a bad heart could get into the woods with a gun. I don't know what Debra told you, but . . ."

"I don't doubt you have angina," Brady said. "But I once filled in for the health reporter when I was on the *Picayune.* We did a piece on heart problems. Angina comes and goes, not like a major heart attack. You know, it was Laverne who said it first; at Dwayne's funeral he said something like, 'She'll probably have an attack now, but not until after the funeral.' It seemed like your ability to manipulate your illness was pretty well known."

"But Doctor McIntire—"

"What was he going to do?" Brady asked. "Turn you out, just because your EKG wasn't wildly erratic? You *did* suffer discomfort, and you had occasional attacks, so Doc treated you on the basis of what you told him. He told you to build up your heart by taking walks."

"So?"

"Penelope Martingale told me she saw you walking past her house. That's half a mile from town. I got to thinking, if you were strong enough to walk all the way out to Pen's, you could have walked from where you parked to Dwayne's camp."

Maud's lip trembled. "But at your house—"

"That attack at my house was purely show. You came over there for the sole purpose of making me scratch you from any possible list I might have. And I've got to give you credit."

"I'm a sick woman," Maud protested. "You can check my records!"

"Sick. Yes," Brady said. "Sick when you saw what your nephew had done."

"He wasn't my nephew," she spat. "He married my niece, but he wasn't my nephew, and he was never good enough to be a part of our family." She shook her head, glowering. "The kind of people who hung around with him. That trashy girl and those men—"

"Those men are what did it," Brady said. "I went out to the camp one more time to see if there was anything I might have overlooked and that's when I saw the deer cutout they'd fished out from behind the range. They were burning it for firewood. But enough of it was left for me to realize what it was. And that's when the little bell made sense; it was one of the decorations attached to the display."

"But you said there was something about buried treasure on Purdy's land," she protested, her voice quavering.

"I had to find some pretext to come over and see you," Brady said. "So I made up that story. The idea was to have the sheriff call while I was there and give me the supposed information that a new chemical test was going to show who'd killed the McInnery girl. I was going to make sure to repeat the story so you heard it, but Debra chased me out of the room and I thought the plan had misfired. Until I heard the click on the line when you replaced the receiver in the bedroom."

"Bad timing," the sheriff admitted blandly.

"Anyway," Brady said, "I figured as soon as you heard that, you'd manage to get yourself put back in the hospital so you could get to the so-called evidence tonight and destroy it."

"What we didn't expect," Matt put in, "was that you'd send Debra."

"I don't know what you mean," Maud complained. "I'm just a sick old woman."

"That, at least, I think is true," Brady said. "But, like Matt said before, Debra's confessed. She says you held her inheritance over her head, said that as bookkeeper, you controlled all the money from the business and if she didn't help you she wouldn't get a cent. She's a pretty scared person."

"She was never strong," Maud said. "But the McInnery girl—"

"Blackmail," Brady said. "She was on the way to the cabin and saw you with Dwayne. She left before anybody saw her and then she asked for money."

"But Miller Purdy's truck was seen at her place!" Maud declared.

"A witness said they saw a blue truck. But what they saw, I suspect, was Laverne's black carryall. He was having an affair with her, too. She was milking both men of every cent they had. According to Debra, Laverne even brought that lawyer to the hospital to draw up a loan agreement so he could get some more money from you. Of course, you both pretended it was because he was thinking of a suit against the Garittys, but it wasn't. That's one thing that increased your resentment of Dwayne; he kept taking more and more money out of the dealership, at the same time your favorite nephew, Laverne, was hitting you up for money supposedly to keep his business afloat. You doted on Laverne, but you hated Dwayne. And when you saw Laverne leaving Jean McInnery's trailer that night, from where you were parked on the road, I think it was her death warrant, if there'd been any doubt in your mind before."

Matt consulted his watch. "I figure right about now Laverne is singing his head off. The feds were working with the Natchitoches Parish people on a drug ring. Oh, you didn't know that, did you, Miss Maud? Well, it's true: Laverne was using the money you loaned him to buy drugs for resale."

"Not Laverne." Maud's mouth dropped open and for a moment a glassiness passed over her eyes. Matt moved forward quickly, toward the call button, but the old woman roused herself and waved him away with a feeble hand.

"No. It doesn't matter now. None of it does. *Laverne.* I was doing it all for Laverne. He was so much like Poppa, you know. If I'd married, had a son . . ."

She seemed to shrink into herself and the two men waited, the only sound in the room her labored breathing.

202

When she spoke again her voice was a dry crackle and they had to strain to hear.

"Dwayne was bleeding the company dry. He was irresponsible and self-centered. Debra tried to ignore what was going on but it was painfully obvious. He claimed to be working late and was with that woman instead. And she was costing him all kinds of money. I called him in more than once, but he wouldn't listen. It was right after Thanksgiving that everything came to a head."

She breathed in and out, as if she were having trouble getting enough air.

"He had shown complete contempt for me up until then. Told me that Debra would never leave him, that there was nothing I could do unless I wanted to hurt Debra and her children. He reminded me that I owned half and Laverne owned a quarter of the business, but that there was nothing we could do about Debra's fourth. And then he did the one thing that made me lose my temper."

"I think I understand," Brady said.

"My father built this business, made it everything it was," Maud went on. "My father was the reason Dwayne Elkins had a job; my father and the traditions he began, the reputation he had for decency and honesty and the way he cared about this community."

She looked away from them, as if seeing something that was no longer there.

"My father started the business in 1925. And he had the Santa Claus display made in 1943, as a way of cheering people up during the war. So many sons had gone over there to fight, he thought we just had to try to keep our spirits up at home. And every year after that, he had the Santa and his sleigh put on the roof the day after Thanksgiving. People came to expect it. It wasn't Christmas in this town without it. Then he added Rudolph when that song got popular."

"And Dwayne didn't believe in that," Brady said quietly.

"Dwayne didn't believe in anything but Dwayne. But I think he trashed the display just as a way to get even, because he knew how much it meant to me. When I heard he'd told them not to bother with it this year I thought I was going to cry. It was like killing a part of my past."

Brady nodded.

"I went to the storeroom where it was kept but it wasn't there. Then one of the salesmen told me he'd taken it out to the camp. I knew I couldn't let it pass. It was a slap in the face of my family."

"You went out there to confront him early Saturday morning," Brady said.

"Yes. I'd lain awake thinking about it all night and when I got up I knew I had to do it. I went over to Deb's and she said he was at the camp, so I decided to go out there. It was raining and cold, but I'd been doing all right lately. I still didn't know what I was going to do: argue, threaten, or what. I didn't know until I got out there and saw what he'd been doing."

Her head went from side to side, as if trying to deny it all.

"The camp was closed up and I knocked, but there wasn't any answer. I thought maybe he was in the back so I walked around there and that was when I saw it: the display, set up as targets on his range. *He'd shot them all full of holes. He'd used my father's Christmas display, one of the historical artifacts of this town, for target practice!*"

Brady tried to imagine the scene: the old woman standing in the mist, the wooden sleigh and reindeer riddled with holes . . .

"I heard something and turned around. And there he was standing there, a smirk on his face, still half-drunk, wearing that orange vest, with that rifle over his shoulder, like he was all set to start shooting all over again.

" 'I figured this stuff wasn't much good anymore,' he said, 'so I brought it out here. Nobody cares about that sort of stuff anymore.' Except he didn't say *stuff*." She looked directly at Brady then. "So that was when I did it. I reached into my bag and pulled out Poppa's old Smith & Wesson Magnum and I said, 'You think it's a joke? I'll show you a joke, Dwayne Elkins.' "

There was a silence while the men waited.

"He dropped down on his knees, but it didn't matter. When he wouldn't look me in the eye I shot him. I didn't even know I'd pulled the trigger. But I must have because the gun went off and he

204

looked at me like nothing had happened and then he just dropped his rifle and got up and stumbled away. At first I thought I'd missed but then I saw some blood on the ground. It started raining harder then and I watched the blood just sort of dissolve and I thought maybe if I just went back to town, it would all be like that: something that never happened at all. I picked up his rifle, put it back in the camp and went home. For a little while I thought it hadn't happened at all. Then I heard about the boy."

"And you decided to let him take the blame," Matt accused.

"He shot, didn't he? He might have hit him? Maybe I missed. Maybe he *did* shoot him. Maybe . . ."

"But the girl saw you leaving the camp," Matt said. "She heard the shot, didn't she?"

"So she said. She wanted money, so I had to get rid of her. She'd already tried to get her hands on some letters she'd written to Dwayne. I guess she was afraid she'd be found out as the greedy little tramp she was. Well, I have news for her; everybody knew."

"So you drove over to the trailer park and knocked on her door and told her you had money for her," Matt persisted.

"Yes. I parked just off the highway and waited. She was such a stupid child. She thought I was old and decrepit. So when she turned around I hit her with my gun. Then I tied her up and looked around until I found some pills. That seemed better than just beating her to death. And more merciful."

"Except that she may have strangled," Brady said.

"Well, she got what she deserved," Maud declared. "After what she did to my family."

"Family," Brady mused. "Yes, I guess it comes down to that, doesn't it?"

"Doesn't it always?" Maud demanded.

Brady gave the old harpy an appraising look and then nodded. "Yes, ma'am, I suppose it does."

Epilogue

IT was the day after Christmas and Brady was thumbing through the *Encyclopedia of Southern Culture* Kelly had given him, not sure whether it was a gentle taunt or a genuine attempt to provide him with a research source. She was overdue, of course, which was beginning to worry him, because she had left again right after breakfast, with the same maddening evasiveness about her destination as before. And just when he thought they had gotten things straightened out. He was beginning to feel hopeless about it, which did little for his disposition, when a horn sounded outside, followed by several more toots.

He laid the book aside and got up, wondering who would be honking in his driveway.

He opened the front door and blinked. At first he thought it was some new decoration, a stuffed hood ornament of some kind, and then he blinked again.

It was a deer, lying spread across the hood of Matt Garitty's pickup, prongs bright in the afternoon sunlight. Before Brady could speak Scotty was out of the truck and pointing to the dead animal:

"I got him, Mr. Brady. I got him with one shot. He's an eight pointer, too. Dad says he's the biggest anybody's got so far this season."

"Congratulations," Brady said, trying to see beauty in the dead buck and seeing, instead, only a vision of Rudolph.

"You should of been with us," Matt said, from behind the driver's seat. "It was something."

"I bet," Brady said. He noticed the blood on Scott's forehead and frowned. "Did you get hurt?"

Scotty laughed and Matt shook his head good-naturedly.

"Pete, you'll never get used to our customs will you? The boy was blooded. The buck's blood was smeared on his forehead. That's what you do when a young 'un makes his first kill. It's an old custom."

Brady nodded slowly. "I'll bet."

The sheriff lowered his voice. "I hear Miss Maud took a turn for the worst."

"Yeah," Brady said. "I talked to Doc a couple of hours ago. He isn't very hopeful."

"Well, maybe it's for the best. What's she got to look forward to but an indictment?"

The lawman shook his head.

"By the way, Pete, you never really explained how you figured Elkins was shot at the camp."

"Just a hunch," Brady said. "And a dirty rifle."

"What?"

Brady explained about the two rifles at the camp. "One was the rifle he used for deer hunting, and it was clean. But the gun he used to shoot around camp with looked like it had been dropped in the mud. Now, for a man like Elkins, the only reason a gun's left dirty is because the owner is physically unable to clean it. It made sense that he might have dropped it when he was shot and somebody else put it back on the rack. I knew Elkins, even drunk as a skunk, wouldn't have put it there in *that* condition. It just took me a while to realize what it meant—the idea of a man going so far with a wound that bad didn't occur until later."

"Good figuring," Matt said. "But how about laying it all to Maud? How did you know about her?"

Brady smiled. "Well, Laverne and Emmett both mentioned that she was a bad person to have mad at you. But, really, she gave it away herself. At Dwayne's funeral she mentioned the Christmas display and what Dwayne did with it. It's funny, all the time my subconscious kept trying to tell me about it, but it didn't register for a long while. Just like when I ran into Jean McInnery at the hospital—she was making sure nobody was at Debra's house. But I didn't connect it and when I saw the map in Dwayne's study I got sidetracked. The truth, of course, was that she was trying to get back some of the letters she wrote him, letters that probably would have showed how much money he'd wasted on her. And that's why she made a trip to the dealership and tried to get into his office. After all, he *was* pretty careless. I even found one of her earlier letters on the floor at the camp."

"Damn," Matt swore. "I'm glad we didn't have to go to court on that."

"Me, too," Brady said. "I was hoping we could trick Maud into making a move. I just didn't count on her putting Debra up to doing her work for her at the hospital."

"No," Matt shook his head. "Well, it worked. But I've got to admit I was saying my prayers when we searched her house. My God, what if we hadn't found a .357 Magnum?"

"You mean a pistol with a bullet diameter about the same as the bullet used in Scotty's rifle? That's easy enough."

"Oh?"

"We'd have been back to *start,*" Brady laughed. "Look, what did they decide to do about Purdy?"

Matt smiled. "Feds are glad to forget the whole thing. It wasn't their fault they missed the burial ground, but they don't want to look insensitive to Native Americans. The person that Purdy called after he left the hearing was a tribal official, it turns out; they were set to raise hell as a last resort."

"That's good to hear," Brady said, then leaned in so the boy wouldn't hear. "Something's been bothering me. About your promise to resign—"

"What promise was that?" Matt asked, his expression blank.

Brady grinned. "Funny, I could have sworn—"

Matt shrugged again. "Better get over to Doc McIntire. I think you may have a hearing problem."

The pickup was disappearing down the street with a honking of its horn and Brady had just turned to go back in when he heard a squeal of tires. He faced the street again in time to see Kelly turning up into the driveway.

She got out quickly and walked over to embrace him.

"Did you miss me?"

"I always miss you," he said. "That's why I hate Jeff Baxley so much—because he sees you all the time."

"Bax?" she laughed. "Well, he and Adrian would be amused to hear that."

"Adrian?"

"His lover."

"You mean Jeff Baxley, your adviser . . ."

"Cross my heart."

Brady shook his head. "I feel like a fool. I was so jealous." He gave his head a final shake, then started toward the house, holding her hand. "So how are things in Jena?"

She stopped short.

"How did you know that's where I'd gone?"

"That's where you went before. It seemed logical."

"You're too damned logical," she said as they walked inside. "You know, seriously, Brady, I think that's one of the things that's bothered me all along."

"What do you mean?" He stared at her, incredulous.

"Well, stand back and take a look: You won the Pulitzer for putting things together on that dope and murder ring in New Orleans. You've solved two separate crimes since you've been in Troy, and now you figure the most harmless person in town was the one behind all this. Can you imagine what it would be like married to somebody who can see into your every motive?"

"That wasn't all there was to my figuring out about Maud," he protested. "As for . . . *married?* Did you say *married?*"

"I said I wasn't ready for it before and I'm not sure I'm ready for it now. But one thing I *know*, Pete Brady, is that I'm not ready to spend the rest of my life without you, either. I guess I knew that all along and it's what was eating at me; I have some hangups and insecurities I need to work out and I wasn't sure I could live with you but I knew I couldn't live without you. So I settled for the best solution."

"Which is?" a surprised Brady asked.

"There was an editor's job available on the LaSalle weekly in Jena," she said. "I interviewed for it the other day. They called me back and I just drove over to accept."

"You mean—?" Brady asked, his mouth open.

"That's right. Please don't hold it against me for not telling you; I was so scared I wouldn't get it and then what was I going to do? Come back here and work for you? We both know we'd fight like cats and dogs if we tried working for the same outfit. So I lucked out and found a job thirty miles away. And you know what? I don't even have to live there. I can drive to work."

"And scandalize the good people of this parish?" Brady asked.

"I have a feeling," she said sweetly, "that as long as you're around you'll keep them pretty busy with their own scandals."

"You amaze me," Brady said, crushing her to him. "You absolutely amaze me."

"I do my best. Merry Christmas, darling," she whispered. "And Happy New Year."